HOTEL ARCADIA

HOTEL ARCADIA
SUNNY SINGH

QUARTET

First published in 2015 by Quartet Books Limited
A member of the Namara Group
27 Goodge Street, London W1T 2LD
Copyright © Sunny Singh 2015
The right of Sunny Singh to be identified
as the author of this work has been asserted
by her in accordance with the
Copyright, Designs and Patents Act, 1988
All rights reserved.
No part of this book may be reproduced in
any form or by any means without prior
written permission from the publisher
A catalogue record for this book
is available from the British Library
ISBN 978 0 7043 7379 2
Typeset by Josh Bryson
Printed and bound in Great Britain by
T J International Ltd, Padstow, Cornwall

For Siddharth, confidante, brother, and best friend

THE ARCADIA
67 HOURS AGO

Sam thought that the first shots were in her nightmares.

She had been dreaming again of places she had consciously forgotten, of people she had chosen to deliberately erase, incidents she had buried deep, never to be dug up again, unmarked even by ephemeral tombstones. No, that isn't quite true. Her photographs are tombstones for those unnumbered, nameless dead. But she files away the negatives and memory cards, never looks at the newspapers that print them, chooses to ignore the payments for them that eventually show up in her bank account, and crams the commendations, critiques and prizes in an ancient, creaking Ikea cabinet in the far corner of her studio.

No, she never thought of bullets, except in her dreams. Perhaps that is why she felt so disorientated when she finally awoke to the screeching of the phone. She had been expecting the sharp cracks, the muffled thudding explosions, to fade as always when she regained consciousness. Instead, as she shook the drowsiness from her mind, the bullet pops continued, punctuated by other more, animalistic sounds: shrieks, screams cut off abruptly, snuffling sounds of herds moving beyond her door, dull thuds of bodies, or something else, hitting the heavily carpeted floors.

'Ma'am,' the voice on the phone whispered urgently, 'I am calling from reception. We have a problem. Please stay in your room. Lock the door please. And please turn off all lights. You cannot let them know you are there. Do not open the door for anyone. Please.'

'What…' she began, but a click had ended the conversation.

Fighting the drowsiness, Sam lay in bed, cradling the receiver against her ear, trying to make sense of the call, trying to

1

remember how long or even where she had been sleeping, even as the sounds beyond her door took on a terrible familiarity. Slowly, the fragments began clicking into place.

She had checked into the Arcadia early in the afternoon, weary and wishing for nothing more than a hot shower and a clean bed. As always, she had sniggered to herself when the taxi had pulled up in the broad driveway. All luxury hotels looked the same to her: obscenely wide carriageways leading up to broad gleaming steps, vast cold lobbies and atria glistening with marble and brass and crystals, the rooms all done in similarly nondescript wallpapers apparently to heighten the sense of luxury, the same large mirrors, the state of the art entertainment systems, and then the only thing that ever interested Sam: a sprawling bed with antiseptically clean sheets and fat fluffy pillows, the kind she would never bother to buy for herself.

She always insisted on staying a couple of nights at one of these at the end of an assignment. In her cynical moments, she told herself these luxury hotel stays were a reminder of all that was corrupt in the world, that the men who invariably bought her a drink at the bar in the evening were also the ones paying for the killings beyond the neatly manicured lawns. She would try to convince herself that she learned as much about the wars plaguing the world in these hotels as she did in the battle-torn jungles, scorching deserts and dusty forgotten villages.

But the truth was simpler, more selfish: she simply liked the ritual of climbing into a clean bed after a long hot bath and drowning herself in a deep bottomed bottle of single malt ordered from room service. And even before she shut the heavy drapes to screen out whatever city lay beyond the double glazed, soundproof glass windows, even before her head, heavy and aching and blurred with whisky hit the pillow, she knew her sleep would be troubled, marred by the images her mind could then not keep out. But if nothing else, the ritual reminded her, after each battle, that regardless of her photographs, her memories, her nightmares, she could still leave the dead behind.

But this time it seemed that the dead had followed her. The muffled explosions and rattles of automatic weapons echoed not far beyond her door. Sam tried to clear her head and focus on that strange abrupt phone call. Then as she began to return the receiver to the phone, a flurry of steps sounded in the corridor beyond her door. Someone tried the door, roughly rattling its ornate handle, knocking impatiently, repeatedly. In an instant, despite the whisky haze clouding her mind, her sense of self-preservation kicked in: the phone call hadn't been a prank at all.

She lay frozen, holding the receiver just above its rest, as if even its soft click would be loud enough to alert the strangers in the corridor. A few more kicks at the door, and then the stranger moved away. Further away in the corridor, she could hear more knocks, rattling and kicks, gruff commands, pleas and shouts, then the spurt and cough of automatic firing, followed by some stray shots. All sounds grew fainter and more muffled as the minutes passed. Finally, breathing out slowly, Sam dropped the receiver on its rest, muffling even the soft click with her palm, wide awake now, the whisky haze briefly dissipated by a familiar adrenalin rush.

Yes, the dead had indeed followed her.

***

Abhi's reaction to the sound of the first bullets was entirely instinctive. He wouldn't even remember it later. All he remembered was Samar's voice in his ear as he hit the floor, 'Little bro, you need to be faster.' Samar's childish laughter seemed to ring louder in his ears than the sound of the bullets and crashing glass.

But he had been fast. Fast enough to duck as the first shots rang out in the glittering lobby of the Arcadia. His had been an inordinately prepared response, instilled by all those war games he had played with Samar as a child, a reaction born of long afternoons of ambushing each other, of practising what they learned from watching the soldiers at drill past the bottom of

3

their garden. 'A soldier must have fast reactions,' Samar would insist with a precocious solemnity that unnerved Abhi even as a child. But this was no child's play, Abhi realised, cowering behind the marble counter, hearing the screams and ricochets ringing in the atrium.

He pulled himself against the counter, curling up on himself in fear. It was that same terror that made him blindly sweep his fingers against the bottom ridge of the counter, till he found the panic button, the silent one that would alert the police. Where the bloody hell was the security, he wondered, even as he pushed the red tab again and again, almost in time with the gun shots ringing out above him.

The receptionist huddled just a little farther along his left. At first glance, Abhi thought she had also ducked and hidden behind the stately reception counter, but the white marble floor around her was steadily staining red.

'Are you all right?' Abhi whispered, trying to reach out and touch her. The new girl. He couldn't remember her name although he had hired her just a week ago. Yet another small town girl, starry-eyed at the idea of working in a five star hotel, thrilled at the prospect of seeing the film stars and cricketers who came through the lobby but never acknowledged her shy smile and wide-eyed wonder, or perhaps simply accepted her adoration as their due. Abhi had been much the same, not so many long years ago – a rebellious army brat who had refused to follow the path laid out by his family, had come to the Arcadia, convinced it offered all that he knew he should not want.

He crawled up to the prone girl. 'Get up, we have to get out of here,' he prodded her shoulder. His hand came away wet and bloodied as she slumped heavily against him. She was dead. Abhi could feel the nausea swell within him, a faintly metallic smell filling his nostrils. Then silently, violently, he vomited, retching over blood spreading over the pale, cool floor, soaking the girl's dark uniform; emptying his guts in painful paroxysms of fear and horror.

Dizzy, sweating, tears racing down his cheeks, he rested his head against a pillar, unable to move, or even daring to open his eyes again. 'Stay still, little bro. We'll hide here.' Samar's voice again.

Abhi stayed frozen, fighting the terror welling up within, knowing his brother was many miles away, off with his unit, playing their childhood war games in earnest now. In any case, they weren't children any more. They hadn't even spoken for years. Not since Abhi had shared his secret, imagining innocently that Samar would understand and accept what no other would.

'All clear. Just two over here. Both dead,' a gruff voice spoke above. Abhi could imagine someone peering over the sleek granite-top reception desk, checking for the slightest hint of life, ready to snuff out any survivor. Not a guest, Abhi knew, not with that uncouth accent. Then, the shuffling sounds faded as someone seemed to move away.

'Take the lifts. You two guard the stairs. Start from the top.' Another voice ordered. Again thick, uncultured. Not from the city. Not native to the spotless marble, gleaming brass and glistening glass opulence of the Arcadia he knew so well.

'Abhi, let's go,' the boyish voice of his delusions insisted again, as silence descended all around him.

He cracked his eyes a slice, averting it carefully from the body lying next to him. Then, as all remained still, he crawled around the counter to crane his neck for a glimpse beyond. Somewhere above him the telephone rang insistently, incongruous in the silence. Abhi hoped it rang in response to the alarm he had raised but he dared not answer it.

The massive glass doors of the main entrance were shut. A length of bicycle chain was wrapped around the golden door handles and secured with a cheap iron padlock. A set of wires ran from the handles across the glass and then past the edges. Abhi suddenly remembered Samar setting up his booby-traps in their home: electrical wire carefully pilfered from the abandoned cottage down the lane, old batteries from their father's heavy military torch, a few firecrackers saved from some New Year celebration. Samar knew how to rig it all together, tightly packing plastic buckets and earthen pots with sand. 'See, Abhi, now when anyone opens the door, boom! They will get a headful of sand.' But the wires running across the entrance looked a lot more sinister than Samar's childish tricks. And beyond the glass, some of Arcadia's blue uniformed security guards lay crumpled and still.

He turned away quickly and almost reeled again. The vast white marble-floored lobby was stained with the blood. Bodies lay randomly, in nondescript lumps, colours bleeding into rusty, dirty reds and browns. He knew if he looked long enough, he would recognise some of those lumps: a white jacketed waiter from Garden Café beyond, the green and gold braided jackets of the bellboys, that red long coat of the stately old man who had been the head porter for decades. But nausea welled again and he forced himself to look elsewhere.

The ornate mirrors along the far wall were shattered, almost as if someone had taken a vengeful hammer to their elegant expanse. On the left, his favourite painting of golden horses running across a crimson field was pockmarked with ugly dark holes. How often had he counted up his monthly salary, fantasising about a time when he could afford to own just such beauty. And now, some madman had sprayed that precious, fragile, gorgeous canvas with bullets! Strangely the enormous chandelier seemed untouched, un-swayed by the carnage below its ten thousand cut crystals.

Abhi stared at the gleaming chandelier for a long instant, his mind trying in vain to make sense of his surrounding: the blood, the destruction. Why? Who would want to kill so indiscriminately? Why had he even been in the lobby? Why had he not been far from the quotidian madness? Not that this was quotidian of course. But he had earned the privilege of his own personal office, stark and minimalist, beyond the constant hum of the reception. In the normal course of events, he would have seen all the chaos on the security camera monitors. But of course, he had been waiting for the international delegation, had come out to the reception to ensure all was in order. Now he prayed that the delegation had not arrived, had been delayed, not caught in the carnage. He could no longer remember anything with certainty.

In all the jumble of his thoughts, one kept recurring, one that he knew well. Hadn't he spent most of his life feeling that way? Hadn't he always known this overwhelming fear of discovery, the terror of not finding a way out, the desolation of fighting all his battles alone? He had always imagined that he had overcome these old enemies, fought his way into a world where he was invincible. But now, in a strange, brutal way, the net had closed once again around him. Once again he was trapped.

THE ARCADIA
66 AND A HALF HOURS AGO

Sam lay in bed, one hand still poised over the telephone, trying to focus her mind to shed its whisky haze, her eyes squinting in concentration. But her thoughts whirled about, jumbled and random, refusing to focus on the present.

She had always had a bad feeling about this assignment. She had no reason to cover the limited conflicts of her homeland when other lands were engulfed in far wilder, brighter flames. In any case, she didn't do peace stuff and God knows there was little by way of proper war out here. Make no mistake, she had explained to the commissioning editor, death stalks her homeland aplenty, and violence borne of poverty, and crime, and hate, and boredom, all the commonplace ways in which humans make each other suffer, was rife. But she didn't cover crime, or poverty, or even the banal quotidian suffering, and there was little of the obscene irrationality that mass violence brings in its wake. Again, as she had done often from the beginning of this trip, she cursed herself for getting talked into an assignment that she should have rejected outright.

But there had been no more excuses, no chance of running away, of looking for something indefinable in foreign combat zones. This time around, Sam knew she couldn't even blame it on being an adrenalin junkie, looking for her next fix in yet another nameless, causeless, futile war.

'Come on, Sam, you have never done your own country. It might bring some biographical interest to your next exhibition,' Stella, her agent had suggested. 'You know how the media works. Give them even one snap, a scrap of personal trauma and they'll love you. They might even stop being bored by the wars and cover the exhibition. God knows the market for your sort of snaps is slow enough.'

Sam had vacillated for weeks, trying to find reasons to refuse. Then one morning she had caught a small online news article: mango harvests were expected to be especially abundant this year. Sudden memories of sticky juice staining her clothes, tangy aromas filling her nostrils, the sweet warm yellow flesh melting on her tongue took her back to more peaceful days. How long since she had tasted a mango fresh off the tree? It was the only thing that ever made her homesick.

Once in the Congo, she had bought a round red, green and yellow fruit as bright as a parakeet, paying far more than the old lady could have named. Her translator had harrumphed his disgust at her sentimentalism: 'You make it worse. Now she will think all foreigners will give her more.' She had hastily sliced the fruit in the car, not even pausing to smell it.

Only to be deeply disappointed.

The sweetness was there, running evenly through the deep gold flesh, clinging to each stringy pale filament that held the flesh to the thick skin. But Sam could only focus on the lack of that hinted scent of bitterness that hid in mangoes from home, the gentle tang of something elusive and unnameable that her palate remembered so well. She had barely finished her slice, leaving the rest for her glum translator.

All right, so maybe she had accepted this assignment out of childish whimsy, out of nostalgia. Or perhaps she was getting just a bit bored, just a little too cynical, because she wanted to want something else. She admits if only to herself that she is addicted. Her body is hooked to the adrenalin rush that surges in her veins when she is in the field. Her body seeks that rush repeatedly, desperately, savouring the powerful surge even as her conscious mind revolts against all that she sees, wants to hide from the destruction. She thinks of her assignments as carefully calibrated hits for a functioning addict, submerging, almost drowning each time, before pulling herself back into iron-willed serenity.

Now the madness has come to her, seeking her with the determination of a spurned lover. For an instant of paranoia, she

9

imagines that the gunmen striding the through the corridors are looking for her, that it is finally her day, the day that she takes the bullet she has dodged for so long, that it is finally payback time for all the dead she has captured, the ghosts she has ignored. Then she shakes herself awake. That way lies insanity, survivor's guilt, PTSD, and a loss of survival skills. She knows the paths too well to let herself go down them. Pushing herself down into the bed, she mentally scans for the slight aching knot in her shoulders, a familiar sign of her fear, and thus of her ability to survive. The sharp twinge between her shoulder blades leaves her momentarily winded, gasping, until she calms herself down, breathing deeply, forcing herself to relax, stretching her muscles against the cool linen.

It is not until she is finally composed that she pulls herself out of her bed, tip-toeing to the door to press an ear against it for noises. For an instant, she wonders if she had hung the do not disturb sign on the door, as she habitually does, a sure giveaway of her presence in the room, but remembers that she had not been able to find it. Now crouching at the door, she notices a red switch, one of the new-fangled techie idiocies instead. She snorts softly, no wonder she hadn't found it, and lucky that she had been too tired to search.

She listens for a long time, her ears straining, her body tense and pressed against the side wall. Finally, convinced of the silence beyond, she gently turns the lock and eases the door open. She peers out, her head low near the floor. The corridor is empty, except for some shattered glass and shredded flowers, the scattered remains of the majestic vases that had graced the long shadowy lengths of plush carpets. After a moment, she slides herself back into the room, locking the door, silently, and with great care.

Her instincts are in overdrive now. She switches on the television, one finger pressed on the volume button, just in case the previous resident has left it dangerously loud. The news channels all have the same shots of the Arcadia, obviously taken by crews positioned across the wide boulevard: smoke puffing out from the occasional window, random shots of policemen crouching behind makeshift barriers. Sam keeps the sound on mute with the banners providing all the information that she needs: gunmen have taken the hotel hostage; there have been sounds of explosions and gunfire; there are reports, or perhaps just expectations, of numerous casualties.

She turns on her laptop, fishes out her phone from her backpack. Thank heavens, she keeps it on silent while working and had forgotten to turn the ringer back on before falling asleep. The screen glows with a trail of missed calls, a string of emails and texts: Stella, her agent, the only one she had expected to hear from; one of the news editors, which makes her realise that this must be quite serious, or at least a bigger story than most; a few journalist friends, most of whom Sam knows have been calling for information, insanely jealous because they suspect that she is at ground zero. There is even a missed call from David, that one she hadn't expected at all. None from her parents, of course, who know never to disturb her while she is working. Almost as if they can ignore any danger to her by not acknowledging her presence in those fields of violence.

She fires off emails requesting floor-maps of the Arcadia, expecting little or no response. The images on the television confirm her belief that the security forces have clamped down on much of the information. But she has seen that before, knows her way around security blackouts. Enough screen-shots from the television coverage will give her a rough outline if not a complete floor-map. As long as she knows the number of floors, potential fire zones and hotspots, and has some idea of the stairwells, she can find her way around.

On a hunch, she dials the reception. It rings and rings, and just when she is ready to hang up, someone answers: 'Good evening, the Arcadia, Abhi Sikarwal speaking.'

How terribly civilised! Sam waits a second before speaking, wondering if she has reached an answering machine. 'Yes, can you tell me where the fire escapes are in the north wing?' she demands.

11

'Ma'am, we have a small problem and we recommend that you remain in your room until further notice,' the voice on the other end sounds slightly shaky.

'I spoke to you before, right?' Sam knows all the tricks of bludgeoning her way past small time managers and officials.

'Yes, ma'am. I am trying to inform our guests of the situation and will call you again with an update soon. For the moment, could I request you to stay in your room? And please try not to use this line unnecessarily.' The voice was beginning to sound exasperated, slightly edgy.

'Yes, that's fine. Just tell me, where is the fire escape in the north wing?' Sam repeated.

'Ma'am, please stay in your room. I will call you the moment I have an update.'

A sharp click ends the call. Bastard!

Well, back to the television and the net. Sam turns back to her laptop and runs another search, this time for requisite local standards for fire escapes in large public buildings. Improvise, adapt, work with educated guesses, she is good at this game. The journalist on the silent television is guessing at about a dozen gunmen. Sam imagines that there must be a couple of hundred hostages in the hotel. Sam doesn't count herself amongst them, of course. But that does mean a couple of hundred potential photographs.

If the dead shall insist on following her, Sam knows of only one way of facing them.

***

For what seemed like hours, Abhi could not move, his mind repeating one sole thought – this was not supposed to happen. He of all his family was the one who had no interest in guns, and bullets, and war. That he could even be hiding from gunmen was really the most ridiculous mischance ever.

It was the fear of being trapped that finally made Abhi move, sliding and crawling back to the door leading beyond. And it was the same fear that drove his fingers across the key pad of the electronic lock, his flesh remembering the sequenced code when his mind remained frozen. Only for a flash, as he shut the reinforced steel door behind him did Abhi hesitate. Was he going further into the trap? Wasn't it ridiculous to go further into locked doors, deeper into a building under siege? Like a wounded animal running itself aground? But then the most pressing need overwhelmed him – all he wanted was to rid himself of his soaking shirt, to wash the blood off his hands, somehow wipe away all he had seen in the lobby.

Nausea is still bubbling in the back of his throat when he reaches the wall of security monitors located in his office. Something acid and choking is lodged in his throat.

Instinctively he checks then bolts the second reinforced door behind him. On his right, the wide window opens into the lawn, and then the city beyond, the greens as serene as ever. As if the madness inside the Arcadia has never traversed its grounds, or has exploded from within. For an instant he is tempted to slide it open, take his chances in jumping the twenty feet down to the north lawn. Then some old memory or sanity kicks in. It is too far to jump, to risk injury and even worse, risk being caught immobile in the open.

On the multiple monitors on the wall, the Arcadia's CCTV system is recording the movements of the gunmen on the higher floors, their moves methodical and controlled, the images, horrible and compelling at the same time. He can't bear to look but can't tear his eyes away from them. It isn't until the scream of an insistent phone cuts into his frozen mind that he can bring himself look away.

'Abhi Sikarwal, The Arcadia.' The words come automatically, even though the voice on the other end seems to be talking gibberish. He tries to focus, identifying the voice on the phone. It's the police chief, the one he tries to avoid if only for his resemblance to Baba. Still his mind wanders, staring in horror as the gunmen rage through the Arcadia.

'Pull yourself together, Mr Sikarwal, you may be the best bet we have,' the voice is insistent, demanding.

'Yes sir,' his response is instinctive, born of memory. 'What do you need?'

'First, stay put. Second, can you get us any information on the situation inside? We have near to nothing right now.'

'Yes, of course sir.'

'Good. And keep this line clear. We are going to need it.'

'Yes sir.' The fog seems to lift from his brain even as the voice continues with familiar platitudes, a security run down to ensure he remains safe, a list of things to watch for and convey. But Abhi knows all that already, has played those games so often with Samar that he needs no instructions.

Hanging up, he notices the stench rising from his clothes, the blood and vomit. Sweat. And something sour. It cuts through the confusion, snaps his brain into action.

His eyes are still fixed on the bank of screens before him. 'OK Abhi, can you identify where those guys are? Just tell me the floors? And stop staring at the screens. Start from the top and make your way down. First across left to right, and then down to the next row. Count to three on each screen. If you don't see anything at the count of three, move to the next screen.' The sound of his own voice in the silent office is comforting, reminding him strangely of Samar in its clipped precision.

He grabs a towel from the supply closet, dampening it with bottled water, to clean himself, his eyes racing across the screens, steadily building a working pattern. Twenty, east. And twelve. The Refuge and the central arcade. The gunmen seem concentrated mostly in the main tower, closest to the entrance, its sea front vistas providing the best visuals for television broadcasts, Arcadia's familiar façade as riveting in terror as it is in aspiration. The Garden Café appears to have been closed off, its heavy double doors sealed shut. Amongst the sunlit tables, he can see the casualties, and the fear, and then with a twinge of pride, the calm organisation by the ageing maître d' moving through the terrified and the wounded, offering aid with his usual gentleness.

Then turning to the hotel exchange, he finds the receiver, his mind racing over the numbers, first the administration desks in the other three towers. On the monitors from the grounds, he can see the police vehicles arriving and taking positions. 'I want you to shut down access between the towers. Now! Yes, I know but just bolt the doors now. All of them. Yes the police are on their way. Just shut off access to north tower.' His voice is more authoritative than he generally allows, and his fingers fly across the keyboard, switching to cameras for the other towers as he watches his staff, receptionists, bellboys, security, even some guests, racing across the restaurants, the gym, the gardens, the courtyards, drawing metal, wood, bronze, doors to the north tower shut. He hopes they will stay safe, that they will be evacuated, even though a part of him is cursing himself for ordering the trapdoor shut around him. There is no way out now for him, no way to leave his office, and he wonders how long, if at all, the re-enforced double doors will hold off the assailant.

'Oh fuck!' As he switches the cameras back to north tower, he notices that that the gunmen have rounded up a dozen guests, just outside the glassed in expanse of the Refuge, renowned for its magnificent rooftop views of the city, packed most nights with the city's finest and most beautiful. Inside the bar, there are signs of mayhem already unleashed, spilt glasses, tablecloths askew, overturned chairs. And at least from some angles, he thinks he can see people scattered on the floor, a man slumped on to a table, one gorgeous woman flung back on the sofa in the corner.

For an instant he feels a panic build. Wasn't Dieter supposed to be at the Refuge? Waiting for Abhi to finish his shift and join him? Abhi scans the cameras, with growing frustration, taps out a quick message on his phone, hoping Dieter will answer quickly, then pushes away all thoughts except the present. 'Focus, Abhi, focus!' he orders himself sternly, his voice a credible imitation of Baba's. Slowly, he can feel the panic recede, his nerves steadying. As he scans the screens, he knows he is even perverse enough to feel grateful that the bar was mostly empty, maybe a dozen guests and a skeletal bar staff.

Some part of his brain is cold and calculating, observing, making sense of the enemy, plotting his own strategy even though he now knows that this was not a military op, just a project to create mayhem.

He scrubs himself with the towel, wiping his hands, his smeared cell phone, his face with it, leaving the pristine white cotton bloodied. Gingerly lowering himself on a chair before the main console, he calls up the occupancy list on screen. He can feel his soaking, stinking clothes sticking to the plush fabric of the chair, the sick cocktail of body fluids seeping into the cushions. He desperately needs to clean himself up. The blood of the young receptionist clinging to his shirt, staining his flesh, keeps him just at the edge of nausea. There would be time for that, he tells himself firmly, systematically calling up each occupied room, beginning from the one closest to the rooftop bar and the gunmen.

LONDON
14 WEEKS AGO

'Did you buy the flat?' David had asked her the last time they met. Such an English question. He had answered it too, 'Of course, your kind doesn't own things,' even before she could frame a response. It was a question she had been asked before, by friends, colleagues, even near strangers. She always hesitates for an instance before dismissing it with some banal answer. But from David the question hurt more.

David's words made her seem vaguely dangerous, foot-loose and irresponsible, like one of those fabled Chelsea girls who live from party to party, or perhaps from one lover to the next. Perhaps a sort of professional mistress, who has sex on demand, is welcoming and sweet, and never asks too many questions, something out of those post-war novels. Perhaps she should spend their hours of lovemaking differently. Just maybe, just once, she should tell him about her work, about the choices she has to make, about long hours spent with developing fluids that leave her lightheaded and nauseous.

Or perhaps she could talk of grocery bills and choosing home electronics. Although in all fairness, she recognises that her home electronic choices are limited; that her grocery shopping consists mostly of frozen dinners and bottles of Macallan's twelve-year-old. She winces, then grins at the thought. Talking of grocery bills would still not make her the kind of woman David has married and with whom he raises his children.

For a moment, she wonders if she should tell him about her images. Would knowing her photographs make him think of her differently? After all, those long years ago, it was David who had pushed her to follow photography as a career. 'You have the talent, so why do you want to waste it?' he had asked her again and again,

17

in that past lifetime. All she had known was that she loved the camera, felt whole, protected, behind the viewfinder, empowered when she could see a snapshot in her mind. She was using her talent, she argued. But that had not been enough for David.

'Press photographs are not enough,' he had insisted, while she collapsed in exhaustion in yet another anonymous hotel bed, the heavy phone receiver pressed between the pillow and her ear. 'You could do better,' his voice would ring over the trans-oceanic static, demanding that she produce new work, that she experiment and develop and create something special. For the world, for herself. And most of all, for him.

She had allowed herself back then to believe that David's interest in her work, her talent as he called it, meant that he loved her, that he loved a part of her she tried to hide even from herself. But then he had fallen in love, with someone else, someone who didn't have to have a talent, someone who would become his bride. So perhaps he hadn't ever loved Sam after all. Or perhaps having a talent was not enough to be loved or loveable.

When she was honest enough, she would also ask herself if she had ever loved David, or indeed any man at all. She knows that she wishes for arms to wrap around her on lone long nights when she huddles in her bed, shaking in fear or sorrow, or just post-traumatic stress. Sometimes, in a rare moment of serenity, when she is on assignment travelling in a far land, she wishes there were someone next to her, a body she could lean against while watching a sunrise. And most of all she wishes that desire would not need to be sated alone, or through dissatisfied fumblings with a stranger. On those nights, she wants a lover who knows her, who can satisfy her without questions and probing and hesitation, a lover whose geography she can see in her mind's eye, even when they are miles and years apart. But then the moment passes and the noise and fury of the world erupts around her. And all she can notice and remember and caress is trapped within her viewfinder, shuddering below her tense index finger.

18

There is no room for lovers on the disaster trail, Sam knows. It is hard enough trying to remain alive alone without worrying about a dear one in the battlefield. When the loneliness becomes unbearable, she reminds herself of the images in her collection: those who have lost a loved one; faces that reveal a silent desolation far greater than any she can imagine.

Sam doesn't use the images of the bereft for her art. Those faces pay her bills at the agency because newspaper readers like to see those grieving relatives, arms outstretched, mouths flung open, tears streaming down from eyes that will never encounter what they seek. A mother crumbled against rubble, only her wildly deranged *hijab* identifying her as Palestinian. Or is it Baghdad? Kabul? No matter, the defeated shoulders, the cracked, dirty fingernails, the tears clearing trails through the grime on her cheeks are eloquent enough.

A man huddled in a watery doorway, his skin melting infinitely into the dark beyond, only identifiable as American by his weight and heavy golden rings on his chubby fingers. Sam sighs in relief, pleased at least some images can be located.

A child covered in blood, screaming silence against a metallic sheet of military green. Where was that? She has no memory around that image. No way of identifying the place or time or disaster that broke that innocent heart. After a while, she had realised, the grieving look exactly the same. Perhaps that is why the newspapers like carrying those photographs.

That is why Sam shoots the grieving to pay her bills, but only uses the dead for her art. For the gigantic canvases that she painstakingly stretches over metres of blank gallery walls: portraits in black and white that obsessively explore the tranquillity death bestows to human faces; scores of close-ups replicated and repeated in minute squares over enormous collages. Despite the thousands of faces and the passage of many years, Sam's art only ever uses images of the dead.

The critics have been kind to her, even from that first exhibition, so many years ago, writing of the political significance of her work, hailing her as a new talent in the field. They praise the composition, attention to details, and dramatic use of light and shade. Though she now takes no notice of the reviews, there was a time, so very long ago, in the years after David's wedding, when Sam had taken the compliments as her due. Each accolade was evidence that she had outgrown her lover, that she had no need of one. After all, hadn't she spent those years traversing the world, arriving in the wake of each fresh disaster? Landing alongside crates of foreign aid, riding on the back of UN trucks, sitting silently alongside yet another forgotten interpreter. She had shamelessly used all privileges that her press card could bring her, sweet-talking her way into hurricanes and wars, floods and suicide bombings. And each time, she scoured the streets for the same missing face, the only one she wanted to find in her pain, love, and loathing: David's blue-lipped, swollen face on yet another cadaver.

In the rush of putting that first exhibition together, Sam had never really given a thought to the way her parents would react to her photographs. All she had wanted was to bask in their pride, share her glory with them, perhaps even reassure them that she was fine, and not nursing a broken heart at all. After all, hadn't she shared the stories of her wild adventures with her father over chilled beers, explaining how MSF or the UN troops had shipped her out on their last plane, last convoy out? She felt a kinship with her father, believed that he understood her urge for adventure, her need to go to that thin edge where a sole second stood guard between life and death.

But what really drove her to farther extremes each time was that lack of understanding in her mother's eyes. She had noticed it early, as a child, when her mother would look at her slightly bemused. Sam secretly called it her mother's ET look. Ignoring her close resemblance to her mother, she fantasised about being an alien changeling, secretly swapped in the cradle, unknowingly fostered by her mother. For many years, as a child, she comforted herself with the fantastic notion that the aliens would one day return for her, that one day that look of bafflement would no longer exist. But the aliens never came, and her mother's bafflement grew alongside Sam.

This is why she had ensured that her parents would be the first to see her first exhibition, in that prestigious gallery that had only ever included a handful of photographers. The photographs would place her, announce her, declare herself to her parents the way her being could not. The photographs would not only speak for her but make them understand.

She had instructed her parents to come over before the inauguration, arranged for her agent to collect and bring them over just after she and the curator had conducted a final revision of the prints. And of course, the ever trustworthy Stella had dutifully brought them over to St Francis-in-the-Field, the ancient church salvaged from realtors and resuscitated as an art gallery, the cavernous apse of grey-brown stone, and half a dozen low-roofed, tiny chapels providing the perfect backdrop for Sam's photographs.

She had told the receptionist to call her out when her parents arrived. She wanted to walk them through the great doors, into the vast vaulted hallway, the innards of the ancient abandoned church dim and eerie, and lit only by the spots that illuminated her giant images.

She had agonised over the selection for the first image, mounted between two pillars, near the entrance to the gallery, at the very edge of the ancient narthex. It had to be the definitive shot, shocking, arresting, compelling, seducing the visitor into the nave, echoing the cleansing agony of the now-erased images that had decorated the stone walls for centuries before.

That first shot had also been the most powerful. She had carefully selected a single shot of that boy in the doorway, his head turned at an unnatural angle, the blacks, whites and greys providing texture and depth. The shadows in the hut beyond the doorway were blurred and squat, like indistinct spirits of the underworld. In blowing up the image for printing on the four metre square canvas, it had lost a lot of the sharpness of the original, blurring the gentle features of the boy, making him seem like anyone, everyone. She had been so very proud of the result.

And she had never expected her parents to be anything other than proud of her. In that first instance, as she had walked her parents through the pillared atrium, Sam had heard a sharp intake of breath from her mother, a reaction that she had to confess she had hoped for. But then her mother's face seemed to crumple as she looked on the boy. 'Oh my poor child,' she had whispered, her hand blindly reaching out for support. Sam's father had immediately taken it in his, comforting and drawing comfort. 'What have we done?' she had blinked up at her husband, his face equally full of horror. Sam looked on, bewildered, as her mother seemed to grow more distraught.

Baffled, she looked to her father for understanding. Yet his face was closed, his eyes blank and distant, staring at the grim cavern beyond the first photograph, perhaps not even noticing the many images, giant and small, solitary and collaged, that filled those depths. 'Sam, it would be best if we wait outside. I think it a bit stuffy for your mother here,' he explained, his voice gentle as ever, before firmly turning his back on Sam's images, leading her mother out. Sam watched them leave, bewildered, bereft and as always slightly envious of her parents' obvious closeness.

'I think that proves our point, my dear,' Stella's clipped voice was approving behind her. 'The most powerful exhibition this city has seen in a while.'

Sam nodded, but still unsure, seeking solace, comfort, once again with her dead. At least they spoke her language, understood her completely. Once again, she thanked the gods, or chance, accident, or whatever stroke of luck that had brought them to her. Since that first meeting, Sam has found herself looking for the dead, finding reassurance and companionship from them.

As she stands in the cool nave, she shudders, at the thought that she had found them entirely by accident, had almost never found them at all, in that tropical village the soldiers had

22

occupied for the night. She had positioned herself on a rise beyond, hiding in the foliage with her guides, ready to run and hide, to produce her press ID in a last vain attempt to escape. She had been young enough to feel self-righteous then and convinced that her photographs meant something. The world would see the images of cruelty, brutality, senseless murders. And the world would intervene to stop these desperate, poorly clad men who couldn't even afford bullets, who did their killing, mutilating, with machetes.

The massacre had gone on for hours, beginning just after midnight and ending just as the first cool sliver of dawn crept through the undergrowth. She had huddled in fear at first, trying to shut out the incessant screams, the two initial shots. 'That is all the bullets they have money for,' her guide had told her. She had disbelieved him for a few brief moments, until the soldiers had begun using the machetes. Through the telescopic lens of the Canon, she had confirmed that disciplined violence, the random selection among victims who would be dispatched with a single well-placed stroke and those who would suffer multiple slashes.

In that first hour, or perhaps it was less, her index finger had pressed on like an automaton, or perhaps the finger that pulls a trigger, clicking incessantly as she focused, captured, shot. She took her eye away only long enough to reload.

The first time she needed to reload, she had made the mistake of looking up from the viewfinder and been baffled by the distance and silence that separated her and the killings. The sounds – the dull thwack of the machetes, the shrill screams, the pulse of running feet – that she had been sure had been punctuating her shots were inaudible.

She always used black and white film, and the sudden green of the foliage, the dull brown of the huts, disorientated her further. A sick taste grew in the back of her throat, a loud wild roaring in her ears. Pushing down the nausea, she had fumbled to change the reel, snapping open the camera by instinct, transferring the exposed film to her right pocket, reaching for a new roll in her left. It had been instinct that had helped her load the camera again, even as the sickness made her light-headed. Had she caught the jungle-fever? Malaria? Last thing she needed now was to be ill.

But the darkness in her eyes had cleared once she lifted the camera and placed her pupil in the centre of the viewfinder. The nausea had receded as the world in the tiny square grew vivid again and the roar in her ears gave way to the now-familiar sounds of murder. Her breath seemed to suddenly flow again, surprising her with the thought that she had been holding it. But the slight taste of sick stayed in her mouth, a persistent reminder not to look away.

She had not made that mistake again, remembering to turn away entirely before removing the camera from before her face. After that initial hour, she had grown discerning, carefully selecting the shots she wanted. Finding faces, bodies, actions that she felt communicated some emotion, some innate aesthetic. Within minutes, she grew, experience transforming her instinctively from the barbarism of the murderer to the ascetic sophistication of the sniper. Steadily, all that she had learned of photography, all the lessons from art history classes, came back to guide her choices: composition, angle, light, shadows.

Slowly, meticulously, she had moved through the mayhem unfolding before her, eventually choosing a particularly graceful soldier whose machete rose and fell with the elegance of a ballet dancer. His slim back seemed to tense with each movement, the darkening sweat patches growing across his dark cotton shirt. His feet, encased in a pair of blinding white sneakers stepped lightly, almost floating above the dirt and gore that was collecting on the ground. He was young, innocent almost, with a smooth baby face that lit up with joy and vitality. Perhaps because he was so alive, so energetic, she had continued to shoot him through the night.

The next morning, when the village had finally fallen silent, her party had walked down, the guides insisting that she needed to photograph the aftermath. How could Sam explain that she had already used up much of her stash of film. With barely a dozen unexposed frames left, she had followed them, only out of politeness.

She hadn't really wanted to look. The flies were already gathering on the dead, making a buzzing sound that was annoying for its constancy. Without the viewfinder, the bleeding colours were obvious, like kitschy travesties of the aesthetic she had encountered the night before: greens, reds, ochres, browns, blacks, all blending into each other. She hadn't really been looking at all, even as her guides ran from one cadaver to another, pointing out the wounds, the mutilations some of the lumps had suffered even after death.

But that was before she had passed the doorway. Just a rough arch cut into a mud hut, with nothing but darkness inside. Spread-eagled across the threshold was a single body, a slight one, like that joyous soldier from the night before; a young man, naked, lying half-turned on his side. The mud floor below had absorbed all blood, so it seemed that he was asleep, albeit in an awkward angle. His arms pulled close to his chest, his head flung back, his legs spread slightly and disappearing into the darkness beyond. It was that fragile plane of his hip that caught her eye; so familiar and yet so alien. The jutting bone pushed against brown skin, gleamed in the growing morning light, the lean plane of his upper leg disappearing into the gloom. Shadows reached up from the depths of the hut and bled into the hollow of his stomach.

She never remembers lifting the camera, or composing the shot, or even clicking that frame. But in her mind's eye, she recalls every frame that she shot of that young boy. And in the story that makes sense of her life, that is the image that marks her calling. She knows now that she stayed long before that doorframe, mesmerised, enchanted, obsessed. Stayed rooted until her guides had called her away, led her away from the village and back into the forest.

'Please make sure the world sees these,' her guide had pleaded repeatedly as he led her back across the border. 'We need the world to help.' She had nodded, silently, in what he had assumed to be agreement. What was his name? Julio? Peter? Ahmed? Some name she has long forgotten.

Guides for death tours are also the same all over the world, she has learned. In the early years, she would send cards, little gifts of gratitude, a copy of the clippings from the newspaper when the photographs were published. Then the list of disasters grew too long and their pleas for help began to wear her down, or perhaps she just grew tired of learning how many of them had died. That is when she began handing out their fees in cash – always local currency, began walking away and never looking back over her shoulder.

They still offer her scraps of paper with their names, addresses, phone numbers, and increasingly, email addresses. She takes those sullied business cards, filthy scraps of notebook paper, gleaming foil from cigarette packets with a smile, always with words of hope and kindness. Always with a promise that she will try to help, send them what they need: a packet of antibiotics, bandages, schoolbooks, Nike sneakers.

The night before leaving for a new destination, she has a final ritual. She spends hours filing her photographs, backing them up on memory sticks, uploading them to a special account online. She packs, still conscientious, even though she knows that she travels light and nothing that she carries is irreplaceable, or even has memories. And then finally, before climbing into bed, she cleans out her pockets, collecting all those little scraps of paper, piling them into a small pyre in the bathroom sink. She sets it alight, always with a wooden matchstick. Using lighters seems disrespectful for what has become her private funeral rite.

The scraps splutter and hiss at first, every time. She knows it's the chemical coating on paper, but the sounds always seem like a protest. When they finally settle into ash, she lets the taps run, letting the water wash away the last of the grey specks. She thanks her fortune that now she can afford to stay in hotels with running water for most part. In the early years, the ritual always required her to sacrifice some of her precious bottled water to wash away the ashes. In a strange way, it had felt more appropriate, the fear of thirst cleansing her with a sense of righteousness as she kept watch over the brief flickering flames. Now, like much else, she feels nothing but a sense of relief when the ashes finally disappear into the sinkhole.

But once the relief is over, when the last speck of grey and black disappears down the drain, Sam is again left clutching the edges of her resolve. That is the instant when a gaping chasm opens up in her stomach threatening to swallow her again in a reminder of that first despair. For an instant, bent over the sink, she too grieves, not emotionally, not even consciously, but in a sudden swell of physical memory where the loss and pain cut through her. Like that very first time she had returned from the jungle, with her very first death mask photo. And in its wake, the obsession returns to grip her again.

THE ARCADIA
64 HOURS AGO

Sam prepares meticulously for her excursion, first painstakingly constructing a functional floor-plan for the Arcadia from all she can find online: maps, photographs, sketches. She scans press reports and tourist brochures for any building quirks that may turn into a death trap, looks through any reports for construction and renovation, making notes of any anomaly that catches her eye. She googles till she finds an initial floor-plan in an architectural archive.

To minimise any noise being heard in the corridor, she moves the printer provided by the hotel from the office alcove in the suite to the bathroom, balancing it over one of the twin glass sinks and prints out the information, taping the A4 sheets on tiles along the giant lit mirror till they are nearly all covered in print, maps, her notes scrawled over the sheets in blue and red ink. The mirror she uses for her sketch, carefully drawing out a working floor plan with the thick black and red markers she always carries with her.

It isn't till she is sure that she has memorised the ground plan that she turns to check for the news updates. Two explosions in the north wing, seemingly over the atrium, are running in a loop on various news channels. Flames leap out from the gaping rents in the glass ceiling perhaps making it easier for the long range pressurised hoses spraying the building from a distance beyond the reach of gunfire. She puts up a red mark on the mirror. Then frowning alternately at the TV screen and her floor-plan, she wipes out a section with toilet paper and redraws the northern wing in black.

Sam ignores the dramatic footage, dismissing it as prosaic, instead surfing rapidly for current news on the tickers which carry the same facts: up to a dozen gunmen, rapidly rising number of casualties, possibly five hundred hostages and the hotlines number for embassies, emergency services, victims information

28

bases. Disappointed but not surprised, she turns online for updates. Logging in to Twitter, she rapidly, steadily, checks her own timeline: nothing incriminating or life-threatening. Her journalist buddies know better than to place her in the Arcadia in such a public forum, even if they know that she's here.

Flicking through the hash-tags, she selects a dozen handles to follow, instinctively picking the ones that seem the reliable, cross-checking their updates against other reports, confirming their reliability against her list of fellow journalists. She sets up a list, desultorily naming it Urban Tweeps, tabbing it so she can update herself in real time. She knows few online will find her with such keywords or indeed connect her list to the on-going attack beyond her door. Then holding her phone in one hand, her hand poised over the laptop, she scrolls rapidly through the Twitter feed, beginning to locate the information on the floor plan on the mirror with bright red x marks.

@_cityboy211 Gunfire in the north wing. 22:15. Looks like tenth floor. Fire still burning in atrium.

@_lovehighheels753 LPC. Terrorists are on the eleventh floor. Shooting randomly, knocking on doors, killing anyone who answers. WTF?

@_Gunnersfan420 Looks like they're making their way systematically down. Gun fire was on 14 about 30 min ago.

@_Breaking897 Terrorist attack at the Arcadia. Many feared dead. Police say north wing has been isolated as they evacuate the rest of the hotel.

@_cosmogirl601 RT @CityNews #Arcadia management warning guests to stay indoors, not open to knocks. Are trying to contact all in the north wing.

@_RussAlexNews263 Reported terror attack at #HotelArcadia. Number of hostages unconfirmed. Unknown number of assailants in the north wing.

She has learned that online is no different from real life where she lets her instinct guide her to pick her translators, her taxi drivers, and fixers. Online she does the same, scanning through the cacophony to pick her guides, following them instinctively even as she consistently cross-checks their updates with other sources.

Increasingly, Sam prefers Twitter contacts to real life ones, picking handles to follow when necessary, choosing a combination of citizen journalists and colleagues, mixing them up with local media and activist organisations. They are faster and more accurate, she knows. Besides, they don't expect payment, or polite conversation, or even sympathy. When she unfollows them after her assignment is over, she feels little more than relief, that it is over with just a few clicks. Besides, she can be invisible with her online contacts, just another follower on a growing list of thumbnail photos and tiny descriptive blurbs, with little or no exchange at all with someone who may end up as her subject in the future. And Sam knows well that invisibility makes for better protection than all armour.

It is not till she has spread out her work kit on the bed that she notices that the red light flickering silently on the phone.

'Ma'am this is Abhi Sikarwal from the Arcadia.' She recognises the voice immediately, feeling slightly annoyed at his persistence.

The voice pauses, as if struggling for words. 'Ma'am, could you please not go out. It is very dangerous.'

'And what makes you think I will?'

'Ma'am, I am familiar with your work. In fact, I love your photographs.' The voice is slightly hesitant.

'Thanks. I would be happy to have my agent send through a catalogue for the hotel.' Sam hoped he could hear the sarcasm despite the whisper.

'Actually, ma'am. That's not why I called. I know you are tempted to go out there, but would you please not do so. Ma'am, this is not a time for heroics.'

'Oh for fuck's sake! There aren't any heroics!' Despite her annoyance, she remembers to softly replace the received without a sound in the cradle.

Instead, focusing on her kit, she spreads the equipment out on the sheets before her: two cameras, the Mamiya and the Canon Eos, extra memory cards, extra battery packs, her phone now recharging to full battery, an extra Nokia loaded with only a half-dozen emergency numbers, nearly weightless, fully charged and set to silent, just in case. And then the Lumix – she has recently been converted to the DMC-LX3, for its ridiculous speed and ease of use. Not great for art, of course, but Sam knows she can get her best on the run snaps with it.

She begins to edit her mental list, removing and replacing items on the bed as she goes along. Not two cameras plus the Lumix. Two would add weight and she doesn't want to carry a bag. So just the Mamiya, with the 150 mm lens. It is better for low lit shots, which is what she expects to take. She halves the battery packs and then removes half the memory cards, neatly storing them back in her bag, zipping it and storing it carefully back under the bed.

Next she pulls out her work clothes: a still filthy long sleeve shirt, the deep-pocketed combat trousers, her usual thick rubber-soled boots. Fortunately she had checked in too late to hand these for cleaning to the hotel laundry! Still the smell of old sweat makes her wrinkle her nose before she resolutely changes into the unwashed gear. Finally she pulls on the black knit beanie, tugging it low on her forehead, pulling it over her ears.

***

Abhi has never been more grateful for the extra set of clothes he keeps in his office as he gingerly drops his blood-and-vomit soaked clothes into the waste-bin, rubs himself down yet again with towels. The stench seems to have seeped into his skin, impossible to wash off, even to scrub off with disinfecting lotion. Be grateful that at least the clothes are fresh, he tells himself, pulling on a clean T-shirt.

The panic he felt in the lobby is receding with each organised step he takes. He has called every room, spoken he is convinced to every living guest. He glances at the clock, twenty-five minutes to go before he begins another round of calling each occupied room, checking for survivors, updating and comforting his guests. He has even patched through to the police headquarters who tell him the re-enforcements are on the way; that a hostage situation needs time to resolve, that they will act as soon as possible. He wants to scream, cry, give vent to what he knows should be terror but something cold and steady seems to have gripped him from within: his voice never quivers any more, his hands are steady as he sips on a bottle of water. Maybe he is more like Samar after all.

Abhi shakes himself alert, chiding himself for letting his mind wander as the external line screeches again.

'Yes sir, from the CCTV, I have spotted ten assailants, armed heavily, working in teams of two.' Abhi tells the police chief, searching his mind for the name, even as he realises there is little point. 'Yes sir, they look trained, maybe military. We may need to consider rations.' Even to his own ears, his voice sounds extraordinarily steady, in control, as he returns to the monitor screens. 'Our guests will only have the mini-bar.' Still he is touched when the police chief enquires about his own rations before hanging up. So perhaps not quite like Samar. At least not yet.

His compassion is instinctive, as he works the internal phone lines, much like being back at school when he comforted and encouraged the younger kids in his house.

'Yes, ma'am, you can use the water from the tap. During emergencies only.'

'No sir, the police are doing what they can, but I recommend you stay put.'

'Yes, of course, I understand you will need your medication. I am sure it will all be sorted soon enough.'

Organising others helps him force down the panic he feels every time he scans the wall of screens. Most are empty of all action, showing nothing but long corridors, empty and desolate. The ones from the Garden Café are full of people, some injured but most huddled and afraid in the corner; someone had been quick enough to lock the heavy carved, metal embellished doors when the shooting started in the lobby. Perhaps it is that same waiter that lies in the far corner, his white shirt stained and ripped, someone constantly bending over to check on his breathing, on the makeshift bandage wrapped around his chest.

But Abhi tries to avoid some of the other screens, even though he knows those are the ones he must monitor most closely. On those screens, men, always in pairs, stalk their prey, methodical and alert. They appear on the flickering squares suddenly, moving into the frame from the lift, or the fire escape doors on the far ends of each floor. They hold their automatic rifles with their right hands, the straps slung across their bodies, ready to fire at the first sign of movement. They knock on the doors, sometimes kicking them repeatedly, as if trying to frighten anyone hiding within.

Initially Abhi had wondered why they had not disabled any of the cameras but now he knows better. Their goal is to terrorise, to give a better show than any the world has seen before. The CCTV cameras are their allies in the grimmest reality TV show ever filmed. Abhi has learned this from the massacre in the viewing gallery not long after he had taken up the monitoring. One of the gunmen had turned to smirk at the camera, flexed index finger like a pistol and mock-shot at the camera in the corner. It was a gesture used by every self-respecting rapper on MTV but frightening in its banality when surrounded by at least a dozen slumped dead and dying. Abhi had vomited again then, barely managing to grab the plastic waste-paper bin under the desk.

He has avoided looking at those screens, glancing only occasionally to ensure that he is still keeping an accurate record of the gunmen's movements. 'Face the fear. Focus, train, act,' he

33

mutters over and over again, bringing up Samar's old childhood chant, breathing deeply.

Finally, giving his head a little shake, he grabs a clean chair, and pulls up the screen with room occupancies again. He has begun an Excel file: those he has located, those he believes are dead, those he has managed to warn, crosschecking against a secondary log on the print out of occupancies before him. Spreadsheets always help him focus his mind, to push out all emotions and replace them with a rational calm. He prays this one will help him keep his fears in check.

After the initial round, he plans to set up a schedule: one round of calls to every occupied room, even those that have not answered, every two hours until midnight. If the situation stayed static, he would then take a break till dawn, even though he already dreads the places where the long silent night would take his mind. The police headquarters are on an exclusive line, calling in updates, asking him for information on the gunmen, the gruff but friendly voice of the chief replaced by far more business-like tones of operational men. How bizarre that he, who can do nothing, can watch the assailants, while those who must act are blind without his information.

Shifting and resettling into the chair, he checks the time: three hours since those first shots in the lobby. Things look grim, but he is pleased that his nerves haven't given way, that his guests are cooperating, that he can do something, anything, to ensure their safety.

All, except that damn photographer in 1402.

He feels nothing but irritation at her. Some people just don't get danger when it smacks them on their face! What kind of an idiot thinks of heading straight into danger? And she is damn rude!

And yet as he finishes his scan, his eyes steadily moving across the wall of monitor screens, Abhi feels an inexplicable need to warn her again, to try to talk her out of her crazy idea.

'Ma'am, this is Abhi Sikarwal from Arcadia reception.'

'Ah. Have you found the ground plans then? Would you email them to me, please.' Her voice is pleasant, low, controlled.

'Actually, ma'am, no. We have a crisis situation and really it would be best if you stayed in your room.'

'Oh! That's fine. Thank you for letting me know.' Her voice is controlled, her resolute tone strangely familiar to Abhi.

'Ma'am, please. I am trying to manage this situation. And you're not making it easier.'

Something in his voice catches her attention. 'Are you alone then?'

'Not quite, ma'am.' Abhi chooses his words carefully, unsure if his words could be overheard. 'I need to ensure our guests are safe.'

'Well, then you should get on with that, shouldn't you?'

Abhi growls an epithet at the dead line. Then punches her number again.

***

As she prepares, Sam ignores the flickering red light on the phone. She knows it is the strangely persistent man from reception set on making her excursion into the action difficult. Instead, she continues to systematically load her cameras with fresh memory cards and batteries, pack her equipment into the pockets of her field jacket, buttoning and zipping as she finishes each pocket.

There is a military order to her preparations, each pocket marked by long habit for its particular use: the top left pocket is for fresh memory cards, the right for the used. She packs the batteries on the mid-right-hand side, the extra Nokia on the buttoned one on the left, even though it makes changing batteries just a little more difficult. Was it Guatemala where she had heard of a photographer who had been saved from a bullet straight to the heart, all because of his cell phone? Probably apocryphal, Sam knows, but it still comforts her to have the old brick-like Nokia nestle against her heartbeat. Her main smartphone will go into the cargoes, set on vibrate against her right thigh, ensuring a quick withdrawal but also no interference with her photo equipment.

35

She catches a glimpse of herself in the floor-length mirror as she zips up her jacket, pulling it up to the dark plain scarf wrapped around her neck: a slight figure, nondescript, unmemorable. Nothing feminine or attractive, more like a boy, all curves and softness of flesh hidden under her utilitarian uniform, even her thin hands are covered with non-skid gloves, with just half-fingers exposed for better handling of her equipment.

She is ready to head out the door when she gives in to temptation. The red light has flickered on the phone, insistently, non-stop for the past half hour.

'What now?' she growls into the receiver.

'Just saying good luck, ma'am.' Abhi's voice is soft.

She is surprised. 'Thank you.'

'And be careful, ma'am.'

'Thank you. I will. And don't call me ma'am.'

'Sure. I will check back. In sixty minutes. Until you are back.'

'Why?' Sam doesn't do check backs.

'You may need to de-brief, ma'am.' Abhi hangs up before she can respond though Sam is sure she heard a chuckle as she slides the receiver back into the cradle.

THE ARCADIA
61 HOURS AGO

Abhi doesn't realise he can watch Sam on the CCTV screens until he suddenly spots an unidentified person in a corridor. 'Oh for fuck's sake!' he begins to swear, another gunman? A guest? Someone he has missed? Then the floor number clicks. Fourteenth. Sam's floor.

She is most unlike what Abhi could have imagined. A small dark smudge on the grainy screen, moving slowly, cautiously, pressed against the creeping cream lilies of the wallpaper. Abhi stares as she fills three consecutive screens, barely visible on the two corner cameras, just a slight, ungraceful smear slowly creeping against the paleness, bleeding into the dark of the carpets.

On the third, he can see her clearly. Her right hand grips the camera that is strung across her body on its thick safety strap, ready to draw and shoot at an instant's notice. She is folded into a half-crouch, with her shoulders hunched a little, her head lowered as she reaches out with every sense. She moves in a crab-like movement, ungainly yet effective as she makes for the fire escape on the eastern edge of the tower.

Abhi is conscious of his disappointment. He knows her photographs, from fat coffee table books, from news reports of far off wars, has read about her canvases in the art magazines he has hoarded for years. He has felt a kinship with her vast reproductions of serenity on canvas although he only knows of them from magazines, of death forced into life, of the vitality of form and composition that taunt the finality of destruction. Even her voice on the phone has been equally vibrant, as if each syllable pushes past an iron dam of self-control, as if once let loose, her passions could sear down the line.

In his mind, he has imagined her as a tall woman, statuesque, powerful, beautiful. With long hair, high cheekbones, and dark

37

eyes. Not a clotheshorse like a fashion model, but full of curves and smooth planes, and light. The furtive creature, nearly willing itself into invisibility on the screens, seems to mock the image his mind has conjured.

But he watches her intently, compelled, terrified, as he glances back at another screen where a pair of gunmen are stalking through another gloomy corridor, with deep dark, plush carpets and shadowed pale walls. He has to check the letters at the corner to confirm the floor. Damn the Arcadia, every floor looks the same.

Abhi has always loved the obsessive uniformity of the lily patterned ivory wallpaper, the deep wine coloured carpets, the gold edged sconces that light the walls as much as they conceal, throwing out swathes of dim yellow light. He has long admired the familiarity of mahogany tables placed precisely at every ten feet, their gleaming dark surfaces each topped by a black glass vase, almost as tall as himself, filled always with even taller stalks of the same lilies that grace the walls. Now, as he flicks his eyes back and forth from the columns of CCTV screens, he swears to himself, his voice low, words forcing themselves out despite his clenched jaws. He can't tell the difference between the floors without checking on the system!

Then he notices! Sam is leaving a trail, setting up a warning system for herself as she moves slowly down the corridor, avoiding the bright patches of light thrown into the corridor from open doors. He punches the buttons on the keyboard before him, his eyes still glued to her slow moving grainy image. He shifts the screens for all the fourteenth floor cameras to the centre of the wall of screens, mentally noting the minor changes she has made, the changes that will let him distinguish her corridor from all others.

***

Sam debates leaving her room door slightly ajar, to hasten her re-entry. She hates the key-cards hotels use, always has to struggle

38

for minutes on end, sliding the card back and forth in the door slot, cursing as the green light refuses to come on.

'Ma'am, you have to be more patient, slower.' How many bellboys, concierges, cleaning maids have said that to her, when she has complained of being given a faulty key? Then they slide in the card smoothly, smiling kindly at her as if at a fussy child when the green light comes on and the door swings silently open.

She knows she will not have any extra precious minutes if the gunmen find her, pursue her. She will need to get past the lock, and fast.

But the thought of anyone accessing her fortress in her absence disturbs her even more. Her hotel rooms, like her flat back home, are special places, secret places where few gain access.

When Sam checks into a hotel, she obsessively follows the same ritual: requesting the desk that the cleaning staff must not enter her room, not even to clean. It doesn't really matter for most part, as she rarely stays on for more than forty-eight hours. In her room, she prepares her fortress just as obsessively, placing the chairs, shoe-rack, the complimentary trouser press in a subtle but effective obstacle course between the door and her bed. Any intruder must surely stumble, and slow down, create a racket, enough to wake her from even the deepest drunken slumber.

From her backpack, she pulls out a packet of small glow-in-the-dark stickers, cut into tiny, abstract shapes, and a spool of thin black thread. Carefully, she strategically places the glow-in-the-dark shapes across the doorway, along the edge of the closets, just under the linens of her bed, visible only to her or another who knows what to seek. Un-spooling the thread, she bites off lengths, placing them carefully on the door, on her backpack, marking her equipment not against theft, but to alert her against any interference. And she double bolts the door every night, propping a chair against the door-knob when possible, just jamming it against the door when she can't.

Over the years, Sam has started doing the same at her flat, although at home she has re-enforced the doors with metal sheets, and added bars to the narrow tall windows that look out at nothing but slim rectangles of sky. She doesn't invite friends over any more, keeping the vast loft with its bare hard-wood floors, haphazardly punctuated by fading, threadbare carpets, scattered with prints and paper and notebooks, entirely for herself. Only her desk in the far corner, near the built-in dark room is meticulously neat: its wide top obsessively organised with to-do lists on the top right, followed by a list of appointments and a desk calendar along the right edge, stationery and office equipment in their specific boxes along the top, her own edited notes along the left edge. The centre is dedicated to her prints, but only when she is working. Otherwise, she covers it with a plain piece of black felt, shrouding the pale pine work surface for long barren periods.

But now she plans to use the spool of thread to set up a network beyond the door, ensuring a warning system in case someone decides to enter her room and wait for her. The stickers she has snipped into even smaller slices, nearly invisible except to the knowing eye, hopefully also unnoticeable for the gunmen dealing in death outside. She hates hotels for their bland décor that disorientate her with its uniformity, confuse her sense of direction and distance, blending everything into one indifferent mass. The glow-in-the-dark slivers will hopefully guide her back, lighting her way to safety, like the shiny pebbles from a fairy story. She likes the whimsy, hopes that the slivers seem like nothing more than a child's lost treasures, even to the most hardened assailant.

She remains divided about locking the door, afraid that her usual inability to work the automated locks may put her at risk. Count till five when you swipe the card, she reminds herself. That is the only way to make them work. Besides, as she tells herself, patting her pockets to automatically check her gear one last time, what if someone entered the room and were waiting

40

for her? That would be riskier. No, she would need to rely on stealth not speed, hope that she could lose her pursuers if they discovered her. With a soft sigh, she slides the key-card into a small outer pocket high on her shoulder and buttons it up securely.

She checks on the dark scarf, feeling the collar of her jacket to ensure all ends are tucked in securely. She tugs on the edge of her cap, covering her bare scalp, the small, delicate ears, pulling it to the edge of the scarf, to cover the vulnerable softness at the back of her head. Then crouching slightly, she slides the door open a crack, listens for a long instant even though she knows from the heavy silence that gunmen are elsewhere, then peeps out. After a moment, letting her eyes get accustomed to the shadowy corridor, she eases herself out, sliding the door shut behind her.

***

'Don't head downstairs, please,' Abhi mutters at the smudge on the screen, automatically checking the occupancy list for the floor that the gunmen are stalking, knocking, kicking at doors. One of them lets off a short, random burst down the shadowy length, shattering a tall vase that shivers and then crumbles, huge shards of glass shattering on the mahogany, slipping silently on to the thick carpet, the lilies spreading like gleaming jewels on the murk.

Eight rooms have guests. He mentally crosschecks his list of calls. He has got through to them and can now only hope that they will hold their nerve. Flicking back up the column of screens, Abhi sees Sam slowly edge open the door to the eastern fire escape.

'Shit!' Sam would be out of visual contact while in the stairwell. He tries to imagine how long she would need to traverse each floor as she disappears into the gloom, the door slowly easing back behind her. Twenty-five steps between each floor, he knows, but that only makes sense when walking or running. He has no idea where Sam will go, or how, or even if she will encounter any of the gunmen. Abhi lets out a string of expletives, cursing himself, the gunmen, Sam, life, everything he can think of and can't control.

On the twelfth floor, the gunmen are methodically covering the passageway. Abhi keeps his fingers crossed as he watches them reach a fire escape without counting any casualties. All doors remain locked, sealed. He hopes there are no sounds that will make them try to break down the doors.

But the relief is short-lived. The E12 on the edge of the CCTV screen is a reminder that the gunmen are heading into the same fire escape as Sam. His fingers curled tightly, Abhi watches as the gunmen let out a final burst of gunfire, then disappear into the stairwell, the fire door swinging slowly till the halfway mark, then slamming shut behind them.

Frantically his eyes race across the screens, looking for that familiar smudge. First across the wall, then speeding down the columns. Then back across again.

He doesn't realise that he has been holding his breath when an almost imperceptible movement locks his gaze. E16. A solitary smudge slips into the corridor, crouching, almost crawling on hands and knees, using shadows for cover. For a long moment, the figure waits, calculating, considering, observing, then slides back into the fire escape.

Abhi lets out his breath, his fingers relaxing slightly. She will go up, he realises oddly unsurprised, towards the carnage.

***

Sam waits, crouched at her door, to get her bearings. Then bending slightly, she places a glow-in-the-dark star against the heavy door frame, burying it carefully in the thick pile of the carpet. Keeping her back against the wall, staying well in the shadows, she makes her way to the nearest table, one of the many that line the corridors. From the tall arrangement of lilies, Sam plucks two fronds of something green and feathery, placing them carefully on the polished dark table top, on the edge closest to her room, their stems facing in opposite directions.

Her senses are taut, her right hand gripping the Mamiya, her finger steady, tense, ready to shoot.

Still silence.

Sam makes her way down the corridor, moving in the slow, ungainly, half-crouch she has used so often in the past. She knows it will give her a back-ache later, but she has learned that it helps her keep her senses alert, lets her move fast, in silence, without attracting much attention. It also masks all trace of her femininity, which is important, for Sam knows that there are things humans can do to each other that are worse than death. And too often, those things happen to women.

Halfway down the corridor, a vase lies shattered, glass spread over the plush carpet, lilies scattered, the water seeping into the floor, staining the carpet a darker colour. Sam snaps a few desultory frames, composing the mess with a wide-angle first, then moving in for close-ups.

Careful not to disturb the mess, she moves a few stalks, imperceptibly changing their positions to cover the width of the corridor, sure to be trod on by anyone who would not be slinking along the walls, anyone who stalked down the corridor to terrorise.

Further down the corridor, some of the doors have been flung open, their doorways throwing out squares of brightness on the dark carpet. She stops at the first, listening carefully, her nerves leaning into the silence before peeking in. Beyond the heavy frame, the carpet changes colour, to a rich cream, perhaps better to show up a thin weaving trail, like a line of ants that ends near the bed, at the lone man slumped there.

Sam's right hand comes up automatically, the viewfinder lining up at the target as her eyes flick over the plain shirt with a loosened silk tie, its pattern barely discernible against the bloodstains, the heavy jowls and rounded belly, all telling of a life lived in luxury. She notes the heavy wristwatch, then the stubby fingers, stained and flaccid, a single wide gold band gleaming on one. Slightly repulsed, she lowers her hand, her finger easing the pressure on the button slowly, gently.

Sam thinks of the dead, her dead, in aesthetic terms, constantly selecting, editing, choosing, judging. This is why she only chooses the very beautiful, the ones left untouched, untainted, un-mutilated for her portraits. The others, the brutalised, dismembered, and ugly, she shoots with disdain, with just enough care to pass on to her sincere human rights contacts, or if they are not too gruesome, to her editor. But she hardly ever shoots the common, constantly seeking the extremes, the beautiful and the grotesque brought together by her viewfinder to form the perfect aesthetic balance.

The man before her, with his overflow of flesh and common-place insignia of comfortable ordinariness repulses her. Even his posture, slumped, half-upright against the still made, pristine bed, is clichéd. No editor would want the shot, bereft of all pathos, replete only in its mediocrity.

Maybe later, once she has seen the other floors, if there are no other options, she tells herself as she backs out of the room, mentally downgrading him on her list. At the doorway, she pauses. Without a glance back at the room, she bends down and places a barely visible length of thread across the doorway.

Sam doesn't bother going into the other rooms, simply peering in from the doorway for confirmation, placing lengths of thread on the doorways, always in a slightly different place, always sure to be disturbed by anyone who crossed the thresholds. Slowly, deliberately, she makes her way to the end of the corridor.

There she stops. Turning, she checks each open doorway, the pattern of lilies on the floor near her room, reminds herself of the shadows the tables throw, memorising the markers she has placed. Then, convinced she has prepared sufficiently for a safe return, she reaches out to heavy fire escape door, easing it open slowly, carefully, pausing to listen for a long moment. Then she slides silently into the gap, sliding the door shut behind her.

SOMEWHERE IN THE FOOTHILLS
MANY YEARS AGO

In his secret dreams, he was somewhere far from their little house in the foothills, far from the cantonment grounds where the black-shrouded trucks seemed to pick a different home every day for their terrible, mournful visit. 'The soldier stands guard on the border, so all those millions who don't even know of us can sleep in peace,' Baba would declare, convinced that his sons were going to someday take over the thankless duty of standing guard. But Abhi wanted to be one of those feckless millions who never had to spare a thought for war.

Instead he had nursed fantasies of a life that was farthest from the dust and dirt, sweat and guns and blood that his brother and Baba so idolised. 'A soldier fights not because he loves to fight, but so that he will never have to,' his father was fond of saying, his bearing as soldierly as ever. Samar had nodded in solemn agreement, listening avidly to Baba's stories, hungrily staring at the military medals that lay nestled in the wood and glass case on Baba's desk, planning wild exploits that would get him his own set. They had all assumed that Abhi, with his quiet, dreamy ways, his blind, unquestioning, following of Samar into all mischief, would be the same. Except Abhi had been different, always longing for things far beyond.

For years, he had nurtured his dream in secret, not even sharing it with Samar. Instead he had played all the games of Samar's devising, crawling through the woods in imitation of proper soldiers, intercepting Baba on his way home with elaborate ambushes from the mango trees that lined the road, and on one wonderful occasion, sabotaging the cook's chicken coop with a combination of pilfered box-cutters and firecrackers. Then later, he had followed dutifully in Samar's footsteps at school: cricket captain, hockey forward, house captain. Teachers all compared him favourably to the elder brother, with an additional recommendation that Abhi was sweeter and more considerate, taking time out to be kind to the juniors who hero-worshipped him, flirting gently but carefully with the girls who giggled at the very sight of him. Besides, as his teachers never failed to point out, Abhi had never been known to set off stink bombs in the assembly or Superglue the headmaster to his chair. He was the 'good' brother. But that was only because no one had an inkling of his secretly nursed treachery.

It had come to light only at the end of that summer after he had finished his exams. Samar had been home on short leave, mostly so he could talk Abhi through the protocols of entering the officers' academy. Already pipped as second lieutenant, his talk when not focused on his fellow officers, on the generosity of his JCOs, and the glorious history of his regiment, was full of the mountains he was setting himself to climb, the complications of climbing ice versus snow, the extra discipline he felt he needed to impose on himself to ensure the perfect climb rate. He would even turn down extra helpings of his favourite roast lamb. He seemed older than his twenty-two years, strangely prepossessed, serious only after three months at his post on the glacier.

For much of the summer, Abhi had debated, feeling increasingly sick with anxiety if he would tell his family about his decision to turn down the academy in favour of a university in the capital. He had taken the letter with his regrets and posted it from the other end of town, unable to face the local postmaster's fulsome praises for yet another of the colonel's sons heading into a life of uniform. He had used a friend's address to communicate with the university, abusing his trust with brutal selfishness, had lied to the teachers for the letters of recommendation, for the extra copies of his school documents. Steadily, secretly, over long anxious months, he had compiled all he needed for the perfect escape.

He did wonder if he could just pretend to leave for the academy and then make his way elsewhere. After all he had secured scholarships and grants, had saved up for the past two years, slowly stockpiling his meagre income from helping other students with their coursework for a time when he would rebel, when he would escape into the exciting beyond. 'This one was born to be a soldier, one of those monk-soldiers from ancient times,' Baba would tease as Abhi denied himself yet another treat to augment his secret stash.

But walking away in secret seemed just too awful, too cowardly a course of action. He may never wish to be a warrior, but Abhi liked to think that there was just enough Sikarwal in him to need to face the music. Although when things finally came to a head, he wished he hadn't.

The conversation with Baba had been short but brutal.

Abhi had broached the topic after dinner, while they all still lingered over conversation and a final round of drinks. Samar had teased him for being withdrawn and silent out of a fear of the 'ragging' he would face at academy. 'Don't worry, little bro, they know you're my brother. The seniors won't be rough on you.'

Finally Abhi had gathered up his courage to start speaking. Halting over words, in broken phrases, he tried explaining his plans, all that he had done in preparation, tried to make the case that he wanted things that may be different but were no less valuable. He had spoken into growing silence as Baba's face grew closed and blank, his pale eyes growing bloodshot with barely suppressed fury. Samar looked bewildered, staring at Abhi, as if he had encountered some strange species he had never even begun to imagine.

At the far end of the table, Abhi's mother – as always immaculate in silks and pearls – had sighed once and then sank back into her chair, her eyes averted. Abhi wondered if she were upset or simply relieved. He knew her well enough to realise that at least she was neither surprised nor disappointed: after all, hadn't she been slipping him a little extra for his 'expenses' for the past year? His mother in her silence was another rebel, except she had accepted that there was no escape, and instead offered herself as the silent martyr.

47

'So you have planned all this?' Finally, Baba asked.

'Yes sir.'

'And you have already turned down the academy?'

'Yes sir.' This time Abhi could sense Samar's exasperation by his side.

'And you are going to this university?'

'Yes sir.'

'Well, then.' Baba fell silent for a long moment. Then abruptly he pushed his chair back to rise. 'You can leave as soon as it is convenient. Do that without any unnecessary drama.'

Abhi had just begun to let out a relieved sigh as Baba walked away towards his study when the final blow fell. Baba had turned slightly, 'And from now, I don't want to know anything more about Abhi. Ever! Is that understood?'

He had nearly forgotten those last days before leaving for university. There was none of the excitement, just a grim determination. The house had been shrouded in silence, his mother preparing his clothes with an obsessive care, as if ironing one last crease in his favourite shirt could change the inevitable. Samar seemed perplexed, 'You're sure you want to do this?' As if repeating the question over and over again could somehow change the answer.

He had never returned home once in all these years out of pride, first Baba's, then his own. Every two weeks, a letter from his mother arrived with news and small inconsequential chatter, all meant to make him feel still loved, hiding any distress she had ever felt about the way things had turned out. Sometimes, there would be a care packet with his favourite sweets, a jumper that was always too small or large for his spare frame, as if in his mother's imagination he could stretch from infanthood to infinity.

And there was Samar, writing, calling, showing up at Abhi's doorstep to surprise him when he had a day or two of leave. He even sent a telegram from some strange border outposts, not because he had to but rather because he could.

Sometimes Abhi wrote back to his mother, trying in vain to put into words a life that was so far removed from all she knows. Eventually, his letters grew just as trite, mere litanies of the progress he had made in his career, promotions and pay rises, material acquisitions and exotic holidays. And every year, he sends them the official New Year's card with a photograph of the hotel on the front, the inside embossed with the corporate logo, printed with his full name and current title. He always addresses it to all his family.

Years ago, when Samar and he were still speaking, his brother had confided that Baba would file away those annual cards in a special folder that he kept in his bedside drawer. But Baba had never written to him, and Abhi, who had inherited nothing else but his father's pride, had refused to take that first step towards reconciliation.

Then that conversation with Samar had snapped even that last tie. Samar had been angry as if it were somehow Abhi's fault. 'Always, always, you have to complicate things. Always be contrary, different. Why can't you be just...' He had struggled to find a word in his anger. 'Just normal!' The epithet had hung between them.

Samar seemed half-appalled at what he had said even in the midst of his fury. But Abhi had walked out before anything further could be spoken, closing himself against any further hurt, holding the word he had so often battled since childhood close to himself for a change, at once a torture-rack and a shield, a prison and a weapon.

Unlike Baba, Samar had tried to make peace but it had been Abhi who held himself away, refusing to answer Samar's calls or emails, rebuffing all apologies. He would acknowledge his brother only in the annual card he sent home, always at the end, like an afterthought, a near oversight, 'and Samar'.

Of course, it wasn't as if he missed any of them. His life is too hectic for missing anyone at all. Hasn't he been building the life he always wanted? The long hours of work, his own first new home all in chrome and black and white more pristinely aesthetic than ever, the car he changes with fastidious routine the moment it loses its new car smell just because he can. His circle of friends is fun and loyal, and if they don't understand his occasional bouts of sadness, at least they care enough not to leave him alone during those times.

Occasionally he takes a lover, someone he has met at a party, or a nightclub, or sometimes even at the Arcadia. He rarely brings them to his flat, choosing instead one of the empty luxury suites he has access to in the hotel itself. For most part, his lovers are suitably impressed with the free mini-bar and room service, and he feels relief at not having to change the sheets or clear the debris in the morning.

His favourite is the one on the top floor, accessed by a private lift, overlooking the wide terrace of the Refuge but splendidly isolated, towering over the city and the luxury of even the Arcadia itself. He brings only special lovers there, the ones that give him a slice of hope of something more than fervent coupling. Lovers like Dieter, who understands his need to impress, are touched by Abhi's gesture rather than awed by the luxury. Lovers like Dieter who seek him out, for conversations about art and books, who return to stay at the Arcadia, again and again, only for him.

Yes, really, Abhi Sikarwal had succeeded. He had not only escaped but landed in a paradise he could never have imagined, where gleeful oblivion is the norm for every night, and shiny, sparkly lives continue in a never-ending twirl all around him. And always with Abhi at the centre of the whirl, clever, articulate, sophisticated; everyone always comments on how Abhi can work his way out of any kind of mess, talk his way out of any jam, negotiate any complicated human entanglement.

And yet, now that a trap of a different kind, more horrible, urgent, bloody, had snapped shut on him once more, all his mind would – *could* – do was to recycle old memories of Samar, of silly children's games.

THE ARCADIA
ABOUT 60 HOURS AGO

Sam makes her way up to the twentieth floor, creeping up the fire escape shaft, her footsteps measured and silent, her back pushed against the wall, against the shadows, her ears straining for all sounds. Cradling her camera against her belly, out of habit, and for comfort, she counts the steps, pressing the memory of each into her muscles, aware of the subtle shifts of smell, the bright sterile light, the rough yet slick feel of fire-retardant wall paint on her fingers; twelve, then a landing; thirteen, and the door into the next floor. She will need to remember the numbers in case she has to run or make her way in the dark. Sam knows eventually the electricity to the Arcadia shall be cut, has learned security manoeuvres from too many places, and that pushes her on, imbuing each careful step with a barely checked urgency.

She edges open the heavy door a crack, letting the cool air of the fire escape creep in slowly and dissipate into the muggy corridor. Her skin reacts, throwing up goose-bumps. She hopes no one else is in on the floor, or at least is not paying attention enough to notice the sudden coolness in air. For a long slow moment she waits, her senses on high alert, leaning into the silence beyond before sliding in, almost crawling, on to the carpeted floor. Same pale walls and plush carpet, as expected, although the corridor is shorter than others. A swathe of marble forms a square foyer before the lifts to her right. On the left are the tall frosted glass doors. Beyond the glass, shadowy tables are lit by gleaming low lights, punctuated by occasional bright spots over the long, well stocked bar, a large one over the piano. And even further away, the muddy urban night hangs over the glass ceiling, the stars veiled by the city lights, the moon blurred by the thick illumination.

51

She had noted the rooftop bar on this floor and is relieved to see that she is right. At another hour, in the evening or night, the bar would have been full. Perhaps, on a less exhausted night, or just a lonelier one, she would have been drinking here as well, sitting as always, alone at a corner table, her back against the wall. She would have been looking out on the city below, sipping her single malt with just a splash of lukewarm water, scanning the crowd for someone, just anyone, she could trust to keep her company late.

But even as the thought arises, she pushes it away. This is not the kind of bar she chooses after an assignment, full of beautiful, glistening, chattering people, slick in expensive clothes, wrapped in cocoons of wealth and distance from the horrors she covers. No, her kind of bar is slightly seedier, even when in luxurious hotels, in places where cars are checked for bombs before approaching their gates, where carpets are just slightly stained under the low lights, where obsessive use of vacuum cleaners and cleaning fluids and air-fresheners can't fully disguise the indefinable underlying odour of vomit and sweat, fear and trauma. No, her kind of bar is full of expats and journalists, security contractors and local fixers, aid workers and conflict zone diplomats, all adrenalin junkies who are hooked on the horror.

Sam had learned about these bars long ago, when she would still try to work with others. 'It's better to work in groups,' someone had told her on an early assignment. Guatemala? Peru? She doesn't remember. She had walked into similar places so often – Sarajevo, and Beirut, and Kinshasa – looking for others like herself, reporters and photographers going to cover the disaster of the day. Back then, she had tried to fit in, drinking with the boys, swearing, playing tougher than tough, swapping stories. Sometimes, she would meet the women, always earnest, nearly always from northern Europe, Canada or America, with shiny hair and wide eyes, and a slight ingrained disdain for the men, for the people beyond, and for her. They never looked at Sam, unless it was a savage glance at the end of the night, when alcohol had eased their self-control, when a flash of jealousy or contempt flared up, briefly though sharply, directed at Sam and whichever of their colleagues was giving her attention. Then the next morning, after coffee and cigarettes, they would retreat into their shells, ignoring Sam, flattering the fixers, chatting up the translators, smiling widely, falsely, at the male reporters.

Perhaps that is why Sam had soon grown bored, or tired, or maybe just realised that she would never belong with the reporters. In her mind, she belongs to the subjects, the photographed and reported on, those without the money or power to fly away from the violence. And she had soon grown bored of repeatedly hearing the same bar stories full of bravado and heroism, as if lies could be turned into truth with lashings of imported whisky.

That is when Sam had started working alone, making her own contacts, beyond the safety lines. The fixers, translators, even subjects, liked her, warming to her gloomy dark eyes, recognising her curling dark hair, hidden even back then under a nondescript cap or scarf, as closer to their own. They thought her aloofness was a measure of her understanding; let her know that they held the flirtations and condescending kindness of others in contempt. Sam's list of contacts had grown, each handing her on to another trusted source, finding in her sharp, darkened face some identification with their own. And through it all, Sam had learned to use these tangles of translations, identities, misunderstandings, for her photographs, moving farther and farther away from others who worked the field, learning first and then loving the possibility of working alone. Now, she trusts her own instincts better, knows her own network is more effective, has learned shamelessly to use her slight, dark, fluid looks that let her blend into the background.

That is why she has stopped going into those familiar hang-outs, always nameless, always similar, the international watering holes of every do-gooder and reporter in town, except when absolutely needed. These days, the only time she goes into the usual watering holes is after an assignment, just when she is ready to wind down, on those nights before flying home when the loneliness grows unbearable and threatens to choke her. On the nights after an assignment, Sam has learned that she will wake up with the smell of formaldehyde clinging to her nostrils, that nightmares will crowd her eyes, leave her shuddering. On those nights, she finds herself a faceless, nameless man, someone whose skin can warm her own freezing fingertips, whose tongue can silence her chattering teeth, whose weight can stop her trembling.

On those nights, she looks up the nearest watering hole for others like herself. There, she finds herself a table, a bottle of Scotch, and waits; scanning the crowd for some company for the night, for a few hours of distraction. She has learned that the company will eventually appear; inexorably draw close, always with the promise of sex, or comfort, always in form of someone with equal degree of PTSD.

Slowly, with each sip of her Scotch, she unfurls herself, making her visible again, loosening the top buttons of her shirt, rolling up her sleeves, stretching into a semblance of womanhood again. Seated at her table alone, she lines up the pair of bottles, of Scotch and mineral water, to her left, meticulously prepares her combination of Scotch and three parts water, not only because that is how she likes it, but because she knows it impresses men. She relaxes once she has chosen the man she wants, watches him as he walks, slumps, drinks, running him against her mental list of risk, reward, desire. She grins at him, friendly, unthreatening, when she catches his eyes, takes note if he begins to look back, is intrigued by her. Then, just perhaps, if he remains alone even after her bottle of Scotch has receded past the halfway mark, she invites him for a drink with a smile that lingers on her lips but doesn't quite light up her eyes.

She always waits till the end of the night, drinking little herself after that initial half-bottle, getting her chosen man drunk instead. She always goes to his room, guarding her own fortress for herself. Sometimes, she doesn't even go that far, finding a dark nook or alleyway for quick, mostly unsatisfactory sex, laughing a little when the men complain that they hate fucking standing up.

But it isn't sex that Sam wants, which is why she performs perfunctorily, or sometimes even hopes that the alcohol is enough to knock out the man. She seeks the comfort, the warmth, of another human body to erase the horrors she has seen. She wants warm breath, gentle lips and a moist tongue against her own, desires strong alive hands that can roam her skin, reminders that humans are also capable of lust, and living, and pleasure. Later, as she lies awake at night, sipping her Scotch direct from the bottle she always carries away with her, her back pushed against the nameless man she has chosen for the night, she likes to feel a pulsating heartbeat against her own. Sam always leaves before she begins to feel drowsy, making her way back to her own sleeping rituals.

But the Arcadia does not have that kind of bar. It is not in a conflict zone, not even near one, unless cosmopolitan desperation can be considered war. The rooftop bar is where glamorous girls with shiny hair and lithe limbs gather, jewels twinkling on their slim throats and bony wrists, their slenderness draped in expensive silks. And glossy, sleek men with money, who send others to wars they pay for. Sam had looked in earlier and decided that there was not nearly enough trauma in the place to try for company. And that is why she had been asleep, mostly drunk, in her own bed, when the gunmen had opened fire here.

Sam brings up the viewfinder to her eye even before she reaches the glass doors with 'The Refuge' etched in tall opaque letters. There is blood splattered against the bottom of the door, smeared along the pale stone tiles beyond. She begins to shoot, her eye engrossed in composition, texture, lighting, even as all her senses remain alert to even a hint of movement.

***

Deep in the belly of the Arcadia, Abhi can't bear to stop watching Sam, revolted and compelled in equal parts. Even worse, he

55

knows she is heading straight for the Refuge, to the bar he has avoided looking at since the madness began.

Abhi thinks of the rooftop bar as his own sanctuary, finding in its shadowy depths and panoramic views of the city a strange tranquillity that soothes him, comforts him when he is at his worst. The city glittering below seems to shout out a welcome, reminding him of those early days when he had just arrived full of dreams and little else. The breeze from the sea always makes him smile, so different from the mountains of his childhood, a smell and tang that is all his own, reminders that he has stretched out and grabbed the chance to live his own way.

He comes to the Refuge most days after finishing work, often for just a drink at the bar late at night, or lunch with friends, sometimes to chat to favourite clients, or to offer that extra bit of attention to the high rollers. He likes to sink into the brocade and velvet Modernist sofas, all lavish curves and dramatic spikes, loves the snowy white expanses of the tables laid with gleaming cutlery. Leaning back, toying with the crystal stem of his wine goblet, he devours the baroque gilt lamps in the far nooks, their sharp edges shining dully, breathes in the white lilies and narcissus in their tall vases that throw mysterious shadows into cosy nooks. Yes, this is his very own Refuge.

And this is where sometimes, just sometimes, very discreetly, he finds someone he can desire, exchanging glances across the softly shadowed expanses, someone graceful and sophisticated like the surroundings, someone with just enough edge, like those baroque gilt lanterns. Someone like Dieter.

No, too many fond memories are tied to the Refuge, and he can't bear to see them tainted. He has deliberately avoided looking at the bar, even though he has diligently dialled the extension on his rounds, unsure whether he hopes someone answers, or prefers the continued silence. For an instant, Abhi wishes he could continue to ignore the Refuge, but now he can't look away. Drawn like a magnet to that foolhardy guest in 1402, that crazy woman who won't stay safe. And also to the inarticulate fear he has ignored since the very beginning.

56

Yet he can't stand the thought of anyone else observing her, targeting her, stalking her. And he feels sickened at the thought of all she can see, as he watches her make her way gently, slowly through the traces of carnage the assailants have left there.

She is already in the centre of the Refuge, calm, collected, her camera now held in position, her finger taut and ready. And yet, somehow, the closer she gets to the carnage, the more she retreats into herself, her crouch becoming more pronounced, her shoulders hunch further, her neck dipping low, almost into her scarf, as if she were willing herself invisible. Perhaps because he doesn't desire her, he can see her gradual effacement more clearly, notes the way her muscles curl into themselves, as if forcing themselves to retract into nothingness. For a fanciful moment, he imagines that she can withdraw completely behind her camera, recede so far into the nondescript smudge on the screen so as to disappear entirely.

But she doesn't vanish from his screen. Instead, she slowly curls herself into something small, unimportant, moving slowly, carefully, never stepping into a pool of spilled drink or blood on the floor, leaving every surface undisturbed. He leans forward instinctively, as if moving closer can stall her gradual effacement, the imperceptible hunching over, her almost ghostly gait. He watches her slide first along the near wall to the corner farthest from the terrace. Then she begins to zigzag, making her away in diagonal paths between the tables across the expanse of the room, shooting incessantly. His eyes flicker to another screen, to one of the assailants moving with similar caution against the pale walls on a floor far below. There is not much difference, Abhi thinks, between the two; both bodies so tautly held as if they would snap at a touch, the senses so alert that the screens nearly crackle with the leashed energy. But he tells himself that Sam is different, finding an inexplicable empathy as he watches her. She moves slowly, deliberately, almost tenderly around the targets, nearly affectionate as she shoots. He can almost feel the camera shudder at strange intervals under her finger, can almost imagine his own arm tingle in sympathy as the shots embed themselves in a memory chip.

Abhi feels bile scorch his throat, swelling into his mouth, as he follows Sam's path, automatically counting off the slumped bodies on the floor, some half-draped on the chairs, one flung across a table, dark hair dramatically spread over the white cloth and shattered crystal. She is following his own well-loved path, the one he uses just before the Refuge flings open its mammoth glass doors, pausing to check each table in the central space carefully, confirming the glossiness of each burnished lamp, the plumpness of the velvet cushions on the sofas in the far nooks. He walks through the Refuge the same way, his eyes scanning from right to left, his steps weaving diagonally across the room, first across, and then back again, pausing briefly, very briefly, when something catches his eyes. He straightens up, pushing back his shoulders, as if to separate himself from the smudge, as if pulling himself upright can distinguish him from the hunched, slightly repulsive figure on the screen.

Still he forces himself to watch, noting how Sam covers the entire room, each corpse. Some she leaves with a single shot; with others, she lingers, changing the angle, finding the perfect spot, composing carefully, before firing off half a dozen, perhaps more, frames.

Even from a distance, Abhi can admire Sam's precision, the careful pauses, the cautious ever alert gait, and the meticulous way she covers the room. She only breaks her path once...to swing behind the tall bar, to try the door into the storeroom half-concealed behind it. She tries the handle once, cautiously turning with her left hand, staying out of the way. When it doesn't yield, she draws closer, frowning. Then she tries it again, pumping the handle carefully, slowly, holding her body tucked against the cabinet on the side.

Abhi scans his list of calls, even though he already knows the answer. There isn't a phone in the storeroom, and no one has answered from the Refuge in the past three rounds. And yet he is sure that some of the bar must be hidden here. Or so he hopes, at least.

He watches, curious, as Sam tries the handle once again and then turns away. For an instant, she balances from one foot to the other, swaying slightly as if torn. Then suddenly, she straightens up, pushing the camera down and away against her hip, her head coming up suddenly alert.

Moving rapidly, she pulls out a couple of bottles of mineral water from the fridge and lays them near the door, flat on the ground, as if dropped in a rush or knocked over. She pushes the base of one with her fist to bend it, damage it just slightly. Slowly reaching out, she grabs a metal basket with small cans of potato crisps and pulls it down, hurtling the cans along the floor. Carefully she knocks some of them close to the door. Finally, grabbing a scrap of orders, she scrawls on it, pushing it under the crack into the store room.

She pauses, waiting, deliberating. Then without turning, she grabs a nearly full, tall, bottle of Scotch – even in the blurred image, Abhi knows it's a Macallan's, finds himself smiling; at least, she likes the good stuff! She takes a sip, her fingers curled around the long neck and then a long pull, tucks it away inside her jacket, the bulge barely imperceptible against her belly. Then, just as suddenly as she had broken out of her path, she curls back into position, camera snapped into place, creeping back out from behind the bar and reverts to shooting amongst the tables.

It isn't until Sam is making her second round, no longer zigzagging through the Refuge, but deliberately, carefully walking to specific tables she has obviously identified on her first sweep, that Abhi's stomach gives a sudden, familiar, lurch.

Sam has been shooting at specific tables, at particular sofas. Her walk is measured, circling slowly around each site, her camera poised and ready as she deliberates over the angles. Beneath the cap, her brow is furrowed in concentration, her shoulders have slightly relaxed. With sudden insight, Abhi realises that she is no longer focused on danger to herself, that she has forgotten about the assailants who destroyed the Refuge, who still hold the Arcadia, roam its corridors at will. On auto-pilot, he dials the extension of the bar, the receiver clenched in his fist, hoping, even though he knows she won't answer. He scans the other screens, frantically, rapidly, his eyes racing in their pre-set sequence, until he relaxes. The assailants have taken up positions a few floors below, are making their way through the balcony lining the shattered central atrium.

Abhi looks back at Sam, to where she is carefully composing a shot, moving around a table, her camera held low while she selects, deliberates. At first Abhi can only see the hastily thrust aside chairs, the snowy tablecloth half-pulled off the gleaming mahogany below. Then, slowly, as if he can inhabit Sam's mind, see with her eyes, he notices a slim hand peeping beyond the edge of a table, resting gently, motionless, on the pristine blankness, as if on a canvas: a man's hand, with a pale silk jumper ringing the bare wrist, a few short curls glistening against the edge of the fabric. The fingers are long, as bare as the wrist, ending in smooth, buffed ovals. Abhi tries to ignore the clench in his stomach, pretends that the recognition is just his imagination, that his memories are misplaced, jumbled.

But he knows that hand well, has held it hard against himself, felt it roaming over his skin, leaving shuddering pleasures in its wake. No, he won't even think of it. The nausea finally wins over his need to watch Sam as he turns away and retches into the waste bin, his empty stomach heaving, his eyes streaming.

THE ARCADIA
5⁹ HOURS AGO

Sam slots in the key-card, counting off the seconds, 'One-Mississippi; two-Mississippi; three…' waiting as a green light flicks on, a barely audible click sounding against her hand, and lets herself back in. She checks automatically for her warning system, confirms the all clear, before letting herself relax, her shoulders slumping.

She pulls out the bottle from her jacket, takes a gulp, feeling the burn slide down her throat as she carefully removes her gear, placing it all in reverse order on the corner table, camera, back-up, batteries, clean memory cards. The used cards she leaves for the last. From sheer habit, she must upload and clear them first before letting herself sink into sleep.

The red button is glowing, flickering insistently, and she answers, surprised that she has been anticipating the call; has even been wishing for it.

'All well, ma'am?' Abhi's voice is thick, slightly choked.

'I told you not to call me that!'

'Yes, you did,' he laughs, but then hesitates. There are no words, no questions that come to him. He has heard of de-briefs, from his father, from Samar, but never bothered to ask any more. He has so many questions for her, but none seem appropriate.

'Looks like they have booby-trapped the door to the roof,' Sam speaks, watching her photographs upload on her laptop. 'Meant for detonation when opened. Or maybe on timers. I didn't go close enough to check. You may want to pass that on.'

'Yes, of course,' Abhi shakes himself, pulls a clean sheet of paper before him to start making notes. 'Did you head up all the way?'

61

'Saw it from the landing below, but can confirm that they look quite substantial. Doubt they plan to keep an eye up there, but there may be more explosives set up at other entry points.'

'How about the Refuge?' Childhood games kicking in again, Abhi realises. He can imagine Samar using the bar's wide terrace to land troops.

'Pretty much all dead, would say twenty, maybe more. Not sure of the count.'

The question that Abhi desperately wants to ask lingers at the tip of his tongue. Then he swallows, 'I mean, on the terrace doors, any other explosives?'

Sam has to flick through the photographs to confirm. She hasn't noticed any, but isn't sure. Abhi has more questions, mostly on explosives placement, but also on the number of dead and their locations. And then, with much difficulty, as if he can't bear to speak it out, he asks her about survivors, the injured. But Sam hasn't noticed, her attention focused only on the dead, her senses alert only for danger.

'That's OK. Can you check that on your next trip?' Abhi's voice is firm now. 'Please.'

Sam chuckles. The last word is an afterthought, a feeble attempt to make an order seem like a request. 'Yeah, sure. Guess you're not talking me out of going out now?'

Abhi's voice is light. 'Get some rest. I will email you the floor plans in a bit. If you're going to be out there, you may as well be useful.'

***

Abhi stares at the jumble of notes before him and begins to unscramble the information Sam has given him, arranging the data by floors, mentally highlighting all that he thinks is important. Only when he has placed the jigsaw of information in a clear semblance of a report does he reach out to the phone, connects to the security ops centre. The first ring is barely complete when someone answers. He realises that beyond the edge of his isolation, security forces are gearing up, planning and preparing; his call is patched through to an army officer, a colonel, instead of the harried city policemen he had been speaking to before.

He winces the first time the colonel calls him son, but then sighs in relief. At least, he is on familiar ground now, reporting the information he has collected, identifying the survivors, confirming the occupied rooms on the ground plans, locating the explosives' positions, and finally the dead.

'And you know this how, son?' the colonel barks down the line.

Abhi doesn't want to tell him about Sam. He suspects the colonel will want to talk to her directly; that they will try to push her to collect more information; that in the cold calculation of success and failure, they may – without thinking out loud, without any words – choose to sacrifice her. Like he has watched them do so often before.

As he holds the receiver, Abhi's mind flicks back to that day years ago when Baba's commanding officer had shown up at their house. He doesn't remember the words, just the grim look on the CO's face; the strange inward crumbling of his mother's shoulders, like a building collapsing partially; Samar's tightly clenched jaws. They had driven to the hospital in the CO's jeep, waited for what Abhi remembers were interminable hours in the hushed corridor, where other officers from Baba's unit had gathered, or at least the ones who were not away on operations.

Samar had put his hand around Mamma's shoulders, his jaws never relaxing, his back ramrod stiff. Abhi had hidden in the background, afraid of what was not spoken, unsure of how to comfort Samar or Mamma or himself. Once, his hand clenched around his brand new Mercedes Dinky car, he had slipped down the hallway. There, just around the corner, more families waited, just like him and Samar and Mamma, but not so groomed, not so prosperous. One of the women sobbed, covering her face with her cheap cotton sari, the glass bangles on her wrists glinting in the light. A boy his own age, perhaps younger, hovered nearby, almost on verge of tears.

One of Baba's officers, one of the young captains, stood nearby, ill at ease, uncomfortable. Abhi had seen him before, at the parties in the mess, or at home. The captain always laughed, noticed Abhi rather than Samar, calling out to him to join him for cricket, always asked what he had been playing. A nice man, a gentle one, Abhi always thought. Yet he was here, standing stiffly before the weeping woman, the scared boy, the others who were grouped just beyond.

'Your husband sacrificed himself for his unit, his country. It was beyond the call of duty. We are all proud of him. He will never be forgotten.' The words seemed broken, automatic, like the final sputtering of a machine coming to a halt.

With a flash of insight, Abhi knew the kind captain was lying, that no one would care about the husband. That he was dead, and the family would soon move away from the cantonment, perhaps back to where they came from, perhaps to one of those sad little houses built for the army widows, with drab yellow walls and tiny windows.

From the shadows, Abhi had watched the captain walk away, the widow crumble as many hands reached to comfort her. The little boy had been pushed aside, thrust out of the circle of grieving by the women. He stood, with tear-smudged cheeks, bewildered, looking about, seeking something.

When their eyes met, Abhi had tried to smile. The boy looked angry, as if wanting to fight, to hit something, anything. Yet his eyes were full of unshed tears, held back only by the strength of his fury. Abhi had walked up, holding his new white Dinky Mercedes out. He had thrust the toy in the boy's hand before racing away, back down to where Samar and Mamma waited, composed, controlled, hand-in-hand.

He had reached out and grasped Samar's hand. Samar had looked at him briefly, then squeezed it back, comforting Abhi, or himself. But Abhi knew they hadn't missed him, hadn't even noticed his brief absence. That their minds were bent on hoping Baba would not have been sacrificed, same as that family of the soldier down the hall; that they would not need to crumble in tears, need to be comforted by the other officers, and their families that were gathering nearby.

Abhi still remembers the terror he had felt in that moment, the clenching fist in his belly that did not loosen even when Baba opened his eyes that first time, even when Baba came home, and all became as before. Or almost all! Abhi notices the dark shadows in Mamma's eyes, the steely determination in Samar's preparation for following Baba's path. And he knows that is when he had begun planning his escape from the life that Samar and Baba wanted and cherished. He would never be a sacrifice, for anything.

Perhaps that is why he chooses to answer the colonel carefully, protecting Sam though he can't explain why; it is for that little boy in the corridor of a half-forgotten army hospital, that Abhi chooses, not a lie, but also not the complete truth: 'From some of our guests, sir. Also I am in the Arcadia control centre. We have full access to our entire CCTV system.'

***

Sam sets her alarm for two hours. She wants to make at least another sortie before the night draws to a close. She removes her boots and her multi-pocket jacket, falls into bed in all her clothes, ready to move at an instant's warning. Her phone is blinking, another missed call from David, even a flurry of emails.

She doesn't really want to talk to him, even email him. She never thinks of him when she is on assignment, when she's working. Even back at home, she never calls him, purposefully erasing him from her calendar, from her thoughts until he gives in and calls her. And then she never answers the first time, letting the call go to voicemail, letting him leave a message that she will save for later, will listen to again and again, finding the comfort that eludes her in his arms in his disembodied voice late at night.

'Never. You never once answer the phone when I call you,' he teases her, only half-joking Sam suspects. She needs time to

65

push away that sudden hollowness in the pit of her stomach on seeing his name flash up on her phone, on hearing his voice on her voicemail, that immediate intense flash of desire she knows well, has resisted for so long, even imagines repeatedly that she has killed and buried somewhere in the past. The sudden desperate need for him despite so many years of resolutely pushing him out of her thoughts, leaves her shaken. She waits, her eyes straying constantly to her phone, until he calls again and the desire to speak to him proves too strong.

When they speak, there is a familiar intimacy in his tone, a strange knowledge of her voice, her breath, her reactions; a surety that he knows what she will say. But perhaps what draws her back into his arms is the recognition of something she never believes him capable of: a faint stain of insecurity, frailty, cloaked in apparent confidence; a barely-concealed fragility that she only notices in infrequent flashes. That shared vulnerability draws her, offering her a promise of comfort that she can't find elsewhere.

Perhaps that is why his unthinking acts of kindness unsettle her. He carries her heavy camera case without asking, without thinking, simply picking it up off the floor as they leave. The same way that he holds her coat for her, amused as she looks for it on the floor. She knows that the gestures are meaningless, routine acts of politeness, yet they faze her. They make their liaison seem untainted, somehow laced with a promise of something deeper.

When David puts his arm around her as they walk back to her flat, she has to force herself not to flinch. She isn't accustomed to walking with another, lock-stepping on the pavement with a body that towers above her, her shoulder pulled hard against his side. Walking with him undermines her courage, reminding her far too sharply that she prefers walking alone, that his large frame seems to blunt her senses, blocking her view, his elusive musky smell dulling her nose. Even worse, the warmth of his body seeps into her muscles, softening her, weakening her, and she knows all too well that the world is not kind to the weak.

She moves her purse, ostensibly to make room for him but also to force a space between them, ducks her head low into her jacket. David remains oblivious to her reaction, teasing her gently, 'I bet you were terrible at school.'

'No. I was the geeky kind,' she resolutely refuses to feed his fantasy, any fantasy. She has enough of those for the both of them, enough to terrify her into frozen immobility if she thinks of him too often.

'The kind that blew up the chemistry lab then?' She shrugs, helpless against his attraction for her, caught in a dialogue that seems to flow between them without really communicating.

'Don't get used to this,' she tells herself sharply, pulling herself inwards, pushing him away, even when they make love, even when he wanders through her bare flat, flicking through her prints, noting each new press clip, his eyes proud and tender, an affectionate smile lingering on his lips. She never looks at him then, closing her eyes, turning away to make a drink, to find an ashtray, to a thousand inconsequential pretexts.

Those silences give her strength, letting her retreat into her fantasy of him, making love to him again and again in her mind when he is gone. She adores him, pleases him, caresses him in all the ways she doesn't permit herself when he lies in her arms. And upon waking, she can be sure he is safe, more than she can ever feel for herself.

She doesn't answer when her phone begins to buzz again, vibrating insistently against the pillow, David's name flashing repeatedly on the screen. Waiting until the call is routed to voicemail, Sam clicks on the text templates.

Her usual answer is saved as template to use each time she receives a worried text, generally from new acquaintances who are sincerely horrified when they see a disaster on their television screens and realise that she is at ground zero. Her parents, even her oldest friends, have learned not to disturb her, trusting in her cat like ability to survive and resurface when the catastrophe eases. Stella, her agent, messages her occasionally but only to pass on news of a better hotspot, or request permission for a new sale, and often to fill her in on the outlines of the emerging press narratives so Sam can better focus her photographs.

Of course, David has never tried to reach her – perhaps because it is easier to thrust her out of his mind, his life, when she is a hair's breadth from death. 'Oh don't be so dramatic,' he had told her once, when she flung that accusation at him, using her PTSD as the excuse to seek greater intimacy. But this time, he has emailed her, texted, even called her repeatedly. This must truly seem horrible from the outside, she knows, even as she smiles to herself, noting the silence on her floor. His concern almost assures her that he cares, that he may even love her. She savours the thought for a long moment, her lips curved into a soft, almost tender smile. Then the panic begins to rise again, along with memories of the dead, and the suffering, and the damned. She can't bear to love him, can't even risk anyone loving her, she fiercely reminds herself. Squeezing her eyes tight, she schools her face back into repose, ordering the muscles to shift, erasing the smile, recovering the small habitual furrow between her eyes. Slowly, surely, the panic ebbs along with the earlier flood of warmth. Sam breathes slowly, forcing herself to remain steady, like a survivor bracing against receding floodwaters. Eyes still closed, she tamps down the emotions, reaching out with her senses, straining to hear into the dark. The occasional explosions are muffled, now on the other side of the hotel, far from her. She feels like the battlefront has passed by, racing past her door, leaving her to pick and choose through the debris as she wills.

Perhaps she is being dramatic as David has accused her, but she sends her template message to almost her entire contact list, feeling the thrill of novelty in that brief crossing from chronicler to potential victim.

Am all right.
Talk soon.
Love,
S.

She likes using the word love in her template, replete with ambiguity. Is she professing it or demanding it?

She thinks for an instant, before deciding against sending the message to David. Instead, dialling her voicemail, she listens to the messages he has left her, his voice insistent in her ear as she drifts off into uneasy sleep, resting her body if not her brain for the next foray.

THE BALKANS
1994

Her portraits have always been about lack, about departures. She finds the faces of the dead curiously mysterious, like deserted train stations, or abandoned towns, the bodies no longer home to that elusive, fragile sense of life. It's as if they have been forsaken by their inhabitants, as if they will lie in wait for whoever has loved and lived in them for eons, and then, in a single instant, without another thought, has abandoned them for eternity. Sometimes, when she is developing her images, replicating them on screen, stretching them on the web of slim wires that criss-cross her flat, at an arm's length just above her head, she thinks the cadavers lie in wait, hoping, wishing, praying that the departed will return, as if they could lie there forever, waiting for that one lost love.

And perhaps that is why she rarely shoots children. She knows others who cover death and destruction find children incessantly, obsessively, attractive; knows well that the editors would much prefer images of the young dead. They sell better, after all. But Sam finds the small bones obscene, the softness of skin unmarked by time disturbs her; the tiny faces seem unloved by that elusive spirit, like a home merely rented and abandoned without a second thought. She diligently turns the lens away from tiny weeping faces, from small bodies contorted in grief, knowing the fierceness of their despair will shatter her completely, even with a single glance. 'You'd make a lot more money,' her agent tells her periodically but Sam plays the bored artist for those discussions, drawling out her words for effect as she explains that she finds photographs of suffering children clichéd, boring, bathetic, and she doesn't do kitsch.

The Balkans had taught her that, with the steady freezing rain, the picturesque villages nestling in the hills savage and

70

brutal. She had spent months travelling, at times with the journalists, at others with the peacekeepers. There had been no rules, no explanation for the butchery, and soldiers, villagers, peacekeepers all seemed to have given up their ice-thin civility to descend into madness. She had stood out, for a change, her skin stark even amongst the grimy faces, her darkness marking her as the foreigner. She had learned to pull her cap low over her face, pull up the collar of her parka high against her throat, and not only to block out the cold rain.

As she moved far into the mountains, the savagery around her bleeding into the mud, she had started wearing her press badge prominently on her jacket, hoping that its flimsy plastic would provide some protection, some measure of distance from the madness around her. But even that talisman had soon failed as the violence around her slowly, steadily numbed her, drowning the adrenalin jolt she always got on assignment. The familiar rush had been replaced with a thick mental fog that seemed never to lift from her frozen, exhausted mind, and forced her to wade through nameless torn villages and shattered icy countryside as if through an invisible sludge.

Just as she was sure she could not even find the strength to raise the viewfinder to her eye, she had found a moment of respite, the only patch of sanity in the madness that had descended on the hills. A doctor she had met one night, in a refugee camp, working tirelessly, blearily on stitching up wounds he had no way of curing, his long pale fingers gentle yet taut as they moved steadily.

Sam doesn't remember his name, knows it is filed away somewhere in her contact list. Even after straining her memory, she can't summon up his face, though in moments of madness, she can still remember the feel of his warm, tender fingers moving over her skin, massaging the knot of pain high in her shoulder. But she remembers sitting with him on the hard cold floor of the makeshift hospital, can still feel the chill climbing up her spine as he mechanically recited all he had seen. She had made notes, and shared the last of her whisky with him, tasting the bitterness of the local cigarettes that he chain-smoked ringing the glass neck.

When the bottle was empty, he had found some local slivovitsa, its fruity clearness burning a trail into her stomach, singeing away some of the haze shrouding her mind. Afterwards, they had watched the sun come up bleakly over the eastern hills, its early red all too articulate of the bloodshed that had gripped the land. She had slept there on the hospital steps, freezing, curled up against him, her hands gripping his, his arms wrapped around her, finding a comfort she rarely encountered, of deep, dreamless, sleep. Sometime in the morning, he had moved her to his bed, the single sparse cot covered with nothing but a ratty blanket, had left her to sleep, assuring her that she would be safe, that he was working just beyond the door, that he would keep a watch on her rest. His voice had barely dented her drowsiness.

And sometime between sewing up wounds, and watching her sleep, he had sown two patches, one on her parka and another on top of her rucksack. Just a red and white square with a single maple leaf. 'It helps to be neutral,' he had grinned, his long fingers gently kneading her shoulders. 'Then maybe, you can thank us Canadians.'

She had smiled back, wishing she could find a reason to stay a bit longer, savouring this instant intimacy of strangers bound by nothing but their refusal to participate in the madness, by their insistence on staying on to bear witness. She had given him her beloved Leica in return, having carefully extracted the last, only partially exposed reel. When he protested, she had told him she wanted him to keep it, that she would rely on her two back-up cameras for the remainder of her tour. He had been delighted, caressing the Leica's black textured case with the same care, same attention, that he had lavished on her skin the night before.

'You sure?'

'Yeah, totally.' She had moved his hands aside, gripping his wrist, avoiding all touch with the Leica he held, and kissed him one last time. Then she had swung up on the truck heading up to the hills, and had not looked back to wave, or to check if he had waited to see her off.

Even after all the years, Sam reaches out to the now filthy patch on her jacket when she is distressed, or terrified, fingering the embroidered edge of the maple leaf like a talisman, or a reminder of that night in the hills, when she had clutched herself, shaking with horror, when not even an entire bottle of slivovitsa could keep her teeth from chattering, when she had bitten through the inside of her cheeks and spat out mouthfuls of blood and bits of flesh.

In her worst nightmares, the ones that assail her at dawn just as she begins to sink into her deepest, briefest sleep, Sam relives that night before she had met the gentle doctor again and again. The drive into the besieged village on a peacekeeper truck, the relief and joy on faces when they had driven to the centre followed by the despair that it was only a mission to gather information, not to rescue any survivors. She had walked around, shooting the village, the scalloped windows damaged by shells shot from far in the woods, the shingled roofs gaping like hungry mouths. She had used only a roll for the people besieging the officers, begging to be taken out, had moved away when their despairing attempts to push their children, infants even, into the peacekeepers' arms had become frantic.

The shelling had halted for the night, perhaps so as not to disrupt their mission, or for propaganda or perhaps because the assailants in the far hills needed a night of rest too. Sam had paid a woman in cigarettes and vodka to let her sleep on the floor of her house. It had seemed the cleanest of all in the village, even though only one room, right at the front remained standing. The rubble of the rest of the house had been painstakingly removed, re-arranged into a semblance of neatness. The lone room was crowded, as if everything the woman had ever owned had been collected there, photographs, pots and pans, clothes, with baskets and chests full of things accrued over a life of family and friends and banality. A bed stood thrust against the far wall, piled high with quilts and blankets and coats and quantities of fabric, all feeble protection against the deadening winter.

Sam had found the translator late at night to ask him about the woman, her round face scored with lines of despair, her watery blue eyes bleak, as she clutched her two children near her. Even to Sam's inexpert eyes, the children seemed small, if not malnourished then somehow arrested in growth, their eyes too large for their faces, their heads balanced precariously on stick thin necks that poked from quantities of woollens that swaddled their tiny frames.

The translator had been brusque, perfunctory. 'Her husband was rounded up and killed months ago. She says the men in the mountains will come finish them off once we leave.'

'And will they?' Sam had asked, even though she knew the answer already.

'Yes, probably even before the end of tomorrow, before we are even off this damn mountain.' The translator looked drained, his eyes as bleak as the woman for whom he translated. He had left abruptly and Sam hadn't followed, merely handing over a bottle to the woman, digging up some chocolate for the children who devoured it greedily, the brown forming a dark, filthy ring around their already begrimed mouths. She hadn't bothered to use the groundsheet, merely huddled in her sleeping bag in the corner, eyes closed against the dim light of the lantern, ears alert for any noise beyond the soft murmurs of the woman, the high-pitched whispers of the children.

The sudden brightness of an additional lamp had awoken Sam, sometime late in the night, or perhaps just before dawn. The woman stood before her, her hands holding out a single small scrap. She thrust it at Sam, again and again, her eyes pleading, her voice rising in terror. Sam's fingers had barely closed around the scrap when the woman turned away. That is when Sam had noticed the preparations.

In the centre of the room, the woman had laid a thick square of blankets and quilts, high enough to be comfortable even on the cold floor. On it she had laid her two children, side by side, fast asleep, covered them with a bright quilt embroidered with the colours and blossoms of spring. The lamps in the corners threw a golden light on the children, and Sam instinctively moved to pull out her camera, tucking the scrap the woman had given her in her pocket, her hands moving of their own accord to pull out the Leica, to adjust the settings, her eye and viewfinder blending into one.

As Sam began to shoot, the woman knelt near the edge, her hands clutched against her full skirts. For a moment, her finger lightly caressing the shutter release, Sam thought the woman was praying. In her head, even as she shot, Sam could see a story unfold: a close-up of the child closest to her, the face as immobile in sleep as in death; the woman, her eyes streaming, face turned upwards, her hands clutched in her lap, like a painting in a church. Sam came to her feet, her attention on the Leica, composing, focusing, shooting on instinct, alone, circling the little group to find the best angles.

Perhaps that is why the next shots came as a shock. Sam had not noticed that the woman held an old M-57 clutched against her dark skirt, the dim steel blending into the ancient folds. Sam was still shooting when the woman raised the revolver to the children, firing twice, at close range, first at the girl, then the boy.

Sam had frozen at the sound of the first shot, so loud in the small closed room, had looked up from the viewfinder at the woman who still knelt near the children. The woman had looked straight at Sam, her eyes bleak yet triumphant. She said something, words that Sam did not, could not, understand. Then raising the revolver to her mouth, she had squeezed the trigger one last time.

Sam had been unable to move, her eyes wide, her fingers gripping the Leica, even when the peacekeepers had burst in through the door. She had stood there, removed from the shouts, the chatter, the warm bodies brushing against her skin as people jostled about.

It was the translator who had shaken her out of her trance, jostling her arm, pulling her out of the cramped little room and into the chill of night. He had pulled out a flask of vodka, helped her drink down some, offered her the courtesy of looking away as the liquid had burned its way down to her stomach and then instantly fought its way back up. Instinctively pushing the Leica to the small of her back, Sam had retched into the dark.

'It's what she had said last night. I wish I had believed her,' the translator was speaking behind her. 'She wasn't going to let them get the kids.'

Sam had tried to pull herself together, forced herself to take long breaths, shaken her head until it stopped swimming. But her teeth would not stop chattering, as the shivers raced up her spine, made her hands shake, turned her legs to jelly. She had gritted her teeth together until she could taste her own blood, swilling the vodka against her mouth until her cut cheeks burned, until the sting brought tears to her eyes. She had stayed there, against the wall, in the dark, sipping and swilling and spitting out the vodka and blood, her unsteady hands clutching the Leica but drawing no comfort from its familiarity.

THE ARCADIA
57 HOURS AGO

Abhi pours a second sachet of instant coffee into hot water from the sink, stirring it to the consistency of weak sludge. Mentally, he counts the remaining sachets in his desk drawer. Enough for three days, maybe four, if he maintains the current strength, possibly less. Even with the preparations to storm the Arcadia, he knows it will be at least another night before they are released.

He runs through the pile of supplies he has on his desk, the low stack of towels, piled packets of nuts and chips, two litre-bottles of Coke and a case of bottled water. Enough, he thinks, to last at least forty eight hours if he is careful. He wishes there were at least a can of beer, a mini-bottle of something alcoholic in the pile, then chides himself for weakness.

Below the high window, the wide lawn lies in the dark. Someone, perhaps the electricity department, or maybe the army has switched off the electricity to the wide roads surrounding the Arcadia. On the sole television screen in the ante-room, the tall towers of the hotel blaze with lights, punctuated with the occasional flash from an exploding grenade. Beyond the glowing perimeter, shadows hulk in the dark, the dull red of a fire engine, the deep blue of a police car.

Even in the relative lull of the night, Abhi grits his teeth, remembering the conversation he has just had with a hysterical guest, insisting that food be delivered to him, that the assailants be removed at once. He has had to use all his patience and tact to calm him down, fearing that much of the aggression is driven by the contents of the mini-bar, hopes that the rudeness will not degenerate into Dutch courage and lead the guest out of the room, and into the path of the gunmen who still roam.

He suspects that the early hours before dawn may be the quietest, that the tempers will fray when the day breaks and the full horror of the siege dawn on the hostages. He knows he should sleep, use this lull for a few hours of rest, but his nerves are on edge, threatening to fray if he relaxes even for an instant.

He has stood often at this window, pleased that its height gives him a clear view across the lawns. He likes to stand in the shadows, the office lights turned off, just like now. The lawn is always lit with myriad golden lights, its shadowy nooks attracting couples looking for a bit of privacy. Far beyond, the hedges screen off the lawn from the busy square. And even farther away, the city lights twinkle, still a siren song even after so many years.

He never brings anyone to his office, uses it as his own little castle, always locks the connecting door to the ante-room when he leaves. He keeps his own supplies here, some changes of clothing, some books, things to keep him company when he is too tired to go home, too alone to bother taking up one of the courtesy suites.

Abhi wants to reach out, race across the lawn, lying so still in the night, its far hedge barely visible, tall wrought iron lamps rising like ghosts against the cityscape, as if promising relief just beyond the large sealed windows. But he knows there is no escape. There is a sheer drop of over twenty feet to the grass below, and he had earlier watched helplessly as the police tried to approach the Arcadia across the vast green and his stomach clenching in horror as two men leading the bunch were picked off by a gunman on some floor high above.

His phone vibrates again, the rhythmic buzz insisting on his attention. Abhi has ignored the calls from friends, acquaintances, even people he knows from the press, focusing on what he needs to do. He scrolls down the call list. Multiple calls from home. And Samar. And then multiple text messages.

He had sent a text to his contact list, just after finding refuge in the office, once the panic had abated, assuring them of his safety, asking for help. He knows he had included both Samar and Baba's numbers in that round. He may be angry, proud, possibly even wrong, but he refuses to be cruel. Yet the calls and texts irritate him. Samar's messages are cool, calculated, full of good advice, some of it ridiculous, though Abhi knows his brother means well. Baba's seem confused, baffled, demanding that Abhi confirm his well-being immediately, telling him not to worry about contacting home and to concentrate on his safety, and tailing off into tangled half-sentences.

He tries to answer back, his eyes staring out into the dark night, barely registering the silence, his fingers tapping, then un-tapping messages. But he can't think of anything to say, more than he already has, can't even identify his father in the strangely confused texts.

Finally, he tucks the mobile back into his pocket, scans the night spreading out before him one last time before turning away to whip up more coffee. Carrying another double sachet offering of caffeine, Abhi walks back to the ante-room, slumps on the chair before the CCTV screens, his eyes gazing lazily, drowsily, ahead as he waits for the night to end.

***

Sam prepares her second foray with her usual automatic precision, her hands moving quickly, meticulously, to stock her pockets. She is almost on her way out when she decides to turn back to the phone.

'Hello, this is the Arcadia. Abhi Sikarwal speaking.' The voice is drowsy, exhausted.

'Hey.' She doesn't really know why she has called.

'Sam? What? Jeez what time is it? Are you OK?' The questions come fast.

'I am heading out again. Will head down to the floors below now,' she tells him, inventing an excuse to pretend even to herself that she doesn't want to hear his voice, that she doesn't want anyone asking the questions he instinctively directs at her.

'Of course, Sam. How many floors?'

79

'Next three down. So let's say until the eleventh. I think I can do those without attracting attention.'

Abhi scans the floors checking for the assailants, who seem to have descended to the lower floors. 'Let me check. Some are occupied, at least on my list.'

Sam savours his voice, concerned, concentrated, soft against her ear. She knows about intimacy born out of moments of extreme stress, or trauma, but this feels different, maybe because she can't see him. Can't even imagine him. In some way, knowing he will wait for her makes her feel better.

He keeps briefing her, counting off the gunmen and their locations from his screen. 'By the way, are you carrying your phone? I am texting you from mine.'

Sam smiles as her phone vibrates against her thigh, even before he finishes his sentence. 'So you got it off the check-in file, did you?'

'Of course! Listen, keep the phone. If they move far, I can update you on enemy location in real time.'

'God, you are a boy, aren't you? Where did you get all this army lingo? I thought you were all so very nice,' she laughs out.

'Army brat! Comes out every so often.'

'Me too, so I know,' her voice drops a notch for the confession.

Abhi can't help but smile at the recognition. 'Who'd have guessed?' he teases.

'Yeah right!' she snorts derisively. She knows she is wasting precious minutes but still she lingers, needing to hear his voice again, drawing an inexplicable, childish comfort from their sudden rapport. 'So what is a nice army brat like you doing in a place like this? Shouldn't you be off playing hero somewhere?'

Even on the phone line, she can feel him tense at her words, unknowingly holds her own breath in response. His words when they come are softer, tinged with emotions she knows well. 'Am the black sheep. Total disappointment to the pater.' His laughter sounds forced.

'Join the club,' she mutters, her words low but distinct, wishing she could find something appropriate to say to him. In her mind, forbidden images float up, of waiting by the door for her father, of his unexplained absences, the olive green of his uniform filling her eyes as she hugged him goodbye. With the memories rise the long buried feelings, her need to prove herself to her father, the desperate training at track and field, and any sport she encountered, the years of being the son her father always wanted. And then that awful, final, day when her father had bought her a dress, something silk and glossy. 'Time for you to be a girl, sweetheart. And you are such a beauty too,' he had told her, his voice full of love and tenderness and something that seemed like awe. She had worn the dress of course. And grown her hair till it swished down her back. And learned to wear the high heels that he said made her a lady. And she had never forgiven him any of it.

'Sam,' Abhi's voice is soft. 'If you are going to have enough time, you need to…'

'Yes, of course,' her voice is brisk, to the point, like always. And yet she lingers, holding the receiver against her cheek.

'Abhi,' she hesitates, staring ahead, a frown deep between her eyes. 'Abhi, will you check? On me. In an hour? I mean, just in case…'

'Yes. Yes, of course. In an hour again, Sam. I will call every five minutes from then till you answer.'

'Thanks, Abhi.'

'Be careful,' he tells her, waits for her response. Her chuckle, when it comes, is low, throaty.

He laughs out loud too. Then just before hanging up, he asks for a favour. 'And Sam, keep an eye out for survivors. Please.'

***

Abhi watches Sam make her way slowly, methodically, through the corridors, one eye cocked scanning the other screens for movement. She enters the open rooms, disappearing into the yawning doorways, sidesteps the closed ones. In most, she spends less than a couple of minutes, moving back out, her twin cameras slung across her neck.

He has watched her make her way through two floors when she suddenly spots a CCTV camera. He watches as she pauses, puzzled, observing the screen carefully. She backtracks to the one on the far end. Close up, her face is angular, with sharp cheekbones, her eyes large and dark and deep, too large for her face. There is a narrow furrow in her forehead, a slight squint in her eyes as she looks up into the camera. She walks slowly, carefully, back into the corridor, away from the lens, as if measuring its range. At the farthest point, she pauses and, turning, she checks the second camera.

Abhi can see her mouth frame the curses, moving silently in the grainy screen. She moves up to the second camera, then back to the first, repeating the steps over and over again, as if confirming its range and reach, her eyes tight in concentration, a frown deep in her forehead. Suddenly, she's out of range. Abhi sits up, even though he knows she has just squatted beyond the edge of the camera. A blind spot! He has not noticed it either. She moves back into the frame again, walking back and forth, measuring, reconfirming the angle, ensuring she has identified the blind spot correctly.

Finally, she turns to face the nearest camera, holds up her hands, palms up, thumbs held out at straight angles. She frames her face with her outstretched palms, moves them gently around as if composing an image for him. Then holding her palms up and outwards, she grins, scrunches her face and sticks her tongue out at the camera.

***

Sam curses under her breath when she realises that cameras are tucked high into the corners. How the hell had she missed them before? She hates feeling watched, even in peace time, always wears wide brimmed hats even through the streets at home, hiding her face, her expressions, herself from the eyes of casual observers who man the innumerable lenses that spy on the streets, shops, trains. At her flat door, she has mounted

82

an extra mirror, its circle angled to replicate the electronic spies in the street. Before leaving her flat, she always checks herself in that, pulling up her collar against her neck, covering the shallow hollow of her throat with a scarf, refusing to let the anonymous watchers catch even an unwitting glimpse of her skin. Perhaps that is why she is so annoyed that she had not noticed the cameras in the corridors before, is horrified that someone, anyone, could have watched her earlier foray up to the Refuge, that someone had noticed her stumble, nearly fall, in the corridor from exhaustion, that anyone had seen her fumbling with her key-card, unable to enter the room, slotting it into the lock over and over again, cursing, even slamming the door with her fist, when she had first checked in.

As her stomach turns and tumbles in panic, Sam wonders if there are cameras in her room. She is terrified that someone, anyone may have watched her set up her warning system, dragging the furniture in the systematic ring along the outer perimeter; hates the thought of an anonymous eye watching her collapse on the sofa, taking gulps of whisky straight from the bottle, her arms hugging herself. She works her way along the corridor, spotting, marking, noting each camera, even as she mentally goes through her list of all the things she has done since reaching her room. First rule of survival, she remembers reading somewhere, is never to let them see a weakness. Has someone seen her weak, collapsed, drunk, weeping, in her room?

Slowly, painfully, she brings her breathing back to normal, forcing herself to breathe through the nose, deep pulls that push at her lungs, fill her belly. She forces the air out the same way, slowly, pushing from the bottom of her unruly stomach, expelling it through her mouth. Again. And then over again. Until she can feel her panic recede, and her mind taking control over the rising paranoia. Of course, there won't be cameras in the room, she reminds herself. There are laws against that sort of thing, she tells herself, even though she knows she will check the room carefully, meticulously, once she returns.

She walks before each camera, observing the angle, pulling herself up as close as possible to check the lens. She walks back and forth, extrapolating its range from her observations to in the corridor. At the furthest reach of the visibility arc, she pauses, frowning, as she works out the possible blind spots. She stands on the edge of the wall, her back pressed against the ivory, withdrawing entirely into herself, making herself as small, unnoticeable as she can. In her mind, she compares the corridor to all others she has seen, knows that the camera placement will be just as uniform across the hotel, that obsessive regularity repeated on all other floors.

Who could be watching her, Sam wonders. The anonymity of the watcher bothers her, even when she has conquered the panic at being watched. As she tests each camera's range, counting each measured step, as she walks back and forth in the corridor, tests every blind spot she calculates, her mind is racing. Her first foray began over four hours ago, and yet none of the gunmen have found her. Surely there are cameras in the rooftop bar as well, and she spent nearly an hour shooting there, enough time for the assailants to find her. She knows there has been nobody else in her own corridor since she returned to her room. She would have heard them, would have noticed some trace of an intruder on the carefully placed debris, the glow-in-the-dark shards, the scattered lilies.

It isn't till she is ready to turn back to the fire escape door, to continue her foray, convinced that she has worked out the camera placements that she remembers the flashing phone light that had greeted her on her return from the Refuge and that confident tone of voice that had promised her real-time updates. Of course! How else would he have known the very instant she had returned to her room. Abhi!

The thought brings an unexpected flash of relief and a kind of comfort that Abhi can see her. Smiling, Sam pushes back her cap a little, revealing a high forehead, letting even a little of the salt-and-pepper stubble on her scalp peek from beneath the dark fabric. Then slowly she runs a single finger under her scarf, loosening it around her throat just a fraction, before turning to the nearest camera. The dark round lens doesn't seem as threatening once she can imagine the steady voice of Abhi behind it. She stands on tiptoe, her sharp-edged face turned up to the lens, her throat elongated and exposed, and gives him a quick, happy, wave.

THE ARCADIA
LESS THAN 56 HOURS AGO

Sam has a rule: she makes no contact with her subjects. She doesn't try to get them help or try to stop them bleeding. Doesn't even make eye contact without her camera blocking out all she doesn't want to see. All those are tasks for others. With her viewfinder before her eye, she sees through a screen and makes sure that she isn't touched by what unfolds on it. For the same reason, she never speaks to her subjects, or hears them cry, talk, scream. Those are sounds she blocks out, in the studio by looping the Doors Greatest Hits interminably on her iPod, and in the field by subconsciously blocking out all sound except what may spell danger for her. Which is perhaps why she doesn't hear the whimpering at first.

From the corridor, through the open doorway, Sam has spotted the first target. A woman lies, her arm flung out and over her head, the other held under her belly, just inside the door, pushed back slightly with the first impact, crumpled just past the dark oak door. She lies with her face half turned up, some stray strands of hair concealing the soft, glowing skin of her cheek, the kind that only very expensive potions and treatments can maintain. A pretty, if not really beautiful, face, at least in profile. She wears the sort of easy casual clothes that shimmer slightly in the light, of soft sensual fabrics, creamy and pale, clothes for a woman who isn't likely to get them dirty, or use them hard, although they are now stained dark red, nearly matching the rich maroon of the wallpaper. Sam likes the symmetry of colour, recognising it as trite, though she knows it is the sort that will sell well for news outlets.

Sam notes the number on the door, drawn into the room, the first she has found on this floor with the doors open. She can see further down the corridor, where light pours from two

86

more doors. What makes people open the door when they hear shots? Wouldn't it make more sense to hunker down? But the thought passes as the doorway beckons, seductive in its promise of images, of possibilities.

Room 1104, she looks again to confirm, a room that mirrors her own almost perfectly, if in inversion. It is decorated in the same tones of cream and maroon, uniform luxury; even the same configuration of the wide bed, the sofa near the window, the wide screen television taking up most of one wall. Except this room is messy, clothes and toys litter all surfaces, the shiny countertop, the floor, the side-tables. Beyond the bathroom door, she can see the marble counter top is almost entirely concealed by bottles and tubes, expensive products for skin and hair, the kind she always associates with unhappy or bored wives of rich men. Near the sofa, a child's cot stands, the linens messy and rumpled, a small brown teddy bear flung forgetfully into one corner. On autopilot, her ears alert for any sound of danger, her eye glued to the viewfinder, Sam shoots off a couple of shots, clicking more for atmosphere than any real value. She knows the papers will pay for it well, exclusive shots from inside the Arcadia, taken during the attack, not later. Hell, with any luck, these could cover her bills for a few months, possibly even for the full year, if they are syndicated properly.

The man lies closer to the bed, tucked into the bed-skirt, far from the door, nearly hidden from view. He is dressed just as Sam would imagine, a light coloured, striped, button-up shirt, the kind that goes under a suit jacket; dark suit trousers; his socks are navy, but with lurid stripes of yellow, red, neon green. Even behind the viewfinder, Sam grimaces at his pathetic attempt at injecting what she knows fashion experts would call 'personality' into his clothes. His head is almost entirely hidden by the fabric of the bed-skirt, his body turned into the bed, as if he had tried to slide underneath for safety, or perhaps comfort. 'What a wuss,' Sam snorts in her head, clicking away.

It isn't until she is almost out of the room that the strangeness of the man's posture clicks. He is too bulky, his torso is too high off the ground for a man of his build. Puzzled, she makes her way back to the bed, peering closely, warily at the body. She knows he is dead, even without checking for pulse or other vital signs, recognises the strange stiffness that marks corpses when life has finally vacated its shell. Suddenly she hears the whimper, barely audible, more of a sniff or sob than an actual cry. Once the sound registers in her conscious, she knows she has heard it before in the room, much like the sound of an animal in distress, dying or injured, but muffled.

From beneath the body, a small hand pokes out, curled on a scrap of the pale striped shirt fabric, nearly hidden from view, unseen by any but the most careful observer. Intrigued, she draws closer, the viewfinder before her eye protecting her even as her fingers manipulate the lens, focusing, pulling in for extreme close-ups. It isn't until many moments later, her curiosity fully aroused, that she pulls back a bit, uses the tip of her rubber-soled boot to gently push the corpse to one side. As the body slumps away, the end of the puzzle emerges. A child, small, tousled hair, lies half-suffocated underneath. Despite herself, Sam feels a tug of sympathy for the man, likely the father, who has tried to protect this frail being that now lies whimpering.

Careful to keep the viewfinder in place, Sam begins her retreat, the Mamiya continuing to frame the child's fragile face, letting it recede into the distance in slow motion. The whimpers have ceased and she is grateful for the renewed silence. It isn't until she is about to turn away that the child suddenly opens his eyes to look straight into the Mamiya. Dark, hazel or brown, almond shaped, full of fear and pain. His sudden movement sends Sam's finger juddering down, unconsciously shooting off half a dozen shots before she can unclench her hand.

'Mr Fuzzy,' he whispers.

Protected by the Mamiya, she pauses, confused. She doesn't make eye contact, she reminds herself. But the dead don't speak to her either, at least not in voices.

'Mr Fuzzy,' the child whimpers again, 'Mr Fuzzy.'

Baffled, Sam begins to retreat to the door, maintaining the dark case of the Mamiya before her face for protection, blocking out the faint whimpers, focusing again on the possibility of other, more dangerous, sounds. At the door, she stops for another sweep, confirming she hasn't missed a shot. 'Mr Fuzzy,' the fading voice is barely a whisper in her head. The viewfinder swings again, moving through the room, until it pauses on the messy cot, the teddy bear, sitting alertly in the far corner.

Without conscious thought, the camera still glued to her eye, her finger moving instinctively on the lens to maintain continuous clarity of vision, Sam crosses back into the room, picks up the teddy, and passes it to the child. Through the lens, she notes that he clutches the toy to his chest, the blue T-shirt damp and dark on one side with blood, his or the father's perhaps. His eyes are closed again, though the frown brought on by pain or distress has eased slightly. For a second her finger pauses midway through pushing down, hesitating, questioning if it should press down, catch the final frame. Then she eases the pressure, consciously, carefully, pulling off her finger back to its rest position on the case.

The child has stopped whimpering, pulling the toy close to his chest, nuzzling his face into the fur. Deliberately she averts her eyes, slowing her breathing to calm herself, an ear still half-cocked for sounds of distress but the child seems to have fallen asleep. Comforted, Sam crosses the room again, her steps slow and measured. She pauses briefly at the open door to check for danger. Then without another look back, she lowers the Mamiya to its habitual rest position, cradled against her belly, she passes swiftly into the corridor.

***

Abhi has watched Sam move through the floors, her slow lurching gait moving along the corridors, focused, determined. He is fascinated by the unobtrusive way she slides out of the fire escape into the shadowed passageways. He finds himself

89

watching for that nearly imperceptible move of the door, the initial sign that she is preparing for entry, then the immeasurably slow curve of the door into the dark abyss beyond. Finally, after having waited, watched, confirmed and reconfirmed the silence beyond, she slides out, her slight frame an almost invisible smudge, bleeding into the dark shadows. She moves so imperceptibly that if he looks away from the screen, it takes him long seconds of scanning to spot her again.

At each closed door, she pauses to listen, her ear held against the oak expanse, then uses her forearm to gently push. Most doors remain shut, and for that Abhi is thankful, both for Sam's safety and for whoever remains inside. She approaches the open doors with even greater caution, sliding along the wall, her tension visible to him even through the CCTV static. After the second corridor she covers, Abhi realises that she has two set times for the rooms, spending just over two minutes in some, precisely seven in the rare few. He wonders how she chooses; why does she need more time, how she times herself as she methodically makes her ways through the floors. He knows that she leaves the latter rooms, happier, jauntier, some indefinable sense of achievement visible in the slight straightening of her shoulders, in the angle of her neck, like a boxer after landing a good punch.

Watching her, he feels a kinship with her caution, with her ability to blend into the background, and an admiration for her ability to nearly disappear. It is a survival skill he has had to cultivate even though he uses it less frequently these days. Sam's skills are far superior, honed in more extreme conditions, but in some ways, they are not so different, this fragile, slight, headstrong woman and he.

It isn't until she exits Room 1104, the door closest to the fire escape that will take her back to safety that he notices a change. She has taken longer in the room, even though he had almost been sure he had seen a shift in light at the seven-minute mark. He checks the stopwatch he's running on a spare phone. Nearly eleven minutes. He wonders what has kept her there, realises she is running behind on her self-imposed hour-long schedule.

90

As she makes her way back to the fire escape, the jauntiness is gone, replaced in those inexplicable minutes with a strange weariness. Her camera is held cradled against her belly, her head bent, even though alertness still tightens her limbs. But a strange lassitude seems to have overtaken her, as if her mind has moved somewhere else, leaving her body on auto-pilot, running only on adrenalin and long held habits.

He finds himself worrying about her, tracking the stopwatch as she seems to linger in the concrete shaft, or perhaps struggle up the invisible steps of the fire escape, far out of reach of all his mechanical eyes. When she slides into the fourteenth floor, he is shocked at the transformation. Her head is bent low, her shoulders hunched. Her feet seem to drag, though still with instinctive caution, on the carpet, as if weighted down. She checks automatically for her trail-markers, the threads, the minute glow-in-the-dark slivers that Abhi can only spot occasionally. At her door, she struggles with the automated lock, sliding the card in and out repeatedly.

'Slow down, let the damn thing read your card,' he mutters, knowing she can't hear him. He thinks she is trembling, wonders if that is just his imagination, or the screen static. Perhaps that is why he waits for nearly fifteen minutes to call her after she finally gets the door open, slides out of his sight with one last enormous effort. Even then the phone rings for a long time before she answers.

***

Sam holds herself together till she gets past the locked door of her room, adrenalin holding her nerves taut, her senses on red alert. Then sliding past the door, shutting it soundlessly, locking it behind her, she makes her away past the short hallway and turns into the room before slumping down. She knows all too well that bullets can slice past even heavy oak doors to leave herself exposed behind one. Holding herself hard against the wall, she lets the customary relief wash over, breathing deeply,

91

eyes shut, forcing her mind to steadily purge all she has seen and recorded.

Her unexpected encounter with the child has thrown her off-balance, she knows, pushing her mind to places she refuses to venture. Sam hasn't shot survivors in years, not since her war brides exhibition, and she knows even those weren't really survivors. Sam always thinks of that exhibition as her most clichéd, most sentimental work, even though it was the only one she sold out in its entirety, is the one that makes her consistent royalties. She tells herself that she didn't shoot the child either, that she eased her finger off even through the shock of seeing him alive.

Yet, as she wilfully deletes the images from her internal memory, Sam is left clutching the edges of her resolve. That is the instant when a gaping chasm opens up in her stomach threatening to swallow her again in a reminder of that first despair. For an instant, slumped against cool wall, she too grieves, not emotionally, not even consciously, but in a sudden swell of physical memory where the loss and pain cut through her as if for the first time again. Like that very first time she had returned from the jungle, with her very first death mask photo.

Over the years, since that first despair, Sam has collected thousands of images, although she uses few of them for her exhibitions and books. She is prodigal when it comes to collection, harvesting the death masks with the insatiable clicking of her Mamiya, even though she has only held it for two years. Before the Mamiya, there were others; the battered old Nikon, the Canon Eos, and somewhere, buried long ago, her beloved Leica that had swung into action just as regularly, always honing in on the perfect images. Ugly, beautiful, young, old, men and women. It doesn't really matter to her out in the field. Out there, there is just her eye glued to the viewfinder, her finger moving like an automaton, her mind filtering and filing and planning without consciousness. She doesn't choose then, but merely gathers all she finds, much like a starving man who can't be satiated no matter how much he eats.

Much later, when she is back in her flat, she will sift through the images, picking and choosing, finding the ones she likes best. She has been accused of picking only the most beautiful of the dead. She agrees, and makes no excuses for it: a young man in the Balkans, his blue eyes wide with innocence even in death; a female suicide bomber, her white *hijab* still pinned neatly in place over her dismembered head, her eyes closed and her lips curled into a smile; a man in profile, his dark hair cropped close to the skull, his dark lashes throwing a gentle shadow on his cheeks.

They aren't faces of the nameless dead to her. She knows which of the thousands of images will be selected finally to be blown up to gigantic proportions, be replicated obsessively hundreds of times on canvases that cover entire walls. She knows that she chooses her favourite photographs because of one single reason: they remind her of David in some mysterious way. She sees him everywhere in her work: in the curling lash on one face, in the enigmatic smile on another, in the shadowy hollow of a neck, or the gentle curve of a shoulder. Her photographs are a living cemetery of all that she wants, a private memorial for all that she can't have.

Which is why she thinks of the years after David's wedding as her death-mask period. She remembers everything of their last days together in ghastly tints of blue-greens. All their time together has been frozen in a series of mental snapshots: the pale of his arm as it curves around her while they sleep; the faded blue of his shirt that wraps her in the morning, caressing her skin with the memory of his; their first argument which was also their last because she couldn't fit all that she wanted to say in that minute; the distant chill of his eyes as he had frozen her out yet again.

Those are the memorised images that drove her to her first series, that very first exhibition. She had even named it Masks, hoping that the deathly chill of her heart would be obvious to those who looked on her photographs. And she opened it with that image from the jungle, of the young man in a nondescript shirt, lying in the doorway, bathed in a ghostly light. Was that a malfunction of her camera, or just the light filtering through the trees? She has never been able to pinpoint the source of that ghostly light. But she knows how to identify it, and to capture it; repeatedly, obsessively, across the world. And she remembers that second photograph when she saw that same light filter through her studio.

She shot it after her return to David, still shaken from witnessing the massacre in the jungle. She had wanted him to welcome her home, to take her in his arms and soothe away the nightmares she had begun having since the jungle, to make love to her slowly, gently. To do what lovers do at times of reunion. She hadn't had words to explain what she had seen: the auto-pilot clicking of her camera, the falling bodies, and sickening smell. And worst of all, she couldn't tell him how she had fallen asleep to the soundtrack of screams punctuated by dull thuds of the machete. Who falls asleep in times of war, she was sure he would question. Would he be disbelieving or merely horrified? But she had fallen asleep, retreating from the killing into the silence inside her mind. And now she felt sickened by her own escape.

Sam had not even had the courage to show him her photos. But then she hadn't been able to look at the photographs herself. She had just couriered them to her editor, keeping only that last black-and-white reel for herself, intuiting even then, without having seen, that those final shots had no news value. Just as she had intuited the distance growing between them, like a crevice that appears from nowhere, gaping and widening with every breath, and had not known how to reach across. How does one bridge a chasm created by the spectacle of death? Or by her own role in that macabre dance? Had she been the spectator? Or witness? Or perhaps retreating into sleep made her an accomplice? That is why David's announcement that he had fallen in love with someone else came mostly as a relief.

Later, on long nights on another airplane bound for another chaos, she would wonder why he had waited until after they had made love to tell her. Why hold her close; why run his fingers through her hair as if she were precious; why caress her skin as if he were memorising her if he had already decided? He told her that it wasn't her, that he took the blame. She hadn't believed him then. And she knows better now: it was her, the whirlwind that insists on racing through the dust, seeking something inarticulate and unknown, leaving nothing but destruction in her wake. Not the kind of woman to build legacies with! And perhaps, that is why she has always kept her second death-mask photograph at the bottom of the cabinet that holds her prints, individually trapped in a sealed brown envelope, always refusing to look at it, resolutely choosing never to exhibit it.

It is a photograph she took at David's request. Or perhaps it just made a more personal wedding present for him. Sam had agreed a shoot for his bride; painstaking, black and white portraits, meant to be a parting gift to him. Later she always wondered what self-loathing had driven her to agree to David's murmured coercion and even much later, on a plane to somewhere far and dangerous, she had caught herself thinking of him as a total bastard for asking it of her. But she stopped that line of thought, mentally reviewing the equipment she had packed, obsessively visualising the cameras, memory cards, extra batteries that lay in the plane's overhead locker until all memories of David, and any pain she had felt, had receded far from consciousness.

She had devoted an entire day, waiting implacable in the shadows as she watched David's bride – Sam likes to call her Lisa, mostly names have a way of blurring in her memory – fuss over her make-up and clothes. Lisa had brought a make-up artist, and a suitcase full of designer clothes that fitted her like a glove.

From the shadows, Sam mentally compared herself to the beautiful woman before her. Lisa was tall and slim, graceful in a way that Sam would never be. And she was somehow innocent and untouched, all qualities beyond Sam's reach, rendered impossible by her intimacy with disaster. Sam mentally photographed her long before reaching for the camera, before setting up the reflectors and lights to highlight Lisa's delicate features. For an instant she found herself seeing Lisa with David's eyes: finding beauty in that fragile face, in those large eyes filled with wonder, and possibly fear. In a blurred reflection in a window, Sam caught a glimpse of herself, the very opposite of Lisa. For a fleeting moment, she wondered how David saw her, why his eyes lit up with warmth when she could be nothing like his bride-to-be, if he had ever wanted her to be the same. An unconscious grin twisted her lips at the very idea of David in his immaculate suits and glossy shoes anywhere near an armed conflict. Sam suppressed sudden giggles, shook her head, and began to click.

She hadn't worked on portraits since her return from the jungle. And the camera felt strange, clumsy in her hands. The lights seemed impossible to control, raking up at odd angles. The reflectors blurred rather than softened. Sam knew even without checking that the shoot would not go as planned. The black and white images would be implausibly beautiful, remote, empty. Soul-less.

Sam has always believed that photographs reveal something of the soul. Even that dead boy in the doorway had held the promise of life, love, kindness amongst rancid death. Even images of arms holding swinging machetes held the possibility of wrapping gently around a swaddled infant, moving softly over beloved skin. But with Lisa, she could find nothing despite all her effort. Sam captured the flawless pale skin, the limpid eyes, smooth cascades of hair; a positive print of the negative she sees in her mirror every morning. She told herself that perhaps it was that photographic inversion that made the positive so different. Filled with stillness, like death or silence.

It was not until the last set of shots that the sun began to slide across the western wall of her studio, lighting up the deep marine blue-green mural, flitting across the floor secretively, bathing the room with the gloom she had always loved. Sam had hesitated, but then chosen to turn off the spots and use that murkiness. In her viewfinder, the light had given an eerie glow to the woman before her. Lisa's eyes had dulled in the gloom, her pale skin growing luminous. A death mask, Sam had recognised. Just like that boy in the doorway. She had only needed to click once.

Sam gave David the prettiest, most pedestrian images, trapped in a heavy, dark frame. His eyes had glowed with pride, Sam never knew whether it was for his bride's beauty or for Sam's skill. She had not cared to ask him further. She knew that even he could not tell the difference between art and kitsch, especially when it came to those he loved.

She had thanked him before leaving, and he had looked momentarily puzzled. 'What for?' he had asked. Sam had shrugged, replicating a gesture that he used often, a swift hunching of shoulders that she had grown to love.

'Does it matter?'

***

He waits nearly fifteen minutes, letting her recover, before he punches her number.

'Abhi?' Her voice is ragged.

'Yes, ma'am,' he teases.

'Told you not to call me that,' she responds, her voice lightening a little as she recognises that he's teasing her.

'You want to talk, Sam?'

'Yeah, yeah.'

'Go over each floor? I have my notes here, Sam.'

'Always the one calling the shots, aren't you?' she says even though Abhi can sense the tension in her voice. He lets her talk, her words settling into cold precision as she describes each floor, each room she has entered, the position and wounds of the dead, her rapid words filling in all he can't see on his CCTV screen. It isn't until she is running out of breath that she stumbles over her words. 'There is a kid in 1104, Mr Sikarwal.'

The formality jars him from his notes. 'What?'

97

'He's alive,' she sounds hoarse, as if the words must scrape their way out of her throat.

'Jesus, Sam! We need to get him out of there. They will kill him on the next round, damn it.' He can feel the panic swell within him.

'I think he may be injured.' Her voice remains mechanical, distant. 'Or in shock.'

'Sam, you have to get him.' Abhi is scanning the wall of screens before him, cursing at his own impotence. Too much open space, too many floors, and far too many gunmen stand in his way to 1104. On a regular day, he knows he could get there in just under seven minutes from his office but now that is an impossibility.

'I don't get involved. I am a photographer, remember,' her words seem to be spat out. For an instant, Abhi is tempted to yell at her, to accuse her of being another heartless vulture profiting from misery, abuse her for her callousness. But even on the phone line, he can hear the strain in her voice, and a fear that he has not heard before. 'I can't get involved,' she repeats, more like a mantra than an argument.

'It's OK, Sam,' his voice is soothing. 'I know...want to go over the other rooms with me? Just in case you remember something else? Something we may have missed?' He can hear her relief as he steers the conversation back to safe ground.

He is glad that she will stay on the line, if only so they can continue talking until her voice grows calm, her breaths come steadily, her nerves grow steely again. Abhi keeps his voice light, interjecting her second round of reports with light-hearted stories about the Arcadia, of eccentric celebrities, wild rock star guests, and secret lovers' trysts in the rooms. He smiles the first time he hears her giggle, the sound so infectious that he rummages through his mind to find more stories that make her laugh.

Perhaps, this is why she eventually begins telling Abhi about David, about how she doesn't return to him out of love, but for the comfort of familiarity. That it is the known quality of his skin, his eyes and hands that draw her back to him after every assignment.

'I wish he could love me,' her voice is plaintive, vulnerable.

'Sam, I am sure he does,' Abhi is gentle and kind and patient, 'probably in his own way. His own twisted way.'

'I wish I could love him,' she mutters, barely audible.

'Don't you?'

'No. Never have. I don't think I can.' Her voice sinks into a whisper.

The moment of confession is too much for her. For long moments, Abhi can hear her struggle to calm herself, to breathe deeply, slowly. Her voice is noticeably lighter, slightly formal, when she speaks again. 'So how about you? Do you have someone? A lover?'

Abhi has been expecting the question, the logical extension of the strange intimacy they have developed in the past hours but still he hesitates. How much can he say? How much will he say?

'Well, there is someone, maybe. I don't think things will work out.' He finally settles on something half-true, half-evasion.

'Why? Did you leave?' She asks, as if that would make everything different.

'No,' Abhi sighs, his mind going back to that painful last parting. 'I think he has.'

She doesn't speak for a long while. 'Men are such bastards, aren't they?'

She dissolves into giggles again. Almost as if there had never been any heartbreak. Or even heartache. As if they were sharing over Saturday night drinks instead of whiling away the long hours of an uncertain siege.

It isn't until she has placed a chair against the door-knob, downed a mini-bottle of whisky, and curled up tight under the duvet, her eyes heavy with exhaustion and lurking nightmares that she realises that Abhi had not laughed at the end, that he had remained sombre despite her desperate final giggles, remembers his last words before he had hung up, spoken so softly that she had almost missed them, uttered after he had bid her goodnight. Words that she would have not heard had she not held on to the receiver for just that extra moment, seeking its warmth on her neck, the strange intimacy it seemed to offer.

'What if you are the only one who can help someone?'

SOMEWHERE IN THE FOOTHILLS
1⁹ YEARS AGO

'Focus on the fear, Abhi. The more you train, the easier it will be to win.' Samar's voice is jagged in his memory. That was the summer when Samar's voice had suddenly cracked, switching unpredictably, veering wildly between his own childish falsetto and father's deep bass midway through a word. The breaking voice had gone hand in hand with an ever growing ferocity, as if Samar could force his body into adulthood, as if he could outrace time to become the man he was so desperate to grow into. His own voice still childishly high, wrapped in growing fears, and desires, and doubts that he could not even begin to articulate, Abhi had idolised Samar even more.

Abhi remembers that summer from long ago, up high somewhere along the border, fondly; the long lazy days of sunshine, climbing the deodar trees so high that his head swam to look down, swimming in the clear mountain lake beyond the cantonment grounds. He had just completed his tenth birthday, just got his swimming certificate, and Samar had told him about the South Sea pearl divers. 'And they just dive, just holding their breath, right to the bottom of the sea, till they find a pearl. They are super-humans,' Samar's voice held a shade of envy, of ambition.

Perhaps that is why they had started taking turns diving in the lake, pushing each other to reach the sandy bottom, with its tangle of green and browns plants. Abhi had tried his best, pushing himself until his lungs felt they were aflame, pushing himself to head straight through the clear waters, his eyes locked on his more powerful brother who always seemed to stay ahead, diving deeper, swimming farther, climbing higher. He would come up for air, his ears ready to explode with pain, his eyes streaming with tears, his lungs bursting, knowing that Samar would remain underwater for many more interminable seconds, a sudden fear for his brother gripping him. When Samar finally broke water, Abhi thought the relief would nearly overwhelm him. He would flash a quick grin, but then turn quickly to swim ashore. Anything but letting his fear, his relief, his love show.

Abhi had been the first to notice the shiny big white sphere at the bottom of the lake. It gleamed like a fairy tale jewel when the light hit it directly at noon, dulled into pearly opalescence with the passing of the overhead sun. Nestled amongst the green algae and chocolate of the mud, it was the size of his fist, perfectly round and pale. In the clear waters of the mountain lake, it shone so bright that Abhi could even see it from the shore; but that was only because he knew where to look. He had been afraid to point it out to Samar, unsure even why he wanted to keep the find for himself. But of course, Samar had noticed his gaze, noticed the longing in Abhi's eyes as they scanned the clear waters.

'Maybe it's a pearl,' Samar had suggested one morning, watching Abhi peel off his clothes, gasping as he waded into the cold waters of the lake. 'We should dive for it.'

Abhi hadn't answered, had pretended that he had not even heard. He desperately wanted to dive for that pearl, knew it was his by rights because he had seen it first. But he wasn't nearly as good a swimmer as Samar, knew he couldn't hold his breath long enough to reach the bottom. Samar would get there first, as always. For the first time, the thought made him glum, made him wish that he could have the pearl all for himself, reach it first, bring it up like a trophy held in his hands to show Samar.

'Actually, you should dive for it,' Samar had said after a while, Abhi's unusual silence rendering him prescient. 'You saw it first.'

Abhi had stared moodily into the water, barely daring to believe, too afraid that he would fail even if he tried. Then he had shrugged, 'You can go get it. I don't mind.'

'We could train for it,' Samar had insisted. 'We have all summer, right?'

Abhi had looked up then, smiling in response to Samar's wide grin.

That is what they had done for weeks, diving into the pond for hours of the afternoon, swimming underwater for minutes on end until Abhi thought his lungs would turn to flames and had to come up fighting for air. Samar always timed him, counting each extra second underwater, each little improvement on his blue waterproof Swatch.

'You're almost ready. Maybe tomorrow you can go for it.' Samar had told him late one evening, his voice as serious as Baba's when he spoke to his junior officers. Abhi had nodded, his heart throbbing suddenly, painfully, with the excitement. 'After I finish studying, we'll go get the pearl,' Samar had instructed, laying out the plans with his usual precision, explaining his instructions to Abhi. 'So RV at 1500 hours, at the usual point, OK? And little bro, you wait for me. You will need back up on this,' he had insisted.

Abhi had nodded, as if in agreement, even though he already knew what he had to do. He knew that Samar wanted to protect him, knew that his brother wanted to watch his back, as always. But increasingly there were days, Abhi wished Samar would not protect him, would let him go his own way.

The next day, Abhi hadn't waited for Samar to finish his studies before sneaking away to the lake. He knew he was ready. And he wanted to try for the pearl by himself, without any help. If he could have said it out loud, even to himself, he would have admitted that he didn't want anyone to watch him if he failed. Not even Samar. Or perhaps, specially, not Samar.

He had dived over and again, almost reaching the bottom of the clear waters, each time getting closer and yet just too far to be able to reach the gleaming sphere. With every attempt, the sphere seemed to glisten more brightly, its smooth curved surface twinkling with an elusive play of iridescence, pink, blue, silver, lilac and grey. Each time, Abhi would stretch his fingers far ahead of him, his lungs close to bursting, his heart pounding in rhythm with the dizzy beat of his head, his legs kicking in rapid determination.

Closer. Just a bit closer. And yet, always, just too far.

Each time, he came up, he had flashed a glance up the hill, checking for Samar's usual loping walk, his jaunty lean figure heading down the path, afraid that all too soon, his brother would emerge along the shoreline. A part of him knew Samar would be angry at him, for not waiting, for trying without back up, for coming to the lake on his own. 'There is a reason soldiers buddy up, little bro,' Samar had explained patiently the night before. 'Higher success rate, and your buddy can pull you out of trouble.' Just like Baba, who had told him over and over again that he was not allowed to go swimming in the lake by himself. 'I want you to make sure Samar is with you. Neither of you are allowed to be in the water by yourselves, understand?' Then Baba's voice had softened, resting briefly on Abhi. 'But I know you won't. You are not the troublemaker.'

Yet, here he was, being the troublemaker, breaking Baba's command, even deceiving Samar, who would probably not even believe that Abhi would come down to the lake by himself. Abhi felt like an impostor most days, these days, hiding what was burgeoning inside him, pretending that he was like everyone else, like all the other boys, like Samar, even when the dark secret threatened to come screaming out from him. After such a big deception, Abhi didn't think swimming alone in the lake would matter, either to Baba or Samar. It was just one more secret, one more lie, one more treason that he knew he would commit, no matter how he tried to stop himself.

Perhaps it was the thought of being the fraud that drove him that final time, or just fear that Samar would find him if he didn't hurry up, that had pushed him that afternoon. Treading water, he had clenched his jaw just like Samar, and his father, and taken huge gulps of air, expanding his lungs to their full capacity. He had promised himself, one more dive. 'I am not coming up till I reach it,' he had growled to the glowing silent sunshine around him.

He had descended straight through the crystal waters, pushing forward with strong strokes, his legs kicking as hard as he could manage. Long before he had hit even the midway mark, his head was pounding, his lungs filling with the first twinge, like a match being lit somewhere deep within. Still he had plunged on, arm stretched, eyes fixed on the glowing pearl nestled at the bottom of the pool, its luminescence stark against the dark mud and green plants. Down, and then further down again. Until the sphere was barely a fingertip away.

His lungs at bursting point, Abhi had pushed one last, reaching out to grab it.

But at the very first touch of his outstretched finger, the pearl exploded. The luminescent fine surface punctured by the first contact with Abhi's grasping fingers. Something slimy had spilled out, spreading into the clear waters, crawled up his fingers, clinging stickily to the skin, as the sphere disintegrated into pale tatters and sticky milky liquid.

Stunned, Abhi forgot to hold his breath and gasped, choking instantly on the water that rushed up his nose, pushed into his throat. Frantically, he struggled to get back to the surface, clutching at nothing, kicking more by instinct, pushing against the weight of crystal waters. His eyes blurry, he pushed upwards, led only by the bright sun that lit the depths of the lake, each passing instant as long as eternity as he could feel his body protest, his lungs clenching and spasming, hacking coughs fighting their way out from somewhere deep within him.

It seemed forever until he broke through, tears streaming down his eyes, choking, coughing, his nose scalded, his eyes streaming, his lungs aching. Later he would only remember that first instant where his head had broken water to finally find clear mountain air, when the suffocating weight of the water had suddenly given way. He would not remember padding to the shore, his body doubling up with the effort, barely able to remain afloat. But he will hold the memory of that grateful moment his toes had finally curled into the muddy shore, felt the warmth of the sun on his wet back. He had barely made his way to the shore before collapsing in tears, and gasps, and painful coughs, on the grass.

Samar found him there much later, his head still buried in his knees, tears finally dried on his cheeks.

'Where is the pearl,' Samar had asked.

'There never was any,' Abhi had sobbed.

Samar had sunk in the grass, next to him. They sat like that for a long time, feeling the afternoon sun hot on their backs, the hoot of the woodpigeons cracking the silence like some indecipherable code, the mountain breeze fanning the heat away.

'Well, at least now you know,' Samar had finally said, putting his arm around Abhi's thin shoulders for comfort.

THE ARCADIA
52 HOURS AGO

Deep in the belly of the Arcadia, Abhi slumps on the sofa, half a bleary eye trained on the bank of screens, his rota of comforting calls to the guests completed once again. He can feel his muscles scream with exhaustion, but his mind races still, jumping from one thought to another, between memory and fantasy, like a crazed junkie. He wants to tell Sam to go look for the whimpering child. That is what he would do. But he is afraid that she would laugh at him, mock him for being such a sentimental fool. Perhaps she would go after all, risking herself not for her own photographs, for her own work, but for his quixotic fantasy. Worse still, he wonders if it would be better if she refused to go at all.

If he lets himself relax even for a millisecond, a sharp planed, familiar face intrudes into his thoughts, the blue eyes sparkling with mischief and promise, the blonde hair spiky and glowing, the lips full and alluring even when curved in laughter. Dieter.

At every thought of that face, Abhi's stomach gives a lurch. He can feel the panic and a growing certainty rise through him, a sorrow that threatens to overcome him if he relaxes his grip on his mind even for an instant. He had planned to meet Dieter in the Refuge, had called ahead to the bar to request them to prepare their special Martinis for him. He had even requisitioned the suite on the top floor, gone up to check that the flowers were fresh, that the bottle of champagne was chilling in the fridge. It was to be a special night, one that had promised possibilities far into the future, of love, of intimacy, of companionship, of a connection to another human being that could grow to encompass his whole world, could finally begin to fill the empty void that threatened to swallow him up on long, dark nights of solitude.

107

He hasn't seen Dieter in the Refuge, even though he avoids remembering that he can't see the carpets or behind the tables. The cameras don't cover all angles, he is beginning to realise, leaving plenty of blind spots, leaving him frustrated at his inability to change their views. Perhaps he should suggest a different set when this is over, cameras that can be swivelled and moved remotely, cameras that provide more visibility. But would he want to see Dieter? Like that? Through a camera? Hurt like that child with his teddy bear? Or worse?

Abhi has not dared call Dieter, or even message him, since that first unanswered text from the night before. Some part of him dares not know. For hours, he has forced himself to not think of him, not worry. When the sudden wave of fear grows to wash over him, leaving him chilled, suddenly shaken, he has called his guests, burying his own terror in offering strangers comfort on the telephone line. Or he has called Sam, instinctively recognising that somewhere she carries a similar abyss within her, the same dark chasm that requires just one small mis-step, one instant of lost control, to suck them into its depth.

But now, in the tedious, ongoing silence, he can't keep his fears at bay. They grow to wrap him, mingling with memories of tenderness, dragging up pangs of desire, melting into sorrow, overwhelming him. He fishes out his phone, the personal one he has ignored for most of the night, ever since the madness began. The one with Dieter's number. And Samar's and Baba's.

There is no text from Dieter. Or call. But there are multiple texts from Samar. And more missed calls from Baba. His father has not quite become accustomed to texts. He flicks to the most recent text from his brother, 'Will you just call Baba, you stiff necked, stubborn little shit? Or text me so I can tell them you're alive.'

Perhaps it is the terrors of the night that make Abhi relent, push his thumb as it races over the screen, tapping a response. 'Love you too bro. Tell them I am fine. Holed up, guiding some other damn uniformed know-it-all who is planning to storm the place. Will call when I get a chance.'

It may be too late to hold grudges, but he is too exhausted for calls. In his mind, Abhi can see Mamma's face, the barely checked tears pooled in the corner of her wide, afraid eyes, that closed blankness that haunts her beautiful features when Baba and Samar are away, or missing, or on operations again. He had promised long ago he would never cause her such speechless agony, would never make her suffer those horrible moments. Another promise broken, he knows.

He dare not let himself think of Baba, maybe because he cannot imagine his father worrying or at least demonstrating it. In his mind, Baba stays seated in the ancient armchair, his legs crossed precisely, his tall body coiled and taut, the tension only revealed in the steady drumming of his fingertips against the dark mahogany arm-rest, in the incessant, regular swinging back and forth of his raised foot. No, Baba doesn't worry. He just waits for the result, Abhi tells himself. Like Samar. He can't see Samar worrying, can't imagine his brother feeling the terror, panic, debilitating horror he has felt in the past hours. He wishes he could have just some modicum of the same strength.

His phone buzzes again, still held in his hand. Another message from Samar: 'Figured as much. We trained you too well. I may just tell the op CO to shoot you when he sees you. Good luck, little brother.'

A smile twists Abhi's lips. Perhaps this is the only comfort he can find. At least until the night begins to die again, until he can drum up the courage to call Dieter, or check on the guests with feigned calm, or at least until Sam is awake to talk away his fears into their far corners again.

***

Huddled in bed, forcing herself out of habit to slowly relax her muscles, Sam does one last scan of her phone. She knows by the silence beyond the thick curtains that dawn is not far off, that the night has turned its inkiest black, deathly still, presaging its own death. She knows she has long hours of tedium ahead, that she won't be able to move nearly as safely through the Arcadia in daylight hours, that she must use the hours to rest herself, to regroup, regain her energy.

She knows her sleep will be troubled, a jumbled chaos of the past and present, reality and fears, jostling against her closed eyelids, careening painfully around her skull. Still she forces herself into sleep, breathing carefully, counting each breath as it flows in and out of her until she can feel the drowsiness grow, a comforting oblivion enveloping her. For an instant, just a short solitary moment she believes, her mind settles into rest, her body relaxing into softness.

Then all too soon, before exhaustion can drain from her limbs, her eyes fly open, her heart pounding at the familiar face, at the horror of the memory she fights so hard to bury, to forget.

Sam has been dreaming of the man with the tattoos, the one they had called The Butcher on the base. In her dreams, even her memories, she has trouble placing him after all these years, confusing Serbia with the Congo, Afghanistan with Somalia, every other army base she has flown through on embedded assignments, covering for a change the killings from the other, more structured side. Every army base seems the same, blending into uniformly positioned prefab barracks, the sandbags and gates, the confining walls with extra barbed wire and watch towers, and those heavy duty gen-sets that always drums up enough power to light up a precise perimeter in the midst of treacly dark.

But she remembers when she had first noticed him, his stride measured, his footfall firm. 'He actually likes going out there,' one of the soldiers had commented, 'yes he does, The Butcher.' She had filed away the nickname, found herself watching him covertly, drawn and repelled in equal measure, wondering what he got up to when he led out the patrols, took the lead on every foray beyond the perimeter. 'He has a tattoo for each kill,' someone told her in the mess.

'So how many tattoos does he have?' she had laughed. Every unit had some crazy legend, she knew.

'Hell, I don't want to know. I wouldn't want to find out.' That had caught her attention, something in the tone perhaps that seemed different from the usual boasts and teasing and banter.

Intrigued, she decided to close the distance, ignoring the aching knot that instantly gathered between her shoulder blades, a sure sign of growing fear. Usually she paid attention to that insistent ball of pain, aware that it was a warning sign for all that she shut her mind against. That knot was a reminder that she was getting too close, was too deep, too much at risk. Normally she pulled out, pushing away the viewfinder from her eye, withdrawing to civilisation. But she was in civilisation, or at least as safe as she could be, on the base. So she had ignored the throbbing and circled the mess, drawing close, hoping that her move would go unnoticed.

From below the sleeve, dark shapes swirled on the pale skin, rippling across his biceps, undulating down his forearms. Fanciful beasts and birds and near human creatures, their limbs curled in agony, or in anticipation of some terrible pain. Or death. She wished, for once, that her eyes could adjust as easily as her lens, cover the distance without placing her at arm's length, or even revealing her observation post. Between the sudden fancy and the pain between her shoulder blades, she hesitated, waiting for an instant too long.

He had looked up suddenly, with an instinct as unerring as an animal's, cutting through the chatter of the mess to find her eyes. She had been too surprised to look away. The Butcher had grinned, his eyes crinkling up. Then he held up his right hand, two fingers held out, thumb curled in, like a boy's pistol, and pointed at her. And winked, the grin still stretched across his lips.

The knot between her shoulders had throbbed with sudden intensity, winding her even as she turned away hastily. She had looked down at the tray of food clutched in her hands, noting their sudden clamminess, and sucked hard on the air around her. She had expected the fear, the terror even. What

111

had shocked her was the sudden clench of her groin, the instant rush of moisture between her legs.

'Don't you want pictures of me, camera girl?' His voice had called after her, raspy and thick, the words as clipped and precise as his stride.

Steadying herself, she marched up to him, 'Not really, but perhaps later, if I need some atmosphere shots.' Sam was surprised at how calm her voice sounded even to her own ears. 'And I don't appreciate that name.'

He smelled of musk and sweat, and the acrid tang of the American beer that was doled out on the base by the crate. The tattoos were even more mysterious up close, dark, pagan, the blues and greens and blacks swirling into dying animals and ancient death masks, their fluid lines as opaque and unfathomable as cave paintings, rippling like living beings over the sharply defined muscles. 'I could take my shirt off if you want to see more, camera girl.'

Sam cursed herself for staring at him. 'No thank you. That will not be necessary.' Now she sounded prissy even to her ears, and she cursed again under her breath as she forced herself to walk away.

'Next time, camera girl,' he called softly. The words sounded like a threat. Or a promise.

There hadn't been a next time of course. For the remaining days, Sam had scrupulously avoided The Butcher, ensuring they would not cross paths until she flew out. She had found herself watching for him, checking surreptitiously for his return from patrols, responding to his throaty laugh in the mess with that same mix of familiar pain and unbidden pleasure.

But The Butcher had come looking for her the night before she was supposed to fly out. She had sensed his presence behind her, even before he spoke. That knot of pain was back, the ache spreading up her neck, shooting down her spine. 'Let me buy you a drink, camera girl.' She had let him, first just one, and then another. But she had also waited to leave, slipping out of the mess while he was at the other end, laughing, bantering with friends.

112

He had caught up with her, before she got back to her quarters. She had let him kiss her, a teasing flicker of his tongue on her lips, had been annoyed to find her own tongue reaching out momentarily to find his. Then that knot of pain in her back had spasmed, sending a shiver through her.

He hadn't pushed further, grinning down at her, his eyes as inscrutable as the tattoos. 'We are not so different, camera girl. Except you wait till they are dead.'

Sam had stumbled away, torn between relief and terror. And grief. She had double-locked the door that night, even though she knew The Butcher wouldn't come for her, and had slept curled up into a tight ball, her sleeping bag zipped up fully around her. Strange fever dreams had flitted through her sleep and she awoke exhausted, as bereft as when she had fallen asleep.

It was still early, she knew, even though the camp lights beyond her window were turned to full intensity, masking the watery dawn she knew must be breaking beyond the perimeter guards. She had stared long and hard into the small mirror in the bathroom, not even noticing the dark circles that gathered below her bleak eyes.

Then using the scissors of her Swiss knife, she had begun snipping the curling tendrils that framed her face, twisting small sections on her finger and clipping them close to the roots. She hadn't stopped even after the floor below was full of the dark locks, gleaming like some wild animal, like many wounded, tortured beasts, torn and scattered across the pale boards. She had wet her scalp, used the hand soap from the steel dispenser attached to the wall, used her razor to meticulously shave off every last remnant of hair.

She thought she should feel cleansed but as she gathered the locks and shoved them into the black plastic lined bin, she could hear The Butcher, 'We are not so different, camera girl.'

'Yes we are,' Sam swore into the mirror. She would find a way to be different.

THE ARCADIA
48 HOURS AGO

The night is beginning to fray against the large glass panes when Abhi gets Sam's call. He has spent much of the past hours slumped on the sofa, trying to sleep. The gruff sounding colonel planning the assault thinks Abhi should be resting. 'Get some sleep, son, we're going to need everyone fully alert once we start to move.'

The colonel doesn't realise that Abhi has come to dread sleep more than exhaustion in the past hours. At least awake, he can control where his mind goes. Asleep, his mind throws up jumbled images and stories, of Dieter, Baba, Samar, forgotten lovers, resentful fights, dredging past hurts and insults, every tiny rejection from all his life. He awakens from his short naps feeling more exhausted than ever before. He welcomes the jangled nerves that come with the buzzing of his mobile.

'Everything all right, Sam?'

'Yes, you bastard!' Her voice is harsh, her words slurring at the edges. 'Where are the fuckers right now? I need their positions.'

The first pinks of dawn suddenly seem obscenely bright outside the window, and he squints as he checks the screens for the gunmen. Beyond the marble sill, the air is so still that not a single leaf stirs in the garden beyond. The gunmen are still positioned along the arcade on the second floor, obviously preparing it as a stronghold against the eventual assault.

'Sam, it is almost daylight. What are you planning?'

'Just tell me where they are.' Her voice has steadied, as if she is willing herself to calmness, or sobriety.

'Still on the second floor. They seem to be setting up there. They haven't gone to upper floors since last night. Can you please tell me why?'

114

'Because I am going to go find that damn kid you are so worried about!'

Suddenly the light beyond seems less oppressive and Abhi barks out a sudden sharp laugh, even though he can hear Sam curse on the line. But then the dread returns. 'You sure you want to go now? There will be too much light soon.'

'Don't have much choice, do I? The kid is likely to be dead by the evening, if we leave him there.'

Abhi knows she is right though he still worries. Not so much about the kid as about her.

'Just keep me updated, Abhi. If they move, I am going to need a lot more notice.'

'Of course. Will do,' he soothes. Then even though he knows it makes little sense to even say the old, familiar words, he says them out loud, 'And Sam, please be careful.'

A soft click ending the call is his only answer.

***

Unable to sleep, exhausted from her dreams, she hates Abhi for not making moral arguments. Those she has always been prepared for, knows how to counter. Instead, she thinks she can hear his horror, a strange revulsion, in that final whispered question. 'But if you are the only person who could help?'

Only once, in a strange moment of weakness, had she asked the same question. They had been covering the retreat of the Taliban from northern Afghanistan. Everywhere in the offices, the bunkers, the huts that seemed to all be equipped with diesel generators and satellite dishes, there had been documents, music CDs that were prohibited to the local population, even photographs in the lost and discarded wallets. The journalists were supposed to hand over all they found to the soldiers, but of course few of them ever did. Instead, they held on to their own personal souvenirs: an internationally famous anarchists' handbook of explosives translated into Dari, a crumpled photograph of an unnamed, untraceable family with half a dozen wide-eyed children, letters written in English, and Arabic, and Pashto from loved ones in a dozen parts of the world, even postcards from picturesquely bucolic Swiss Alps and silent Virginia hills. Who delivered the mail in such realms of hell, Sam had wondered, knowing full well that there would be post boxes and far flung post offices that would hold the mail. It had been much the same in the Congo, and Bosnia, and in Somalia, and Guatemala. The urge to communicate with loved ones is one of the indefatigable drivers of the human species, one that never ceases to amaze Sam.

Charlie, a freelancer, had found a letter, in one of the hovels. It was just a fragment on a dirty sheet of lined paper ripped from an exercise book. Yet the handwriting had been unusually elegant, making the same point in delicate looped letters, the points precise and neatly spaced, on both sides of the paper, once in English and then again in Urdu. A beautiful woman's writing, Sam had thought when Charlie held it up for her.

'This is bizarre, Sam.'

She had read the incongruous letter, hidden perhaps in an unseen crevice in the mud, shaken loose by the weeks of bomb and shells.

'I was taken from my cousin's wedding in Darra Adam Khel. If you find this, please for Allah's sake, inform my father that I was alive on 23 July 2003. We are on the move again, if God wills, then perhaps even across the border.'

An address in Lahore appeared at the bottom of the page.

For a moment, Sam had reeled at an incongruous thought. What if she were the woman leaving such a letter for her loved ones? Had the woman been kidnapped, as the letter made it seem? She had a sudden unfamiliar image of her father waiting for news from her, from each war-zone that she chose to cover.

'Will you post it?' she asked.

'No ways! This one is for my collection.' Charlie was tucking the letter in his little notebook that he carried in his field jacket.

'Maybe you should drop the family a postcard?' she had said much later.

116

'You still thinking about that letter? You women! You know that it is probably a code to trigger off a whole wave of attacks on us?' She hadn't contradicted him. But Charlie hadn't relented, teasing her incessantly. 'You getting soft, Sam? Or is it that time of the month?' he had sniggered until she was forced to punch his arm. Hard.

'Fuck off, Charlie. It could have been a great human interest story.' She had an out clause. As always.

But if she were honest with herself, that pilfered letter had bothered her long after. Once she even found herself driving through the upper middle-class neighbourhood of Lahore, wondering if she could find the house from the letter. But then her mind played tricks, all those long combinations of numbers and alphabets that marked the residences got jumbled up, and all memory of the address was irretrievably lost. Finally, after gazing at the curtained windows and immaculate lawn of one house after another in the colony, she told her driver to return to the hotel.

But Abhi's question brings back the dilemma. What if she had found that letter? Would she make the same decision? And worse still, now in the Arcadia siege, isn't she the only one who can help, perhaps even stop the whimpers in Room 1104? Worse still, she has been trying every trick she has learned over the years, to distract herself, to shut out the memory of the child's soft whimpers in her ears, the sudden sign of life that she had spotted in the viewfinder.

'Damn! Damn! The manipulative fucker!' She fishes out her personal supply of the Auchentoshan single malt she carries, buried at the bottom of her backpack, for moments when all other alcohol stops warming her up. For an instant, her eyes linger on the red and white maple leaf sewn to the canvas top and a bitter smile twists her lips. What would that young medic think of her, bitter, fucked up, and now on a stupid mission for nothing? Or perhaps he would understand her. Absently she runs a finger along the edge of the maple leaf, knocking back a good inch, neat, straight from the bottle.

'The bastard is going to make me play Florence Nightingale.' Another half-inch, except this time she rinses her mouth with the viscous, warming liquid with each mouthful before swallowing it. She feels her belly warming up, and holds up the bottle to consider if she should take another gulp but eventually decides against it. God only knows how long this siege was going to last and she was going to have to ration supplies if she is to hold on to her sanity.

Grimly, she puts away the bottle. 'Let us see if Dutch courage actually works,' she announces to the empty room, before heading to the door.

Wide awake, suddenly energised, Abhi has positioned himself before the screens. His eyes scan for the assailants, returning to the fourteenth floor to check for Sam's entry. But over and over, his eyes return to the Refuge, gleaming now in the morning sun, the glass fronted terrace now stark in the light. He knows the far screen holds that slim hand resting on the table, tries to avoid looking at it, even though he can feel his eyes drawn repeatedly in its direction.

An inexplicable exultation fills him. Perhaps he isn't trapped completely, he tells himself, if Sam can check on others for him. The thought rises unbidden, accompanied by an image of a laughing Dieter. If she can pull this off, perhaps he can ask her to check the Refuge, check for Dieter, even if it only means he can grieve in private, in this hidden dungeon where nobody will hear him scream.

He spots Sam as soon as she steps out of her room. She seems disorientated, her arms folded tight before her, her head ducked nearly into her chest. As she creeps along the corridor, she hesitates with each step, lacking the surety, the confidence of her usual crab-like gait with her camera clutched before her eyes.

'Damn it, Sam, watch where you are going,' he spits out loud as she crashes into the table, sending a massive vase of lilies careening to the floor, the crystal thudding down to the plush carpet, the white and pale green blossoms arcing across the floor in a dark puddle of water. She stands with her hands pressed against her injured hip, rubbing it, her head swivelling to check around her. She looks a lot more vulnerable than he has seen before, a tiny figure, shorn of its only shield, conscious of her own fragility, afraid of the world that has expanded beyond the missing viewfinder, the missing grids on the square no longer available to guide her steps.

He nearly texts her, to tell her not to go further, to return to her room, to safety. After all, there are other victims in the Arcadia and he feels less kinship for the unseen child in 1104 than with the small woman he has laughed with, got to know, teased into going into danger. He feels a pang of guilt, but then Baba's stern voice cuts through his head, rising from long buried memories, 'It is our job to watch over the weakest. And that means sometimes sacrificing some who are stronger.' Staring at the screen, Abhi crosses his fingers tightly, hoping, praying that he has not sacrificed Sam. At least not this time, at least not yet.

'Come on, Sam, you can do this,' he coaxes the still figure, as if she can hear him through the screen. 'Come on.'

It takes him a moment to realise what she is doing, but then he can't stop grinning. Fishing out her phone from her pocket, she taps quickly, and then raises it before her, her arm half-extended, her hand entirely steady. Even on the screen, he can see her eyes are locked into the faintly glowing square before her. Confident, sure of the world as it shrinks to fit her view, though perhaps not as cocky as when her camera is held before her face, she swiftly moves down the corridor, crushing the scattered lilies underfoot, and disappears into the fire escape.

***

Sam feels naked without her camera as she makes her way down the corridor again and she feels its lack acutely, as if she is missing some vital limb. Without the habitual Mamiya clutched in her hands, part talisman, part compass, she finds herself stumbling, hesitating, questioning her sense of direction. The dim, golden lights are unlit now. She knows Abhi has turned them off from the main board. His attempt to give her cover, even from his far-away little mouse-hole, comforts her as she makes her way down the corridor, finding safe spots in the deep doorways, using the enormous occasional tables for protection.

With the Mamiya excised from her hands, prevented from shielding her eyes, every sense seems to be in overdrive, hyper-alert, picking up sights and sounds and smells that she would ignore otherwise. The corridor feels musty, stuffy, over warm with stale air that pushes against her, caking the skin on her face, creeping into the tightly wound scarf to finger her throat. She knows that the air-conditioning has been turned off from the mains and is aware of the absence of the low distant hum, conspicuous more for its lack than the perpetual white noise. Without the constant renewal of air, the corridor smells dank, and she can feel a trickle of sweat slide her back.

Sam shudders in distaste, wrinkling her nose, pushes back a knot of bile rising to her throat, as a familiar smell rises even through the muggy heat. She realises that there is blood on the carpet on her floor, enormous quantities, as if bodies have been dragged across it. The red pile is flat and moist in parts and squashed as if wounded. For a long instance, Sam stares at the stains. Then she bends down, reaches out with a fingertip to touch it gently. The finger comes away wet and red. She lifts the finger to her nose, sniffing it carefully: metallic and yet vaguely musky. Definitely blood.

Abhi has told her that north wing is nearly entirely fire-free. 'There were some explosions on the third floor about an hour ago but it doesn't look like they were trying to set it aflame.' But in her nostrils, the scent of smoke is stronger this time, she is convinced, knowing that the gunmen have been setting parts of the Arcadia on fire, spreading panic or just putting on a better show for the cameras on the outside. Her eyes tingle and water, her skin feels warm and itches. Her nose is full of something acid and burning.

What if he was wrong, she begins to panic but then forces herself together again. She realises the sourness in her nostrils is not really smoke. The corridor is full of other smells: urine, excrement, blood, vomit, a fierce melange of terrible, living, human odours that insist on lingering even after life within the bodies has been forced into a rout. As she accustoms herself to her hyper-alert senses, she imagines she can differentiate the scents, like colours: the floral lightness of a vain beauty; the oily richness of a middle-aged businessman; something spicy and elusive and glamorous; the brutish musk, perhaps one of the gunmen? Her own body smells sour to Sam, like something left in the heat for too long and edging towards rot. Can they track her by her scent, she wonders momentarily, then blinks her eyes, squeezing them tight, reminding herself to remain focused.

Worse, her mouth feels dry, sour, with a sweet hint of whisky that has turned cloying on her tongue. She shakes her head slightly to clear it, wishing she had brought at least a miniature bottle of the shit in the minibar with her, then sternly pushes the thought away.

It isn't until she crashes into a long table, slamming her hip hard against the polished surface, sending her head spinning, with pain and alcohol, that fear rises in her throat like vomit, the knot in her shoulders spasming in conjunction with the fresh pain in her hip. She stands for a long time, bewildered, frozen into immobility with panic and, for once, unable to find comfort or even safety in a viewfinder. It is more instinct than thought that makes her pull out her phone, switching on the camera, pulling the world back into focus within a clear rectangular boundary. The phone camera is unwieldy, unfamiliar, and she struggles to hold it at the correct angles to guide herself, and yet slowly the world begins to contract into some semblance of order, folding itself into pixels before her.

Rubbing her aching hip with her free hand, aware that her hyper-alert senses are still overflowing beyond the ineffectual rectangle of her phone camera, Sam pushes forward through the corridor. The phone will not protect her as efficiently as the Mamiya but perhaps that is better if she is to make contact with a subject.

LONDON
24 MONTHS AGO

At the beginning, Sam had regularly invited David back to her flat. At least for those first times when he had found her again, after years of silence, just after her Wedding Albums exhibition, just as she had known he would.

Many years ago, she taught herself to not wait; to never watch the phone willing it to ring just so she could hear a much-loved voice; to never stare out the window waiting for the post to arrive. Over the years, she has refined that initial lesson, never waiting or even wishing for what she cannot have. She has made herself into a fortress, a woman to be briefly desired but not loved, not the marrying kind. She has built up an intricate maze in her mind, secreting the gnawing kernel of doubt in its unreachable core that perhaps she is incapable of loving, of being loved. That is why she is shaken to find that it only takes him a single voicemail to rip apart the barriers she has built up so meticulously. It isn't even what he says, at least not in that first message. It is just the sound of his voice: 'I call you after all these years, and you won't even answer the phone.' There is laughter in his voice, and maybe even affection.

The sudden hollowness in the pit of her stomach on hearing his message, that immediate intense flash of desire she remembers so well, has resisted for so long, even imagined that she had killed and buried somewhere in the past; the sudden desperate need for him after so many years of resolutely pushing him out of her thoughts. She drops her head between her knees, forcing herself to breathe slowly, reverting to a childish stratagem to calm herself.

She decides to not return the call, but then he rings again. This time she answers. Desire always overwhelms rationality when it comes to him.

There is a familiar intimacy in his tone, a strange knowledge of her voice, her breath, her reactions; a surety that he knows what she will say, despite the distance, despite the fact he knows nothing of her life. But perhaps what convinces her to see him is the recognition of something she has never imagined him capable of: a fragility that she has never noticed before.

Yet the truth is a bit more selfish, at least before that first moment of re-encounter. She wants him to regret leaving her. She wants him to see her – confident, successful, worldly, everything that she had admired about him so long ago – and wish that he had chosen otherwise. And she wants to demonstrate that she has caught up with him; that she is no longer the naïf, the innocent with little knowledge of the world or life. That she can be as jaded, as cynical, as world-weary as he had been. If she could be honest enough with herself, she would confess that she is also a bit curious: would she still find him attractive? And perhaps equally or even more importantly, what would he think of her now?

Perhaps that is why she dresses with extra care that day, picking out her favourite dress, one that reminds her of childhood dreams from well before she had met him. The dress is a lure but mostly a shield, encasing her in a confidence she doesn't feel, wrapping her body like a present; a present not to be opened, at least not by him. Just a small reminder of what he can't have.

She wants to keep him at a distance, and deliberately picks a bar where she is a regular, knows the staff. A safe space, she tells herself. A place where he can't get past her armour. When he suggests a different venue, she refuses: her space or not at all.

She arrives before him, giving herself time to settle into her favourite seat, orders the single malt she has cultivated a taste for in the years since they last met. Her choice of drinks has been another distancing mechanism: long ago, together, they had always drunk beer or wine; swigged tequila and Cuba libres. Her studied fastidiousness about single malts is intended to erase that woman she had been with him, a woman who was too vulnerable, too fragile, too loving; to replace her with a new construction, replete with strength, impervious to sentimental assaults.

As she takes the first sip, hoping to steel her nerves, even before she has the time to pull herself together, he walks in. A part of her wants to rush over and hug him, hold him, but she forces herself to remain seated, aloof, watching, noting every detail, as he walks over: the familiar stride, the knowing smile, that well-loved tilt of his head. She feels an instant surge of the emotions that she was sure she had outgrown, but she pushes them away, forces herself to remember the devastation instead.

She had planned to offer him her hand, perhaps her cheek for a polite kiss, but he moves to hug her, holding her tight, too close, far too long, as if what they had shared really meant something to him, as if he has missed her. For an instant she lets herself believe, but then the memories come flooding back. She pulls herself away, holding herself at a safe distance. She's not that woman he remembers any more: starved for his approval, striving always to please him. Now she listens with a disbelieving ear to his compliments, ignores his obvious pleasure in seeing her, refuses to notice the warmth in his eyes. It no longer matters, she repeats to herself.

And then just as she is beginning to convince herself that their meeting is over, that she has nothing more to hear from him, nothing she wants to say to him, he leans over to snatch a sudden, flighty kiss. His mouth tastes hers for an instant. She flinches at that first touch, pulls back. He doesn't push further.

In that instant she changes her mind. Not because of the kiss, or the memories it sparks. Instead, it is his smile, like that of a little boy secreting away something wonderful and forbidden, a smile full of mischief and want and pure joy, something much before hurt and loss, even before a sense of right and wrong. She wants to share that innocent pleasure that lights his eyes, wants to be able to claim things, people, places, without hesitation, without even asking.

125

Memories of The Butcher still haunt her, his taunting eyes rising unbidden in her unguarded moments. Despite all the pain, she thinks of David as safe, as comforting, far removed from the world outside where a single bullet can shatter a universe, where every bullet comes with a name inscribed on it and nobody knows which one is meant for them. She finds his slight effeminacy attractive, the flowing walk in absolute contrast to the men she shoots, men like The Butcher who stalk like beasts of prey, men who march straight into oblivion. David makes her feel that innocence is still possible, that somewhere beyond the edge of her vision, a serene quietness can exist, where none of the horrors of the field can ever reach. If only as an illusion, by a determined denial of all that exists beyond his safe world.

Yet a part of her is annoyed, wanting to protest the unfairness of it all. Just as she has finally achieved the worldly confidence he had worn so lightly in the times past, he has moved the goalposts. He has moved to a new space, somewhere full of innocent pleasures. A place where a brief snatched kiss can provide intense joy. Once again, she will have to struggle to catch up with him, this time shedding her hard earned, paid-in-blood, cynicism.

Perhaps that is why she is unconvinced, not only that first night, but for many nights after, remains doubting despite all his efforts. 'So why are you here?' she had asked the first time they had sex, on the duvet he had pulled off her bed and spread over the ancient silk carpet on the cold floor. They had sipped the champagne he had brought from chipped coffee cups Sam had hastily rinsed out.

'I hope you don't expect me to answer that?' David had said, pulling her closer. It is the answer she had predicted in her mind.

He doesn't answer her questions but she doesn't mind living without answers, at least until the nights when the uncertainty and doubt overwhelm her, when memories of things she has seen rise from the dark to smother her. In the early days, it was enough that he was close, his arms wrapped tight around her, his skin warm against hers, their mouths glued together. She thought it strange that he had found her again though she had been excited by the tumultuous mingling of knowledge and ignorance, as if reading a beloved book that has been rewritten in one's absence. So many things that they knew of each other: insignificant details of what they like and dislike; flashes of memories, of tales shared and half-remembered; and an odd new understanding of quirks that had baffled in the past.

The first time they made love, she had made a mental inventory, noting the minor transformations of his body, lingering over the familiarities, teasing him about what she remembered, all she could not recognise, and hid her confusion at her half-knowledge of him in cloaks of assumed confidence and levity. Yet David's assurance bewildered, unsettled her. His eyes didn't linger in puzzlement over her body but simply claimed their pleasure. His fingers didn't hesitate over her skin, roaming confidently, finding nooks and secrets that make her gasp, moan. His mouth slid over her skin, always unhesitating, leaving her shivering and shaken. It was as if he had long visualised her in his mind, as if his fantasy, memory, was so comprehensive that he needed no reality to complete her.

She had protested his familiarity. How could he treat her with that same offhand affection after so many lifetimes apart when he had never known her at all? So many injuries had healed while they had been apart and left nothing but imperceptible scars. They could let their fingers roam over the sites of old disasters, but they had missed the initial moment of offering comfort. Now they only devoured – with their eyes, hands, mouths – the transformed geographies of their mutated selves.

'You still know nothing of me,' she later whispered inaudibly against his throat, shaken by the instant intimacy they had seemingly achieved again.

Even the banal after-sex rituals were familiar, easy. She found him an errant ashtray, lit a candle to cut the smoke, climbed back into his arms. He lay back smoking, holding her close against himself. The conversation had flown smoothly, of lives lived apart, of disparate memories of shared moments, of work and daily living, of the universe and all else.

And perhaps that is why she was horrified when she had woken up hours later, still in his embrace; sleep has always been very private for her, even more intimate than sex, a secret she keeps to herself. She was annoyed to realise that she was rested, that even in sleep she had moulded her body to fit his, had held him close against herself.

'What do you want to know?' His hand had moved to cup the back of her head, making her feel fragile yet safe.

'When is your birthday?' A safe question, one to which she had already known the answer. She had circled that date in her diary many years ago even though she never sent him a card or made a phone call. But that was long ago, when she was naïve, sentimental. Just a test, she had sternly told herself, to see what other lies he could tell.

But he had answered truthfully. And perhaps that is why she continued to see him, occasionally, before setting off on her assignments, finding him again and again, before weeks in the field, if only for his familiarity, and the lack of danger.

David always tells her bits of himself: his work, family, travels, fragments of information so inconsequentially intimate that for a short while she can imagine that they are just another couple discovering whimsical, mundane details of each other. Just another couple falling in love. Except she hardly ever tells him anything at all, only asks him questions that let him talk, fill their moments together with his slow, drawling words.

'Is it worth the risk?' The one question she never asks him, afraid that it will remind him of the consequences of their liaison. That such a question will bring to an end even these clandestine trysts. It is also a question David has never asked her, even when she leaves for another assignment, even when the dark hollows under her eyes grow darker, flesh falls off her bones.

And because that question is never spoken, she hides from David's probing as well. When he asks about her life, she tells him that she has enough friends and lovers. 'But what about love?' he asks. Is it his arrogance seeking a confirmation, she wonders, that she has loved no other? A judgement maybe that she can love no one? Or is it perhaps competition, a showy game of which of the two has failed or succeeded? Later, in his absence, she will nurse a flicker of rage against him, for turning to her for a safely controlled injection of excitement into his life, against herself for playing along with his games. There is no love between them, she tells herself fiercely. Just convenience, and many layers of betrayals.

'So what about love?' he insists.

She hides further, throwing up translucent veils of fictions and facile opinions, soft words that conceal the solid barriers she places around herself. She doesn't tell him about the heartbreaks and the tears, doesn't share the bruises and scars from her past. Not even the ones he had left. Such confidences are for those she trusts. These are secrets to be shared amongst those who are truly couples, intimate not only physically and intellectually but also emotionally. And she knows he isn't really intimate with her. His emotions are saved for the house in the country, for the woman who makes that ancient structure his home, for the legacies he has created there. Her own legacy seems to be caught up in nightmares, in doubts, in half-remembered lovers and frightening half-buried spectres.

And because that question is never spoken, Sam stops inviting him to her flat after the first few trysts, choosing to meet him in undistinguishable hotel rooms, at hushed private clubs where rich or famous men take their mistresses. She prefers to think of herself as just that, the mistress not the wife, finding both comfort and revulsion in the word, relieved that it serves as a shield against her ignored, inarticulate desires.

Her home remains hers own alone, cold, comforting, safe. Except of course on that one special night, each time before she leaves on assignment, when she invites David for take-away food and wine drunk from plastic cups, for making love on sheets that remain reeking of him after he leaves for her to savour alone.

She doesn't change the linen before she leaves, leaving the bed unmade, rumpled, scented with their lovemaking, leaving it unchanged until she returns from assignment. Then, putting down her backpack, before even she unpacks, before even she strips off her thick rubber-soled boots, fighting off the bone-deep weariness, she strips the rumpled bed down, replaces the linens with an identical set of freshly laundered ones, creating a fresh start for herself.

But on the last days before she heads into the field, as she prepares for an assignment, meticulously reviewing her notes, maps and data, checking, cleaning, sorting her equipment, packing her small backpack of personal essentials, she will sleep on the sofa. The bed she leaves, unmade, still smelling of David, and the hours they spent on it, the sheets rumpled and untidy, with books piled as if for a child's play-castle, or a nest. In her allotted hour of fantasy, she climbs in the midst of that nest, curling herself into a tight ball with her limbs pulled close together, her chin tucked deep within.

In her loneliness, and growing dread, she will snuggle under the covers, her face pushed against the pillows, to breathe in his elusive scent, to close her eyes and imagine him lying there, just out of reach. She will deny herself – in her fantasy – the pleasure of reaching out and stroking the body she has known so well: the lean arms, the wide chest, the oddly vulnerable roundness of the back of his head. And then, with a sharp jab of desire, that smooth plane angling up his hip, a strangely fragile vision of male beauty.

'Hold me,' David had whispered the last time they had made love. Was it a command or a plea? She was sure she had not heard him right. She watched his mouth as he repeats the words, convincing herself that he meant it before moving to wrap her arms around him, pressing herself close. She had savoured his words later, when he had gone, leaving her trapped between satiety and terror, when she doesn't know when he will return, or if she wants him to.

And in those final hours before an assignment, she obsessively reads love stories, piling them in untidy stacks on her bed, happy ones on the side he takes, automatically, when he visits her; the sad ones in a higgledy-piggledy heap on her end. She sleeps curled on her sofa, close to her improvised dark room to be able smell the chemicals. She surrounds herself with prints from whatever assignment she is finishing, from the exhibition she is preparing.

She knows that the happy love stories are only so because they end with the first consummation. Those aren't really love stories but rather tales of chase, of gratification delayed, a bit like the Boxing Day hunts when the promise of blood is never really fulfilled. It's the tragic ones she treasures, the prolonged agony of separation, the fear of loss, and finally loss itself.

They remind her of what she shares with David, an endless cycle of the same pathetic story: the sudden excitement when he calls; each meeting feels like a new beginning, always with the promise of a different ending, always with hope: this time he will love her; this time he will stay; this time he will not abandon her. And then the clenched nausea of anticipation as she waits for him, a gnawing fear in her belly that he will cancel, that he will have forgotten, that he will have changed his mind. The fear keeps her desire at bay, only to rush to the fore when she sees him, desperate with need, racked with the desire to touch him.

That is where she ends her happy love story. Later she will draw out memories of his smile, of his eyes resting on her, she likes to imagine, fondly. She will remember the weight of his arm encircling her, his hands warm on her skin, his mouth moving slowly, tenderly against her flesh. She resolutely closes her mind to departures, to that terrible sense of loss that engulfs her every time they separate, even when it is her mind that withdraws first. Worse still, she allow herself to, at least briefly, wallow in the loathing she feels for herself each time he leaves her, taking with him all illusion of loving her, of being loved by her. She forces herself to not look at him as he walks away, forces herself to turn away first, ensuring that in her mind she will never see his departures. And she refuses to think of what he does on the many days he isn't with her. Those partings, separations, betrayals, are for the sad love stories that she keeps like talismans on her side of the bed, to shield her not from the terrors of the dead but the living.

THE ARCADIA
48 HOURS AGO

The child is conscious and whimpering in her arms by the time Sam gets back to her room. She can't figure out if he is fighting or merely trying to escape but his struggles remind her of a gangly puppy. Lucky that she knows dogs, even if she understands little about children, and so she just tightens her hold on his arms and legs to prevent them flailing, hoping that the noise he is making is not loud enough to attract attention.

Opening and closing the door to her room is not only difficult with the wriggling bundle in her arms, but trying to do so silently is utterly impossible. Finally, she just dangles the child with one arm as she clicks the door open, hoping that the trail of blood on the carpet is profuse and confused enough not to attract attention to the slim new thread that has trailed in their wake. The towel she has held against his shoulder is soaked and dripping.

She puts him on the sofa at the far end of the room, because it seems farthest from the door and half-hidden from the entrance. If they are discovered by the gunmen roaming the corridors, he may have a slightly better chance than on the stage-like bed that dominates the room.

'So, what's your name?' she asks, slightly awkward, wondering if she should ask his permission to check for injuries.

'Billy,' he whispers after a long silence, his eyes huge, wary pools of tears.

'OK, Billy, we're going to get you clean and put on some fresh clothes.' Sam hopes she sounded business-like and credible, instead of just plain queasy. 'And we'll put something on that shoulder to make it stop bleeding. All right?'

'It will hurt,' Billy protests. 'Medicines always hurt.'

133

Sam knows he's right. Except of course, she doesn't actually have any real medicine to give him. 'I'll find something that won't hurt so much,' she promises.

She wanders about the room, trying to compile an impromptu medical kit. One sheet to be cut into strips for a bandage. She suppresses a nervous giggle as she pulls out her trusty Swiss knife; who'd imagine that those damn old romantic novels would actually be lived out in her own life! Billy's eyes are closed again, although Sam knows enough to recognise that he's in shock, his frail body shivering and shuddering every so often.

She wonders if she should use any of the bottled water from the mini-bar, but then changes her mind. Best to conserve that in case they are stuck for a while out here. Instead, she throws out the flowers from the large vase, cleaning it with a bit of shampoo and filling it with hot water from the bath. Enough fluffy towels for swabbing, padding, cleaning, even if she sets aside the one she has used earlier.

Antiseptics are more of a problem. Many years ago, a lover had shown her how to use urine to clean a nasty cut she had acquired while covering rebels in the Horn of Africa. But the idea of using her urine for a child seems somehow way too intimate and she is sure that Billy wouldn't let her use his own even if she could get him to pee into a cup.

She finds herself back at the mini-bar, weighing up whether gin or whisky or vodka would make the best antiseptic. 'I always knew dogs were better,' she mutters, 'kids are just bloody trouble.' Well, she will just have to sacrifice a miniature bottle of vodka! Then she could give him the orange juice and keep the tonic for herself. 'Bollocks!'

Finally, pulling her supplies together, she makes her way back to the sofa. Billy is half-awake, looking up at her warily. 'OK, this has to be done, except you can't make a noise,' she warns him. He nods, wide-eyed, in agreement.

But he is whimpering softly even as she begins cutting off his T-shirt. 'Look we just have to do this. Come on now.' Sam wishes her mum were here. Or one of those crisis junkie doctors who always seems to know what to say to people to calm them down. Someone like the man who had given her the maple leaf to carry on her backpack, on her jacket, someone who had almost been able to soothe away her worst waking nightmares.

By the time she begins cleaning the gash on his shoulder with a towel, Billy is sobbing, each garbled intake of breath and tears getting louder. Lucky, Sam sighs, it's just a scrape rather than a proper bullet wound. Sam imagines that the father's body had fallen on him and had stayed there for hours until the child had managed to wriggle out a little, that it had perhaps limited the bleeding, perhaps even helped the clotting. The move up the stairs has started the bleeding again, though, and his wriggling is not helping. Billy knocks her hands off a couple of times, splashing the water from the vase over her. 'Look this has to be done,' she tries to reason, not sure if children are capable of reason at all. But he pushes her off once more, this time accompanying the defiant gesture with a definite 'No!'

His voice sounds loud in the silent room, disrupting the hushed atmosphere of whispers and measured steps. Sam jumps up instantly, cocking an ear to the door, wondering if even that small voice has somehow travelled through to danger. Billy's eyes grow sharp. 'I don't want that,' he speaks up again, in that same tone, raising the volume by a fraction. With the unerring child's instinct, he has understood that he can control her with the threat of sound.

Sam stays still, listening for sounds in the corridor, cursing the moment she had allowed Abhi to talk her into this. She has a sudden flashback to a friend's picnic last summer, one of the few occasions when she had let herself be talked into a family gathering. A child had fallen over and scraped her knee, then a little later, another had dropped his ice-cream. In both cases, she had been stunned to note just how piercingly loud children could get. Bloody hell, she's sure that if Billy emitted one of those, he would be heard not only down the corridor but a few floors down. Enough to bring the whole lot of gunmen roaming outside to her room!

For an instant, she wonders if she could just turn him loose in the corridor, or maybe she could take him back where she had found him in his own room. The thought is tempting. She could go back to what she did best: recording the horror instead of trying to patch up little brats.

Then Abhi's horrified reaction cuts into her thoughts. 'You can't leave him out there. You must try to get him safe, Sam. Please.' Damn, she must be getting sentimental or seriously post-traumatic, if some fucking stranger on the phone can manipulate her into acting like this. Keeping her ear to the door, she eyes Billy carefully. Well, she knows puppies, or at least had known them long ago. Kids couldn't be that different.

Billy watches her warily as Sam strides back up to the sofa. 'Come on,' she half lifts him off the sofa, settling herself behind him. He struggles as she gently, quickly, cleanses the shoulder. Then before he can begin whimpering, she has twisted her legs around his, pressing his uninjured arm tight against the back of the sofa. She brings one of her hands up to his mouth, clamping it tight against his lips, using the flat of her palm to hold his jaw shut. Billy struggles frantically, trying to get free.

But Sam holds him tight, using her free hand and teeth to open the miniature vodka, easing the fiery liquid over the gash in the soft flesh. As the first drops fall on the wound, Billy goes rigid, his throat contracting in a strangled scream. But Sam holds him tight, pouring the entire bottle slowly, deliberately over all of the tiny shoulder.

Then as she turns to grab a hand towel for padding the wound, Billy finds his opening. Finding the pressure on his mouth ease fractionally, he bites down as hard on her hand as he can. Sam's reaction is just as instinctive: she cuffs him soundly on the side of the head – 'Stop that, you little shit!' – and tightens her grip on his jaw again, cursing fluently under her breath. She holds the folded hand towel against the clean wound, pressing harder than is strictly necessary.

'I am going to remove my hand,' she growls. 'If you make a sound, I will open that window and throw you out,' she tells him.

136

Billy, apparently convinced that anyone willing to cuff him is also capable of throwing him out the window, nods in acquiescence, copious tears streaming down his cheeks. Efficiently, silently, Sam finishes bandaging his shoulder, sponging the rest of him carefully to get rid of all bloodstains, and eases him into her sleep-shirt.

'Here, you should be comfortable now,' she tries to inject some gentleness into her voice as she lowers him on to the pillows she has gathered to cushion his shoulder, covering him with a doubled up duvet. His teeth are chattering and the shivers have grown, but he refuses to look up to her, tears still rolling down his cheek, albeit slightly slower than before.

'Be quiet, OK?' It is part threat, part instruction as the phone on the table lights up again.

'Abhi,' she grabs it at the fourth blink of the red light.

'Yes, Sam,' the voice is as calm as before. 'Are you all right? And the kid?'

'Billy,' she automatically corrects. 'Yes, yes. He is in pain, though.'

'Well, I am sure you will think of a solution.' There is relief in Abhi's voice.

'I know shit about kids. And he just keeps crying. And I am sure I won't be able to keep him quiet once the pain really hits,' she whispers.

'Oh, I am sure you'll think of something.' Abhi's voice holds a now familiar trace of laughter. 'I'll call soon,' he promises. Sam sighs, hoping that her silence would somehow extend the call.

On the other end, Abhi too holds on for an extra second. 'Oh, and Sam? Good job!' Then the phone clicks dead. Sam hangs on to the receiver for an extra moment, her lips twisted in a ghost of a smile. Then she turns back to Billy, eyeing him speculatively.

'So, you like chocolate?' she asks, her voice barely above a whisper.

He nods, refusing to meet her eyes.

'What about liquid chocolate?'

'Hot chocolate, you mean?' he scoffs, holding his voice as low as hers.

'No, actually liquid, sweet, cold chocolate,' she insists.

He is intrigued despite his earlier shock, watching her as she goes into the bathroom to mash up a couple of tablets of paracetamol and one of her usual post-trip Valium into a glass. It isn't as if she is going to get much more sleep. She hopes that she isn't overdosing him. What the hell are dosages for children, she wonders, shaking her bottle of prescription Valiums: all the label says is to keep out of reach of children! Next some sugar from the tea tray, and finally a topping of half a miniature bottle of Baileys: that should keep Billy out of pain, and quiet, she hopes.

He looks at her warily as she approaches with the concoction in one hand, a Milky Way from the hotel's snack stash in the other. 'Yes, you can have both of these. First you drink this, then you can have this,' she holds out each to him in turn. Reluctantly, he takes the glass, sniffing it hesitantly before taking a small sip. 'Ew, not really chocolate,' he screws up his tiny face in disgust.

'You know how they give medicines to puppies?' Sam asks, meditatively looking at the pile of blood-stained towels piled at the end of the sofa. Billy's eyes are wide as he looks up. 'You just have to hold their mouths open, and pull the neck up so it is straight. Then you close their nose and pour the medicine in. And zoom, all the medicine goes straight into their stomachs.'

Horrified, Billy drinks down the Baileys fast, spluttering and coughing as the alcohol burns his throat, bringing fresh tears to his eyes. 'Well done,' Sam commends, holding some bottled water to his mouth. She gives him the chocolate, even gently helping him rip the wrapping off.

Yes, she grins. Not so different from puppies.

THE ARCADIA
ABOUT 45 HOURS AGO

Sometime in the morning, when the air-conditioning has been turned off for hours and oppressive heat grows thick and heavy both in and outside the Arcadia, she calls Abhi.

'Is it Billy?' he immediately enquires.

'No, he is asleep still.'

They both fall silent, nonplussed by the shared moment of incongruent domesticity. As if they were just another working couple worrying about an offspring. The thought makes both of them laugh.

Inconsequent chatter, of friends, of childhood memories, of anything that can distract them from the insanity beyond their doors. 'Think the rest of them have gone to sleep. The switchboard has been completely quiet for the past hour. For the first time since this began...' Abhi tells her, explaining the ease with which he can converse.

'Yes, the magic thirty-six-hour mark for exhaustion. No one can really keep fretting much longer beyond that.' Sam is wise in the ways of danger.

'Is that really true?'

'No, I just made it up. It happens to me, though. I can manage a day and a half, and then I must sleep.' She laughs.

'We haven't passed the magic hour yet,' Abhi reminds her.

'Yeah, I know, I am still totally wired.' He wishes he could confess that sleep has evaded him too for the past hours.

'I think they are planning to move, but not sure when,' Abhi ventures, after a while.

'Tell them to get moving. I am getting a bit bored up here.'

He laughs. 'What? The adrenalin rush wearing off?'

'Nah, just not getting any with all this babysitting.'

He laughs. 'And how is that going?'

'He's asleep for now.' She feels that Abhi would probably not approve of her giving Billy alcohol or Valium.

'Good. They heal better that way,' he sounds so confident that she nearly believes him.

'How the hell would you know?'

'I don't. It just seems like what I should tell you.'

'Always working, aren't you? Managing crisis, soothing people, God help us! I can't figure out if you're playing me or actually being nice.'

He doesn't answer her, perhaps because there is no acceptable answer. Just before she is about hang up, he speaks out.

'Sam, have you eaten?'

'What?'

'You are going to need food. Not only for yourself now, but also for the kid. Have you eaten?'

Despite her unfamiliar irritation, she is touched. 'No, there isn't a whole lot in the fridge. Just booze, and chocolate bars, and a couple of those weird cup things, puddings or something…' she scans the room, checking the tea-station. 'Oh and what looks like biscuits and a pack of chips. I am not going to eat any of that shit!'

His voice is calm, reasonable. 'Well, first you are going to need to eat something. We are now going into nearly a whole day. Don't think the army is ready to move in yet. My guess is they will try to exhaust these guys, move in maybe tomorrow night. So that makes it how many hours? You'll be ready to drop. You need to eat, Sam.'

'Gee thanks for the concern,' she snorts. 'You want me to order room service then?'

He chuckles. 'The kid will probably be OK with the stuff you have. Look, we did room service just before this kicked off. One on your floor, two on the floor above. There are others, but those are the closest.'

'You bastard! You actually have this information, don't you? Remind me never to stay at these hotels ever again. Cameras, activity log, fuck man, you might as well be the panopticon.'

140

'Or just a really good business.'

'Fine. I am going to work for a bit. I will call you a bit later, and we'll do a forage trip,' she concedes. It is as far as Abhi will push her, knowing that she is still pulling herself together after stepping so far from habit.

'Will do, ma'am.'

'Don't call me that,' the response is automatic.

'Sam, you did good. With the kid, I mean.'

He hears the now familiar derisive, dismissive snort, a low muttered 'fuck off' before the line goes dead.

***

He is so engrossed in identifying the rooms closest to 1401 on the room service records that he doesn't notice the time slip past in silence. Nothing exists except the squares of light flickering before him, the CCTV bank, the television on silent in the far corner, the laptop propped on the desk before him, his two phones flashing occasionally with messages. Perhaps that is why he doesn't notice the initial movement in the Garden Café.

He has run up Sam's room service order, a single one for dinner from the day before, a Caesar salad, a plain chicken soup, a lot of whisky. 'You don't eat much, do you?' he mutters, letting his own voice fill the silence that engulfs the Arcadia. He is cross-checking what he is sure are her preferences against room service orders delivered to the nearest rooms, when the sudden movement in the café catches his eye.

The army has breached the Garden Café, entering through the far off delivery gates, the ones he can't see on his screens. External gates are monitored by the security post near the driveway. Abhi can only hope that the gunmen have ignored that, that the army has found the gunmen's blind spot into the Arcadia. Approachable from a backstreet, he had identified the delivery gates as a possible entry point hours earlier, had briefed the CO on the multiple casualties inside the café, the need to evacuate them at the earliest.

141

He can see the cautious silent evacuation, the uniformed armed men hustling away hysterical civilians, carrying the wounded, the weak. In the café, he knows the doors have been bolted from the inside, by a smart thinking guest or perhaps one of the waiters. Perhaps even the ageing, slightly officious maître d' Abhi has always found annoying? Perhaps the wood podium gave them cover when the gunman had first burst into the lobby? Perhaps the glass doors had given the café those precious, extra few seconds?

Hours ago, he had spoken to the shift manager, knows there are multiple dead and injured there, but far fewer than if there had been slower initial reflexes. He had even considered the possibility of evacuation, using the delivery gates nearby, even though he knows they are locked, are too high to scale for most of the guests trapped in the café. He had told them all to stay put, assuring them that the security would rescue them as soon as possible. 'You are likely to be the first ones out of here,' he had reassured, just a few hours ago.

Hope flickers wildly as he watches the army move in, and with it, the possibility that perhaps it will be his turn next. On a normal day, he takes less than three minutes to cross from the café, through the small foyer, across the lobby, to the reception and then into his office. He knows the assault will take longer, but can't stop feeling a sudden elation. In the tight square before him, the men move carefully, administering first aid, separating the wounded from the healthy.

'The bronze doors lead to a foyer, sir. Yes, about six feet by eight, leading to the lobby. The lobby side has a second set of doors, mostly glass. Yes, sir, the second doors open straight into the lobby.' He remembers the CO asking questions, asking Abhi to walk him through the floor plans. 'Yes sir, the first set are locked now. Secured from the café side. The gunmen can access the foyer from the lobby, though.'

He feels a sudden pang of nostalgia, of homesickness, of sudden powerful love as he sees the uniformed men take up positions, placing themselves in formation near the doors to the lobby, instinctively identifies the young officer who seems to be the fulcrum of all activity, the one who will lead from the front, when the assault begins, the one that reminds him of Samar. The officer has taken the lead, positioning himself to the right of the double doors. Even in the small square, Abhi can feel the officer's muscle tighten, his entire being coiled like a spring, ready to burst into the lobby, and into whatever it holds. Exactly like Samar.

Perhaps it is the nostalgia that makes him look away, tearing away his suddenly blurred eyes from the screen. That is when he catches a glimpse of the television screen. The news channel is beaming new images of Arcadia, taken from a rooftop somewhere along the backstreet, images of the ambulances pulled up, the fire engines waiting along its length, of armed men in olive green moving purposefully to the delivery gates that he knows lie now open just beyond the camera's reach. Then in the far distance from the live broadcast camera, figures supporting huddled evacuees, bearing stretchers, carrying wounded.

'Oh fuck! Wasn't there a news blackout?'

Turning to inside the Arcadia, he can now see two sets of movement on his screens. In the café, the soldiers have completed evacuation, are taking up positions near the door, upturning tables and moving furniture in an arcane obstacle course. But on the screen above, the assailants have suddenly sprung to life, galvanised by some unheard instruction, moving from the arcade overlooking the lobby, down the steps and then across to the wide bronze café doors.

For a long moment, he watches the two sides dance in near perfect harmony, both sides with weapons held in readiness, silent feline steps, muscles tense in anticipation. On both screens, the men advance towards the heavy bronze doors separated only by a few paces, elegantly mirroring each other, in some trained, learned dance, where guns and crouches, swivels and measured gestures seem more like seduction than a threat.

Then the dance subtly changes pace, the soldiers moving across the café with the same steady pace, while the assailants have sped up, their movements deliberate, sinister, rapid. A team of two drops their automatics, placing them carefully against a marble pillar. They purloin one of their backpacks, searching for something Abhi cannot see, their backs hunched, their faces bent close together in consultation. He punches through to the army ops room, 'They know you're coming. From the pictures on TV, damn it!'

He can hear the CO swear, graphic, fluent.

Unlike before, when they had rampaged through the Refuge, stalked the corridors, when they had shot and destroyed for the cameras, the gunmen have now turned away, blinding him to their actions. It isn't until they move past the glass panels and up to the double doors, their stealth and care strangely different from the swagger they have shown till the moment that Abhi begins to worry. They place the unidentified packets against the bronze, taping nearly half a dozen dull, clean rectangle bricks to the heavy oak lintel. Understanding comes to Abhi almost too late, only when he sees the assailants move swiftly back into the lobby, begin to help the others to push the heavy antique armoire against the glass doors.

'Get your guys back, they are rigging the doors to the lobby with explosives,' Abhi's shouts into the receiver before even the CO can speak. Before he can finish the sentence, the gunmen have retreated across the lobby, far from the newly barricaded glass portals.

'We've allowed for that. Our boys know what they are doing.' The voice on the other side is unflustered, frustrating in its similarity to Baba's. For an instant, Abhi feels like a child again, trying futilely to explain some small defeat to his father. On the screen, he can see the soldiers take a step forward, can see the young officer, the one who reminds him so much of Samar, inch along the wall, barely a few inches away from the doors.

144

'These are different. Not grenades. These are new ones, additional ones…' The first blast takes him by surprise, flashing on to the screen in a sharp blinding burst before the camera blows out. He can feel the thud reverberate through the building, shaking the walls, Arcadia's very foundations. On another lobby screen, he can see a fire spring up around the bronze doors, can barely see through the smoke and steam.

In the café, the soldiers have crashed to the floor. The young officer is huddled against the wall, a hand held up to his ears, his body hunched away from the flaming, gaping hole in the wall. Abhi feels relief course through him as the officer gestures to his men, pulling them back from the spreading flames, shouting into his headpiece, can see some of the others move forward with extinguishers.

He can hear the CO still, cursing softly on the line, his trained calm fragmented for an instant. 'Tell them to stay put. Nobody goes forward until we know what else the sons-of-bitches have,' the voice on the line barks, probably to a subordinate. When the CO reverts to Abhi, his voice is quiet though strained, his emotions barely in check, 'Thank you Mr Sikarwal. These bastards are really well prepared. We'll need all information you can give us.'

Abhi sinks back into the chair, his heart pounding, as the flames spread in the café, fighting the soldiers and the extinguishers. Though he can't see it, he knows the foyer is blocked with debris, barricading the entry into the lobby. The sprinkler system has kicked in, spraying the blown out doors, the charred space with water and fire-retardants and steam.

The assailants have retreated back into the lobby. They are busily setting up obstructions to use for the final assault they know will come soon. Abhi watches them move heavier cabinetry against the shattered glass doors of the café foyer, rigging the furniture, and door frames with further explosives.

In the café, the troops are moving to secure the space, directing the fire extinguishers at the blaze, setting up firing positions. A breach has been achieved into the Arcadia, but anything further will need more time, more cover of darkness. Hope that had flickered is smothered by exhaustion. Slumping back in his chair, he swipes a hand across his eyes, wearied even more by the realisation that he's unlikely to be sprung from his trap.

THE ARCADIA
12 WEEKS BEFORE

Sometimes Abhi is jealous of his brother, of the iron discipline Samar can impose on himself, the self-control that leads his every desire, as if the uniform he wears in life is forged in his soul. On nights like this, when Abhi finds himself distracted, desire running through every millimetre of his body, pulsating like some barely leashed wild thing, he wishes he could borrow some of Samar's self-control.

All it takes is Dieter's name to flash up on the guest list again to send him into turmoil. They had met three months before, at Arcadia's reception. Even at that first moment of eye contact, there had been a mutual recognition, a flash of desire that refused to be tamped down. Abhi had lingered behind the reception desk, watching the tall man check in, taking in the tasteful clothes, the sharp planes at the base of his throat, the soft glowing curls that shone on the back of his hand. He knew the attraction was mutual, as Dieter had kept throwing questions at the increasingly befuddled receptionist, insisting politely, gently, that he needed more information. Finally, Abhi had stepped in, much to the receptionist's relief.

'Of course, sir, we will be happy to take any special requests.' His dark eyes had risen to meet Dieter's smiling blue ones, and an instant hot flash had swept through him.

'That would be most kind of you,' Dieter's voice had been low, intimate. They had woven their words, inconsequential, practical, public, in a secret dance, making plans, plotting the venue, seducing each other with nothing more than eyes, and brief smiles, with words that meant little except for the warmth of voices that bore them. His eyes had followed Dieter's progress to the lifts, had grinned in response when Dieter had suddenly turned and flashed a smile, had felt an instant tightening of his cock.

When Abhi thinks about it, he knows he had been lost from that first instant, floating through the rest of the day in a dream state. From his office, on the bank of screens, he had watched for Dieter, noting when he left the hotel, his suit indicating that he was here for work much to Abhi's relief; his return to his room for a shower and change of clothes, the ascent up to the Refuge, first for dinner, then for cocktails, perched at the glass and granite bar.

Abhi had finished work, telling himself that he was just checking in at the Refuge for a last round, to circulate and greet the regulars, to mingle with the city's celebrities and powerbrokers who kept the Arcadia in the news and comfortably in the black. He had felt Dieter's eyes clock him from the instant he had entered the bar, knew they were locked on him as he walked through the perfumed beautiful crowds, had felt the growing tension at his core, the pleasant ball of nerves at the base of his stomach.

He had not approached the bar until he had finished his rounds, drawing out the anticipation as long as he could, letting the desire and nerves build to a crescendo. When finally he had leaned over to request his usual beer, he had been close enough to Dieter, to catch his cologne, something musky and spicy. Abhi had noticed the soft luminescence of the silk jumper, the cuffs pushed back just enough to show off the muscled forearms, the elegant wrists, the long tapering fingers, all sprinkled lightly with wiry golden curls.

'So is this the time to make a special request?' Dieter had said, his voice low under the hum of the talk and the pulse of the music.

'Oh, I think this would be an excellent time for special requests,' Abhi had flashed a smile, still leaning on the bar, feigning a confidence he had not felt.

They had talked of inconsequentialities then, in a dance of seduction unseen and unremarked by others in the Refuge. Not for long, though, as their mutual need grew too overwhelming for extensive preliminaries. Abhi had discreetly slipped across

148

the key-card for a room he used on nights he stayed at the Arcadia, always picking one on a floor that would be mostly unoccupied, on a floor where he had carefully turned off the CCTV cameras before leaving his office.

Dieter had left the Refuge first, finishing his drink quickly, flashing a grin at Abhi, nodding at the bartender, weaving his way through the half-drunk crowds without a backward glance. Not that Abhi would have seen that glance, as he hunched lower over his beer, refusing to let his muscles relax, just in case the temptation to turn and see Dieter walk away grew too overwhelming. He had waited there for nearly half an hour, finishing his beer at a forced, deliberate pace, counting slowly to sixty between each sip. The bartender had hovered, swiftly producing his usual shot of cognac just as he drained the beer.

Abhi has long been a creature of habit, another vice he blames on his upbringing. But some habits are well cultivated, and the bartender knows that he likes a final drink before retiring for the night. He always drinks a VSOP, one of his many indulgences, another sign to himself that he has succeeded in building the life he has dreamed, has always wanted. On nights when loneliness grows too overwhelming, when he wishes he could share the successes of his life with someone, with anyone, the cognac helps him put his thoughts to rest. On those nights he takes a bottle to bed, glugging the amber liquid until his dreams grow blurred. But on that first night with Dieter, he had only had that one nightcap, swallowing the shot in a quick scorching gulp, thanking the bartender, and headed out swiftly.

In the room, Dieter had been waiting, impatient, passionate, wanting to please. They had made love repeatedly, discovering the secret places that made them sigh, moan, gasp. Later they had fallen asleep almost at the same time, their words drifting comfortably into the night, their limbs intertwined, comforted by the feel of a living heart beating steadily under their outstretched fingers.

Abhi had woken up early, roused from sleep by the eastern sun streaming through the windows, to the slightly acid, male smell as his face turned into Dieter's armpit, to the bitter-sweet taste of skin he thought he could grow to love.

For many long moments he had watched his lover sleep, memorising the fringed half-moons of his closed eyes, the gold-brown curling hairs, the wide planes of his chest, the play of muscles under the expanse of skin, the occasional punctuating sunspot. He had wanted to draw close, feel the fresh stubble on Dieter's chin against his own, feel the sandpapering on his lips, but had held himself in check. Instead he had observed, overlaying memories of the way Dieter had moved his hands in conversation, how he had run those same gentle, strong, fingers through his hair and rubbed his eyes when tired.

Abhi still savours the memory of that first moment they had seen each other in the Refuge, when an involuntary delighted smile had curved across Dieter's lips, when his eyebrows had shot up briefly, anticipation, desire, attraction all contained in that fraction of a second, in that most innocuous of gestures.

In the lazy silence of that early morning, Abhi could have almost said out loud what he never admitted even to himself, that he desperately wanted to love someone, that he wanted a lover who would reciprocate his passion, his love, his kindness. A lover that would be more than a fleeting interlude, someone he could call his own; or just call, especially in moments of loneliness or sadness or anxiety. Dieter seemed to hold that promise behind his softly curving mouth, under his shut half-moon eyes. In that hushed dawn, Abhi desperately wanted to believe that he too could find a safe haven all his own.

Perhaps that is why he had lingered, waited for Dieter to awaken, staring out into the rising sun, weaving fanciful impossible dreams and plans. Perhaps that is why when Dieter woke, he had remained to cuddle, to chat and giggle over instant coffee drummed up from the tea station, to luxuriate in a moment of unfamiliar intimacy, looking constantly into a future that promised more of such mornings, and more nights of urgent desire.

And perhaps this is why Abhi had promised to stay in touch, to email and text, to meet the next time Dieter is in town, to meet for a proper date, with dinner and drinks, maybe even champagne, before they made love. And also maybe this is why when Dieter finally left, he had felt bereft, wishing for something that could delay the life that swirled beyond their rumpled bed, that threatened to whip them back into the whirlpool of daily responsibilities.

Loathe to give up on some strange inarticulate dream, Abhi has repeatedly risked his heart, emailing Dieter, texting him and calling him. Not daily, not even weekly. He is aware of the need for dignity, the need for keeping a safe distance, at least safe enough to retreat should Dieter wish to turn him down, so he gives chase from a distance, maintaining contact but never closing in for the kill.

But on many nights, alone in his bed, the pristine ironed white sheets stretched without a wrinkle across the wide expanse, Abhi summons up the memory of Dieter's last kiss, not the penultimate one. He cherishes not the full passionate ones, but the very last flickering touch of their tongues, their lips separated only by their breaths. 'Next time, I promise,' Dieter had breathed, his eyes warm and glowing.

THE ARCADIA
37 HOURS AGO

She is hunched over the laptop, sorting and labelling the photographs, readying them for dispatch when the knot between her shoulder blades throbs again, painful and insistent. Winded, Sam looks up, forcing her breath to slow down, willing her heartbeat to stop hammering. On the sofa, Billy sleeps uneasily, murmuring softly against the pillow, his small face contorted in pain, beads of sweat glistening in the furrows of his brow.

Sam turns to the single buzz from the mobile on the table. A text. From Abhi. 'Stay in. Cameras show they are on your floor.'

Beyond the door, she can hear faint footsteps, men moving carefully, purposefully, pausing to knock on doors. She jumps up, grabbing the mobile, ready to move to Billy, her hand poised to cover his mouth, the pain making her giddy and breathless. 'You may as well stop,' she tells herself sternly, willing her body to obey her mind. 'There really isn't anywhere to run or hide this time.'

The footsteps come closer then stop before her door. A knock. First gently, then a loud hammering. Billy's eyes fly open, wide with fear. Sam holds a finger to her lips, grateful he hasn't cried out. She tiptoes to the sofa even as the coarse voice outside shouts, 'Hotel security, open the door.' Sam shakes her head at Billy, holding her finger tense against her mouth, mouthing a silent *shhh*.

The hammering on the door sounds nearly as loud as her own heartbeat. Or Billy's as he slides closer to her, his fingers curling tight on Sam's arm. 'We'll be fine,' she reassures him, her breath soft against his ear, as rough voices spoke from beyond the door.

'Nobody in this one. Keep going. Check the other rooms.' After a last flurry of loud knocks on the door, the footsteps move away. Sam holds her finger up in another warning to Billy, straining her ears to hear as the danger moves further down the corridor. 'Shhh…' She hears hammering, then more voices, a short burst of gunfire. Her nose twitches, alert for any hint of smoke, any suggestion that the gunmen may be speeding up to the end game.

It isn't until Billy sobs softly, the barely audible whimper drawing her attention away from the noises beyond the room that she notices that she has placed herself to cover his slight, shaking, huddled body, hugging him through the bulky duvet she had wrapped around him. 'Oh, for fuck's sake!' she tells herself under her breath, noting that his trembling has spread to her own limbs. He is sobbing now though no tears leak from his closed eyes. But his breathing is ragged, punctuated by the shudders that shake his small body.

Sam hesitates for a long instant, then carefully moving him on the wide cushions, she eases herself next to him. Wrapping the duvet tightly over him, avoiding any contact with his warm, feverish body, she wraps her arms gently around him, hugging him close, forcing her body to be absolutely still, hoping that some of her steadiness, if not calm, can transmit to him. 'We'll be fine, kiddo. Promise…shhh.' She searches her mind for words that can comfort the child and can find none, just a half-remembered lullaby with few of the words. So instead, she just holds him tight, hums tunelessly, softly, her voice barely above a whisper, until he falls asleep again.

***

The fire-fight at the café has left Abhi a nervous ball of energy, the long lethargy of the confinement disrupted by a surge of adrenalin. He paces, trying to walk off the sickening rush, his mind in a jumble of random thoughts. 'Focus, Abhi,' he tells himself again and again, muttering the words in the same tone that Baba and Samar use, hoping that the command will eventually sink in.

153

But the calm doesn't return until he notices the gunmen retreat to the second floor, leaving the lobby an obstacle course of upturned furniture and rigged explosives. Abhi notes that this time the explosives seem intended to cause delay rather than damage, notes the locations and passes it back to the CO, wondering what the gunmen plan. He knows that they can't bring down the tower with those, can't even delay the soldiers for long. He marches back and forth before the wall of monitors, his mind barely registering the gunmen moving in the arcade, his eyes hardly registering the stasis on other screens.

It isn't until the gunmen split into teams of two, four staying to guard the arcade and the lobby, the others moving to the lifts, guns held at the ready again, that he moves, punching in Sam's number, needing to warn her, protect her, first.

He watches as the teams exit the lifts, each taking a floor, beginning with the Refuge, again stalking the corridors, hammering at the closed doors. The team in the Refuge seems to be the most desultory, peeking into the bar, one of them letting off a random, short, burst of gunfire at the bar, laughing as the bottles burst and shatter. Like little boys running wild, Abhi suddenly thinks, slightly repulsed. In his life destruction comes with discipline and this sudden breach from the gunmen bothers him.

On the other floors, Abhi can see the gunmen knocking on the room doors. He is beginning to tell them apart, can see the ones who knock politely, softly, hoping to lure out any guest hiding within; the ones who hammer on the wood with their fists, shouting, kicking at the oak. Despite his revulsion, he can feel a grudging approval of the first, if only for their ability to think through what will be more effective.

He hopes that none of the guests will be tempted, or scared, enough to respond the gunmen. He has already done the rota, over an hour ago, warning the guests, reassuring them, updating them. 'Yes, sir, the army is trying to evacuate as quickly as they can…ma'am, please, I don't know when you will be able to leave. For the moment, please don't attract any attention to yourself…

please do not open the door, no matter what.' Now he knows he can't take the risk of a ringing phone sounding out in a room, even though he has warned all guests to turn the room phones to silent. He can only hope that they will follow instructions, that some instinct for survival will win over fear, and the innate need to obey commands.

He feels increasingly frustrated, furious as he watches the gunmen range through the Arcadia, no longer concerned with only their human targets. This time, they seem weirdly energised, slightly cocky, letting out sudden bursts of laughter. Two of them, on the eighth floor, joke and laugh, firing occasionally at the ceiling, into open doorways, posing like actors in action films, until one of them accidentally shoots out one set of cameras, leaving the corridor half-blind. The others on other floors are just as highly strung, firing random bursts at mirrors, smashing the tall vases with the butts of their assault rifles. He wonders if they too are feeling the adrenalin rush from the fire-fight earlier, then suddenly catches one staring into a camera. Abhi recognises that tense, wired, wide-eyed look. Speed. That is what they are popping to stay awake. As if things weren't bad enough!

Despite telling himself repeatedly that he is equally responsible for all the hostages, Abhi can feel his eyes flicker back constantly to the fourteenth floor, hoping against all odds that the gunmen will miss it, that the speed high may mean they will count wrong, or that identical corridors will distract them, convince them that they have already covered it. For nearly thirty minutes, he is almost vindicated, as the corridor remains clear, its shadowy length comforting in its vacancy. Then suddenly two of the gunmen spill out of the lift, stalking through the shadows, marching purposefully to one end, towards 1402, too close to Sam.

His breath caught in his throat, he watches them hammer at the door he has seen open and close repeatedly over the past hours. Unconsciously, he clenches his fingers further in his fists, his eyes glued to the pulsating square of light before him. 'Just

155

keep her safe,' he mutters, repeating the words like a mantra, unaware that it is the closest he has come to praying in years, that he is invoking a deity he denied long ago. He stands still as stone, heart pounding so hard that he can feel it shake and shudder against his ribs, as the minutes creep by.

The two gunmen are efficient, albeit loud, hammering on the doors, kicking them hard repeatedly. Abhi's nose wrinkles in disgust as one aims a playful flying kick at a door, not Sam's, but one just down the hall. 'Grow the fuck up!' he growls, startling even himself with the gravel in his voice. The corridor remains safe, the doors shut against the intruders, as the men rage its length, trampling the lilies that Sam had arranged in a deliberately artless pattern as her warning system, unseeing of the small glowing markers she has embedded into the thick pile. Then bored, or tired, or perhaps just following instructions, they punch the button for the lift.

Abhi sighs, letting relief wash over him, lets his eyes flicker to other floors. Perhaps that is why he misses that first sliver of light that slices across the shadowy corridor. A door slips open, not 1402, but on the other end. Instantly the gunmen are alert, turning back from the lift. Then the younger one smiles, crouches for an instant and breaks into a sprint towards that slim slice of light that carves the dark carpet. Just before he reaches the dark oak panel, he jumps into his signature flying kick, slamming with his full body force into it. Lights blazing in the room, so long held in check by the heavy door, burst fully into the shadowed corridor.

That sudden change in light is what pulls Abhi's attention back to the fourteenth floor. The gunman has dragged a man by the collar into the corridor. The victim is young, perhaps younger than Abhi, perhaps less than a dozen years older than the gunman; and portly, fleshy in that sedentary well off way of young businessmen, his rounded belly signalling too many expensive dinners, too many nights of drinking, too many hours spent in a comfortable chair. Abhi remembers him from earlier in the week, can hear his querulous voice in his head, recognises him as the big spender at the bar, desperate to impress the women, or just anyone who would watch. Even then he had seemed too small for his enormous bulk. He seems even further reduced now, on his knees, crawling, struggling as the young gunman drags him along the thick carpet.

The second assailant, still poised before the lifts, calls out something, gesturing forcefully. The gunman, dragging the victim, laughs in response. He pulls the begging hysterical man, grabs a hunk of hair, pushing a soft weeping fleshy face up to the lens so the camera can catch the hysteria, the wide-eyed fear, the glisten of drool and tears and sweat on the victim. He grins up at the camera, his eyes bright, laughing, for an instant. Then he pushes the barrel of his rifle up against the man's head and pulls the trigger.

'You bastard! You bloody fucking, fucking bastard!' The sudden fury that races through Abhi is unfamiliar, cutting through the horror. He can feel the blood race to his head, bashing against his skull, a red haze filling his eyes, filling the screen that has gone suddenly opaque before him. For a long instant Abhi is lost, as if drowning in a wave of bloodlust he has never known before. But then a sharp pain jolts up his arm, piercing the edge of his palm. When he looks down, clearing his head with a shake, he notices he has been punching the table top before him.

The pain in his fist calms him down. He looks back up at the screen and can only be grateful that the blood spatter covers the lens, blurring the view of the corridor, of the body now slumped on the floor. On the second camera near Sam's door, still feeding a clear image, he watches the gunmen disappear into the lift.

It isn't until he sees them reappear on the arcade below, confirms that the gunmen are regrouping that he punches the number to the ops centre. 'We have another casualty, sir.'

***

Beyond the closed curtains, Sam knows the sky is growing dark. She has not felt so wound up, afraid even, in many years. To calm herself, she reverts to the ritual discovered so long ago, the simple act that she approaches with all the solemnity of a sacred rite, the one thing she can do that she has learned will calm her down regardless of all else.

She sets up her flashlight in the shadowy bath, more to be able to see her tools than to illuminate her reflection. She is so accustomed to the act that she needs no visual guide. She wets her head with lukewarm water, rubbing her palms over the increasingly grey stubble.

She isn't particular about the lather, using whatever she can find, just like that first time. The variety is oddly comforting as she spreads the liquid soap from Identikit dispensers or those small bars provided in hotels that melt like so much viscous butter. She always lathers up the soap on her palms before spreading it over her skull, relishing the slickness spreading between her fingers, creeping up on the inside of her wrist.

She uses a silver and pink four-blade safety razor, finding every last patch with her fingers. She isn't particularly fond of the nauseous colour but she has learned that the head swivels just right, making it easier for her to smooth the back of her head. Each measured stroke removes the stubble down to her scalp. The years have turned the stubble grey, giving her a strangely lightheaded look, the grey making her dark eyes stand out even more starkly, emphasising the fragility of the sharp cheekbones.

She never repeats the promise she had made that first time, preferring to erase the moment entirely from her memory. Instead she stares into the mirror, not seeing her own image, letting her hands roam her skull. In her mind's eye, she sees only the images she has chosen not to capture, all the snaps that she has let go before her finger could tighten. The ritual is comforting, reminding her of the ways she has chosen to distinguish herself, of her choice to honour the dead if only by choosing to shoot them most aesthetically, and at times not at all.

'Who died?' Billy's voice is tremulous.

Her hand pauses mid-sweep as she tries to refocus her eyes, blinking to push away the images in her mind, before angling the shaving mirror to catch him on the sofa behind her.

'What...?'

'Isn't that why you are shaving your head? Because someone died?'

'Nobody has died.' Sam sighs, all too aware that he will eventually learn of her lie.

'When grandpa died, daddy shaved off his hair too. Everyone did. Well, not me, but all the men.' Billy was insistent, his bleary eyes trying to remain focused.

'Go back to sleep. You ask too many questions.' Sam's voice is brusque, though she is annoyed only slightly at Billy. 'And no, nobody died. OK? Now sleep!'

Sam can't bear to look at him, even in the mirror. Someone will have to tell him who had died in that room where she had found him. Some day. But first he had to survive those who were stalking the corridors with guns and grenades. Sam's mouth twists in a grimace, she has to make sure he survives. Just so he could find whatever heartbreak lay in the future, just so he could learn who had died. Because life just makes so much fucking sense sometimes.

THE ARCADIA
33 HOURS AGO

Slumped back in his chair, Abhi just wants the nightmare to be over. He can smell the slightly rancid scent from himself, or perhaps it is from the refuse collecting in the trashcan in the far corner, even though he has tried to cover the top with plastic folders, ensures that he seals the empty Coke bottle he has been using for urine. Still the sour smell hangs over the room, invading his nose at unexpected intervals, triggering a wave of nausea each time. Even in his exhausted slump, his face twists in disgust as he sniffs at his shirt. His fastidious side is offended by the forced uncleanliness. He has always prided himself on his neatness, ensuring that his clothes are pristine, his desk clear, his home ordered and disciplined. 'Little bro, admit it, you let Baba get to you,' he can hear Samar's teasing voice in his head. 'Either that or you are seriously OCD, and I don't know what is worse.'

Abhi settles for OCD, stripping off the soaking shirt, spreading it out in a corner to dry out, willing it to stop stinking. Grabbing a towel and bottle of mineral water, he wipes himself down, scrubbing hard to rid himself of not only the sweat and bile and fear he feels, but also the rage from the fire-fight, the gun-smoke and acrid chemical smell of explosives. He rubs down his close-cropped hair with the damp towel, and is surprised when it comes away as clean as before. He had almost expected it to be covered in the soot and dirt and blood he has been following on the screens.

The magic thirty-six hours that Sam had mentioned will soon pass, he clocks, counting back to last evening when the first shots had been fired. The air-conditioning has been turned off from the mains by security; maybe for the silence, or maybe to make things uncomfortable for the gunmen, Abhi can't be sure. In a flippant moment, earlier in the day, when the low machine hum had fallen silent, he had wondered if those trained, grim men terrorising the Arcadia would even care for air-con. His office is sweltering, the air heavy and oppressive and stale, despite the tiny crack in the opened corner window. The night fallen over the city offers little respite from the heat and humidity.

Staring at the console before him, he knows the assailants are equipped with phones and laptops. Much like him, except, of course, for the guns and grenades, and the neatly packed explosive bricks. The key accessories for the modern terrorists, or the urban guerrilla, as Samar would say. His brother is as precise in his thoughts as Abhi is with his appearance, and so much better prepared for this madness. Abhi wonders about the instructions the gunmen receive, who gives them out, how they plan to get out of the mess. For a flickering second, he even wryly compares himself to them. Both are like automatons, acting on whatever a strange voice on the phone tells them, except the gunmen are free, like Sam, able to move, change positions. Unlike him. What is he then but a spider weaving a web, and not even of his own material or plan. But perhaps it is an even sicker game, of hide and seek, of I-spy, or just blind man's bluff, where those who can move cannot see, and those who see are cursed into immobility.

And now he can't get the fat man out of his mind, his eyes drawn again and again to the same square, opaque and peppered with thick dots. Abhi remembers that he was annoyed with the fat man, first at reception for his ridiculous demands, then at the Refuge for his insistence on buying drinks for a woman who had rebuffed him, then even on the phone when he had been warning the guests to stay in. The fat man has insisted that Abhi give him more information, had later called and blamed him and Arcadia for the attacks, had demanded that the security get him out in time for his flight in the morning. 'I know people, do you understand? And I expect this to be sorted soon.' His voice had been slightly nasal, demanding, each word beautifully enunciated. 'I plan to sue your asses for this, I hope you know that. This is utterly unacceptable!'

161

Abhi remembers hanging up on the fat man, cursing him, 'I hope they shoot you first, asshole.' A throw-away line that seems to have come true. His eyes flicker back to the opaque screen, making him slightly queasy. He resists an irrational urge to reach out and wipe it clean just as he resists the urge to look at the feed from the Refuge, hoping against all reason, that what he knows rationally, what he fears most, is false.

'Brains,' Sam tells him laconically, when he calls her. 'Turn that camera off. The lens is probably covered with bits of that bastard's brains. And blood. Either way, that stuff sticks to glass so unless you are planning to clean it off, you won't see shit.'

'Are you always so…' he isn't sure of the words, unwilling to offend her.

'What? Brutal? Honest? This is my world and it is what it is,' she snaps back. He almost hangs up, but then her voice softens. 'Stop thinking about it, I mean it. There is nothing you could have done. And you can't let your mind keep going back there.'

Of course she is the expert, he reminds himself, so like Samar and yet so unlike him. 'I just wish,' he begins to protest.

'Wish what? That you could have done something? That he hadn't opened that door? He made his choices. We all do, OK? And sometimes when the choice is stupid, the consequences are, well, not great.' Her voice is harsh again.

He knows she is right, at least rationally. But thinking of the fat man leads his mind to other terrors, to the certainty of the one loss he fears most, feels most guilty for. 'But what if…' he trails off, unable to articulate what he refuses to think of, that Dieter must have been in the Refuge when the attack began, is perhaps still there, discarded on the plush carpet, just like the fat man. For an instant, a familiar much desired face floats up in his mind, hovering for a brief second before Abhi can push the thought away, bury the grief that he knows will eventually rise to engulf him.

'Abhi?' Sam's voice is soft, hesitant but enough to remind him that he can't let himself fall apart. Not yet.

162

'Yeah, I know.' He forces himself to sound calm, even cheerful. 'You want me to run you through the room service info so you can head out to get food?'

***

Sam hugs the Mamiya close as she makes her way through Abhi's list of rooms with possible food supplies, checked off against his roster room service orders, cross-checked with open doors to ensure access.

'I have been called a vulture before,' she had quipped, 'just never thought it would be quite so literal.'

'So now you have qualms about taking from the dead?' Abhi had been equally, if more unconvincingly, flippant.

As she creeps down the fire escape to the eleventh floor where two rooms lie open, she feels a strange elation, as if a weight she didn't know she carried is lifting from her shoulders. She doesn't pause to think, savouring the sudden surge of inexplicable happiness. Not the usual adrenalin rush, she recognises, that pulses through her body, that keeps her mind alert, but leaves her emotions as dead as ever. This time, she can feel her limbs relax, the habitual knot in her shoulder melt away almost entirely, replaced by an exuberance she had forgotten long ago. She hasn't worked with a partner in a long time, but she knows this is different. She has never taken a friend into the field, knowing she would die of anxiety if she put anyone else at risk. Yet Abhi is different, not quite a partner, but also not just a friend. He can watch over her, even fear for her, warn her, but she never has to worry about him. The best of both worlds, she tells herself, a sudden smile lighting up her eyes.

In the first room, a couple lie silent, the woman flung back from the open door, on to the carpet, the man half-slung in his chair, as if caught by the bullets as he rose. Not particularly interesting she notes, triggering off a couple of desultory shots. Middle aged, or perhaps not so much older than her, but in that nondescript, grey manner of lives of comfortable boredom.

Funny how the women always seem to rise from the meals, from reading, from bed, to answer the door, she thinks, remembering other rooms. Some sort of domestic habit deeply inculcated.

The table is set with the Arcadia's usual ivory and gold china, the gold-leaf cutlery gleaming against the snowy linen. Covers have been pulled off the dishes, and food sits cold and lumpy on the plates. 'For fuck's sake, Abhi. How am I to carry spaghetti Bolognese back up the stairs?' Although she feels none of the anger her words shape. She notes the red stains on the white linen, clumps of crimson on the bone china, spatters of similar colouring on the carpet and curtains and silver.

The sudden rush of energy is making her a bit giddy, reminding her of her earliest trips into the field, before the joy had been sucked out of her, when life still held all possibilities, when each moment alive seemed a victory against whatever chaos had been unleashed beyond her viewfinder. Sam finds herself taking pictures of the table, the cold pale pasta, with slivers of pale congealed fat nestled amongst the red of the sauce. 'Just for you, Abhi. You get my very first still-life.'

***

Abhi is watching Sam on the cameras, slipping in and out of the fire escape, moving down the hallways, framed briefly in the open doorways he has identified before disappearing into them. Something seems to have shifted though he can't identify anything particular. Her hunched posture has straightened imperceptibly, the shuffling, slightly awkward walk has a slight bounce, as if she can barely keep her energies in check. Even the nondescript knit cap pulled low over her head seems to have a jaunty angle. Watching her makes him smile, filling some vacuum within that he never knew existed, though he worries about her, keeps a wary eye on the gunmen still holed up in the arcade. She seems more complete to Abhi. A lot like Samar. Both are people who know what they want, never once doubt their ability to get what they wish for, are never paralysed by indecision.

164

After the first room on the eleventh floor, she turns to the camera to give him a thumbs down, her mouth curled downwards in an exaggerated frown. Surprised, he looks at the room service list. Surely, they couldn't have finished the food so quickly? The meal had been delivered less than five minutes before the attack, the waiter had been one of the fortunate ones, escaping the initial carnage because the service lift took him straight into the kitchens. The people in the room had not been so lucky, and the open door and unanswered phone are ample give-aways.

He flicks back between the cameras and the roster, puzzled. Of course! The room doesn't have portable food, she can't carry any of it back. How did he miss that? He scans the list again, then quickly taps out a text, 'Sandwich assortment in 1109. And club sandwich on your floor.' He can't number the latter room yet, but knows Sam will identify it as the fat man's, will have to step over his corpse to enter. Just the thought makes him queasy.

On the screen, he watches as Sam checks her phone, nods up at the high camera, then strolls down the hallway to the second open door, the bounce in her step making her seem slightly cocky. He counts off the minutes she spends in the room, watching her in his mind, almost as clearly as he does on the screens, his imagination rewriting the earlier memory of her in the Refuge. He knows she is circling around the room, careful not to disturb any evidence, circumventing all debris, her camera held before her face or cradled lovingly in her arms, her right eye squinting slightly in concentration, almost as if the viewfinder were still glued to it. He knows she will take photographs before she picks the food, hopes that she will remember to collect what she can of the remains.

When she emerges, he sees her posture has changed slightly, a new bulge in her field jacket. The pockets are full too, zipped up over the contents to ensure that nothing is lost. She grins up at him, giving him an excited thumbs-up before patting both sides of her jacket. Even though Abhi knows she can't see him, he gives a low whoop, and flicks up his own thumb in response.

As Sam makes her way back up the fire escape, the sandwiches wrapped in napkins feel odd tucked into her jacket, squishy and soft, warming up with her body heat. Sam can smell the ham, the scent wafts up to her nose, sets her stomach rumbling with long ignored hunger. She can hear the faint tinkling of the miniature booze bottles she has swiped from both the rooms, picking up the Baileys for the kid's pain, vodka and whisky and pretty much everything else for herself. One never knows when one will need something for sleep, or just sustenance. For an instant she feels a flash of anxiety, that the tinkling may give her away, but then her mind kicks in, reminding her that her heightened senses are magnifying the sounds; that Abhi has told her that the gunmen are nowhere close; that the sounds are so faint, they would dissipate even down a single flight of stairs. Even so, she hugs her arms close.

On her own floor she pauses, staring down the shadowy corridor where a doorway lies open, the light from the room throwing a bright square on the carpet outside. To one side lies a lump, misshapen and dark. She knows she doesn't need any more supplies, even knows that the corpse lying before Room 1410 is not really the kind she would shoot, not even for the news photos. Still, in her strange euphoria, she needs something more, needs to push forward just a little more.

She has to step over the fat man to enter the room, carefully avoiding the growing patch of blood and bits of brain on the floor. The wallpaper, even the camera lens nearest the door, are spattered with bits of him, both more obscene, and less aesthetic, and yet fitting for what she decides was a life lived the same way.

The room is pristine, the bed neatly made, clothes piled still in the small suitcase. In the bathroom, the leather kitbag holds expensive products, stacked neatly. On the table, she checks the silver covered plates. Yes, the bastard had ordered club sandwiches all right, she snorts. But not a single crumb remains on the plates, not even a sliver of lettuce. Sam moves quickly, emptying the fridge of the chocolate and alcohol again. She is leaving when a single bottle of wine on the desk catches her eye. A business gift, she thinks, eyeing the red and black print label, the vineyard etched in grey on top. L'Eglise-Clinet, 1994. She is impressed despite herself, pursing her lips to let out a silent whistle. It is a year she remembers well, a year of slivovitsa and madness, being frozen and soaked up in the mountains. There had been not much wine there, at least not of this quality. Unconsciously, she raises a hand to her head, rubbing her bare scalp through the knit cap, a gesture that comforts, pushes back the nightmares that live in there. She grabs the bottle by its neck, and heads out, back down the corridor to her own room.

Just before entering her sanctuary, she raises the bottle in a mock toast to the unseen man she has begun to think of as a friend, holding it up so he can see the label. 'The bastard won't miss this,' she mouths, sticking her tongue out at Abhi.

YEMEN
10 YEARS BEFORE

She has only shot personal photographs once before, nearly a decade ago, on a solitary trip to Yemen. Photographs that she had never filed, never even printed, just shot for grieving relatives, for a single old woman for whom she had felt an inexplicable empathy. Sam no longer remembers the name of the village. The images are in unmarked memory cards, packed away in sealed off boxes.

She had been alone, covering an out of the way funeral of yet more numberless, nameless dead. Killed from somewhere far away, a missile strike or bombs dropped from an airplane flying far above, or the new unseen drones, managed from even farther away, by people who would never need to see the impoverished, dusty villages they demolished. She has learned that it no longer matters if death comes up close and intimate or is rained down from far above and impersonal, only that it is a special privilege for those it takes with speed. She no longer dwells on the survivors, the mourners, who seem to blend into each other, the same loss etched on their faces, the same bereft shadows in their eyes. Sam's eyes only seek the dead, searching only for that final moment of lack, that elusive mystery when a living being becomes a shell of itself, emptied, vacant, and yet whole. Like a skin that is shed and yet remains unshed.

She drove back to the funeral only because she had passed through the village a few days before, remembered watching the narrow streets where the people went about their business. A tall thin house of ochre near the centre was being decorated, with strings of paper flowers of gaudy colours, with plastic palm trees in colours unimagined by nature. Like the rest of the village, its blind windows loomed high over the narrow lanes, fanciful patterns of white painted fresh along the edges of the frames, the painted arches much like shaped eyebrows of the mud-brick homes. She had stretched a finger to gently touch the smooth brown wall, soft, glowing, like skin stretched over blood, and flesh, and bones, not so different from her own hand.

Some children played just beyond the door, winding bits of discarded tinsel on door handles, tree trunks and on themselves, trailing streams of paper flowers in their wake. The house seemed to revel in its gaudy decorations, standing out amidst the dusty streets. She thought she had seen shadows in the higher windows, sensed eyes that watched her from behind the ornate floral shapes of the windows, one more veil in a land of veils. She had felt suddenly vulnerable, feeling more exposed in a land where she had seen few female faces. To her the house had appeared alive, pulsing with something defiant, as if calling out a challenge.

Her translator had told her something about a wedding coming up in the next few days, had introduced her to the villagers, telling her the usual story of his own links to the people, pointing to cousins, uncles, complex family alliances, that she only noted out of politeness, interested only in the strange house that insistently called her eye back to its decorated façade.

She had taken a few photographs, desultory, pretty, only to show the children who clamoured around her, using only her Canon EOS, just forgettable images that she had deleted once back in the car. She had not shot a single frame of the house, embedding it in her memory instead, repeatedly summoning its parched, striking image in her mind even when the car had driven away, moving from the dust of the desert to the verdant of the mountains. Even in the cool air of the high reaches, she remembered the sense of being watched, had been surprised that the thought did not disturb her. Instead she found it strangely appealing.

When she had heard of the strikes, she had wanted to know about that strange house with its tawdry decorations. For once, she had wanted to shoot a building, something entirely

169

inanimate, instead of a person, to see for herself the ochre mud and plaster skin broken and mutilated, perhaps still tangled with garlands of paper flowers, gold tinsel.

The village had been full of people, not deserted like the first time, when Sam returned. They had been hushed but friendly, welcoming her as the only journalist to care enough to shoot their tragedy. The survivors had led her eagerly through their few streets, as they so often did, irrespective of geography and language and history, with that familiar mix of anger, grief and confusion. They had pointed out the damage, pulled at stunned friends and relatives, shouting out names, insisting that the mute speak to confirm their stories.

Sam had diligently taken notes, taken her photographs, even though the main strike had left nothing but charred rubble. Sundered limbs, fragments of bone and hair and flesh flung far apart were the only evidence of casualties. The strike had not hit the tall house but the one adjacent, and the precision of the destruction shocked her despite all she had read and heard. The tall house, her house as she had begun calling it, stood intact, its tinsel glowing in the afternoon sun, the paper flowers dusty but still wrapped around the tall metal gates. The white painted curlicues were dimmed and smudged, some of the delicate window screens had been shattered and stared blindly at the afternoon sun. Much of the plaster had been ripped off, exposing paler, narrow mud-bricks beneath, bones jutting from the ochre skin charred black.

Someone, perhaps her translator, had led her inside, speaking excitedly, pointing deep inside, tugging at her jacket. She had instinctively stepped up the narrow stairs, heading she believed to the *mafraz* on the top, to be given the sickly sweet tea while the men of the village clamoured around to give her the details of the story. She didn't really want to know more, didn't think she needed any more, but the translator had insisted, gently, politely. 'They have no photographs,' he had murmured, stumbling only slightly over the words. 'They want you to take one.'

She had been confused. 'But I can't give them my pics.'

'*La, la.* No, they don't need the picture. They want you to take one,' he had explained, only adding to her confusion. Then as they reached the second landing, a small square resting patch of ground, flanked by doors, he had stopped behind her, stepping down a few steps to give her room. She had stopped too, wary at the way he had fallen back, noting only vaguely that the other men had remained below, that none had followed her up.

She had found herself before a doorway, partially covered by a curtain of some shiny cloth, a cheap version of an Arabian Nights fantasy, something that can only be shot in black-and-white, its sheen and tone too jaded to be caught in colour. Briefly she had wondered about the soft murmurs beyond the doorway, had noticed that the voices of the men below had faded. Then before she could turn, or even speak, she had found herself pushed by unseen hands into the doorway. A slim hand had slid aside the curtain, making just enough room for her to step inside.

The silence in the room had hit her with the force of a blast. Illuminated only by light filtering in from narrow, high windows, the room was full. As her eyes adjusted, Sam could see huddled, shapes swaddled in dull colours, broken only by glints of gold and silver, flashes of brightness from a stone, or cloth. Women were gathered there, grieving together, their arms ringing each other.

Someone moved, an older woman, her back slightly hunched, her eyes dim. She tugged at Sam's hand, pulling her to the centre. There, on a solitary, narrow bed, on a dull cloth of some nondescript colour, was a lone figure. A young woman, much younger than Sam. She was almost childlike, her skin pale, her eyes closed, her dark hair clustered around her forehead in tight curls, a slender silver and turquoise jewel gleaming in their midst.

The women had cleaned her, had dressed her as a bride. Her dress was satin, heavy with gold and silver embroidery, and fine

171

lace shaped into flowers of myriad colours, jarring in their clashing exuberance. A veil of some pale, translucent cloth covered her head. Thick ropes of gold covered her throat and chest.

The old woman tugged at Sam's hand, pointing, talking, insisting. Sam had nodded, raised her Canon, begun to shoot. First medium shots, then close-ups, shifting to black-and-white after a few minutes. Then, moved by aesthetics instead of veracity, Sam had suddenly found herself missing her beloved ancient Leica, wishing she could hold it once again, even though she knew she could not bear to shoot with it, that she had excised it from her life, from her hands, deliberately, so many years ago. A flash of memories threatened to overcome her. A village in the forest, the taste of slivovitsa, a little crowded hut with two children, another old woman with eyes much like a crone, or a witch, filled with suppressed rage, or horror, or pain. Sam could feel her mind grow dark, her eyes blurring as she put away the Canon.

Beneath the tightly wound headscarf, her scalp itched, the freshly shaved stubble crackling an instant reminder, a warning signal that she must pull her mind back from the pathways of memory. Forcing herself to breath slowly, deeply, she had shaken her head, slowly, deliberately, blinked her eyes to clear them, until the memories receded and the shadowy room came back into focus. She had pulled out the Mamiya AFD instead, its bulky case still unfamiliar in her hands, the difference in weight like a new lover who can heal a loss but never quite fill the space of a lost love.

She had wanted something different in the final shots, something not meant for the exhibition she was planning, or to send off to news desks for their banal sentimentalism. Unconsciously her hand had risen to the red and white maple leaf sewn on her jacket pocket. The sudden flash of understanding had stunned her, sending a strange exhilaration through her veins, as if a light had gone on in her mind, banishing the habitual shadows to the very edges of her conscience. She finally had a word for the warmth that had drawn her to the Canadian doctor so many years ago, the strange troubling flickers that curled occasionally in her belly when she was covering a particularly brutal conflict, even the rare wet film that glazed her eyes on nights when she was entirely alone. Empathy. That awful, terrifying, human fragility. For an instant she savours the knowledge, and then carefully, deliberately, she pushes it deep into the dark recesses of her mind. Empathy is a trait Sam has little strength for.

Before her eye dropped back to the viewfinder, she looked at the old woman, caught an inexplicable glow that sent a shudder down her back, even as it pushed her to deliver the perfection she wanted in the final shots.

The old woman had watched Sam change her camera, had let out a deep sigh, and signalled to the other women to pull away from the bed, leaving her alone with the bride. They had collected near the doorway, watched in silence as Sam moved around the bed, framing, aiming, composing, each move as slow as if she were underwater. Sam had taken her time, composing each of the final twenty frames with painstaking care.

Then at the end, she had sat down amidst them, packed away the Mamiya, slowly scrolling through the screen on the Canon, letting them see the bride, the graceful repose, the fading sun sneaking past the slits in the wall to light the veil with a hint of gold, the absolute serenity. They had stared hungrily at the screen, unnerving in their silence. When Sam rose to leave, they had nodded at her, holding out their hands, muttering softly, caressing her hands, her shoulders, soothing her with unfamiliar words. Finally, the old woman had pulled Sam down, planted a heavy kiss on her forehead, had led her back out of the house. No further words had been spoken. Neither had Sam looked back as she drove away.

And all through, the bride had lain silent, unmoving, her veil trembling occasionally with the weak desert wind that wound its way through the window.

173

THE ARCADIA
26 HOURS AGO

It won't be until morning, after Abhi has called the rota of guests to assure and update them, spoken to the CO in the ops centre, and confirmed with Sam that she is headed straight to sleep and will not be venturing out again, that he will force himself to curl up on the floor, a towel under his head, hoping that sleep will fill up some of the tedium of the long hours stretching ahead. But in the grim hours before dawn, he can barely push down the panic bubbling in his belly.

He tells himself that he ought to be grateful that there has been only one casualty, though the thought does not comfort him much. His mind flickers back to Sam, telling himself that at least he helped her save one life. Perhaps he has even helped keep her safe, although that may be a stretch too far. Something tells him that she would cling to life, even at the edge of chaos, coming out of the madness, brittle, broken, but somehow still alive. And then, there is the thought at the edge of his consciousness, pushed back repeatedly, consistently, into oblivion, the one thought he refuses to let into the light, steadfastly denies existence.

The thirty-six-hour mark Sam had joked about has come and gone. His back seems to have frozen despite the frequent stretches, the base of his neck aches steadily. He has run on instant coffee and biscuits from the tea station piled up in his office, but his stomach growls for proper food. His mind seems incapable of settling, racing from one thought to another, between memory and reality and fantasy. He forces his eyes shut, hoping to at least rest his body. Through the thick carpet, he can feel the hard floor, the concrete pushing against his bones, and fidgets in discomfort.

He knows the assault is coming, starting with the skirmishes early the next evening, mounting to a full assault before dawn.

The gruff army voice on the phone has not told him that of course, but he remembers enough from his childhood games with Samar to put the puzzle together. The power mains to the Arcadia will be switched off, he knows, cutting off the television in the rooms, even the lights just when they would be most comforting to the guests. When dusk falls again, there will be no illumination, except what sneaks in from the city beyond, and from the dim emergency bulbs lining the corridors. He has informed them that emergency lights are powered from the solar grid, just like his cameras, the ones he has come to rely on with growing desperation. 'As you have CCTV access Mr Sikarwal, you can update us in real time if there are significant changes,' the CO had told Abhi even though, despite his best effort at civility, his voice reveals his distaste at the thought of a civilian watching the assault.

In his dreams, Samar's voice blends into Baba's. They shout directions, laugh, talking as they always do, so caught up in things that matter to them that he feels invisible. 'Come on, Abhi, you know that is not true,' Samar chides, his voice as sure as ever, even as he turns back to joking with Baba, never noticing that Abhi stands as isolated, as alone as before.

His mother seems to hover just beyond the edge of his dream, beautiful, loving, her perpetual anxiety for the men in her life betrayed only by an almost imperceptible frown line that stretches like a faint scar through the centre of her forehead. Long ago, Abhi had wondered what she thinks of him, so different from Samar and Baba, unlikely to come home with broken bones, or bleeding, or in a coffin. But she hides behind an impenetrable wall of silks and perfumes, pearls and cossetting, loving and yet so distant that he can never bridge the gap.

So different from Sam, he thinks for an instant, with her bravado and focus, and unpredictable flashes of mischief. It is pleasant to think of Sam, not of the fear he feels for her when she is wandering through the hotel, heedless of threats, her camera an extension of herself. He prefers the Sam he has talked

175

to about nothing and everything during the long boring hours of waiting, the one he has told things he never mentions even in his dreams to Baba, or mother, or even Samar.

'Do you talk to others like this?' Sam had asked him, her voice suddenly full of doubt. 'I mean, to others in this place.'

There had been a teasing note in Abhi's voice. 'Why? Would it count as adultery? You know we haven't even met.'

Not knowing him makes Sam bold. 'Actually, yes. It would be like adultery. Or worse.'

This time he did laugh. 'No, Sam, I don't speak to others like this. Most of my guests are staying put in their rooms until the commandoes secure the building. None of them are wandering through the corridors, playing hide and seek with armed nut jobs.'

'Good,' Sam had retorted, her voice suddenly vehement. 'Maybe someday, we'll mean something, this will mean something.'

Her voice thickens in his dream, deepening to Dieter's, startling him, jolting him awake. He stays there, his eyes wide open, sweat soaking into the carpet, his heart hammering.

Dieter! The one casualty he has been trying to ignore, the one that matters most, at least to him. For a long disorientated moment, he can't place where he is, can't remember why he is curled up on the floor. Then it rushes back to him, the siege, the madness, the fear, the boredom. Slowly Abhi tries to bring his racing heartbeat back under control, willing the roaring in his ears to recede back into the deep. But even as his heartbeat begins to steady, the tears begin to fall, gathering slowly in his burning, exhausted eyes, leaking one by one from the corners, until the stream grows so steady, so full that he can only bury his face in his hand, feeling the tears drip down his wrists.

There has been complete silence from Dieter's phone, not a single response to his texts. Every time Abhi has gone through his phone rota, he has diligently called Dieter's room, even though he knows that there will be no answer. Each time, a knot in his stomach builds, only for Abhi to deliberately ignore it. With each hour, a growing despair that he has lost Dieter forever. And with the darkness comes the guilt, the knowledge that Dieter only came to the Arcadia for him.

'I made sure Arcadia is now on our corporate roster,' Dieter had twinkled, not so many weeks before, 'our preferred business hotel in the city.'

Abhi had laughed, raised his glass, his stomach fluttering with nerves, anticipation, with dreams he had woven in the past weeks. 'Yes, thank you. I oversaw the price documents, we will do very well from your company.'

'And I will see you every three weeks,' Dieter's voice had dropped a notch, turning husky with desire. Abhi had felt a flash of happiness. He had just smiled back, telling himself that he deserved the joy, at least the possibility of that joy, that he would let Dieter see past his reserve.

But the moment had passed, and they had reverted to their usual games, building familiar patterns of the lover and the beloved. Abhi would keep his distance, always kind, always charming, replicating their initial courtship. Dieter had chased him then, for months, with charming texts and inconsequential, chatty calls, and funny emails that only hinted at their growing intimacy. Abhi had started really looking forward to their monthly elaborate game of seduction, waiting at the reception on the flimsiest of excuses each time Dieter was due to arrive at the Arcadia, prolonging that first moment when their eyes would meet across the lobby. He was even growing accustomed to the shared rituals, the late night drinks at the Refuge, and the long nights of lovemaking.

It isn't until the long shadows have nearly filled the lawn beyond the window that Abhi can begin to check his tears, can begin to collect his thoughts. It isn't until he has stared blindly at the growing light that he suddenly realises that his mind can't seem to recall Dieter's face. There are slivers of beloved memory, of voice that makes his insides clench with ferocious desire. There are even flashes of Dieter's loose-limbed gait, the triangle of curls on top of his chest barely revealed under a pale shirt, the sharp angle of his collarbone. Some memories are intimate, strangely distorted by imagination, of their lovemaking as if Abhi had stood outside himself watching instead of participating; Dieter's soft moan of pleasure that he has come to recognise well, can summon up at will, their lingering closeness the morning after.

Yet as he stares out at the lawns, Abhi can't remember Dieter's face. He races through what he knows: pale eyes, long dark lashes, full lips, high cheekbones, strong jaw. But the list seems finite, lifeless, a list of physical attributes that could be anyone, could even not be Dieter. For only an instant, he tries to remember if he has a photograph before discarding the thought. Abhi doesn't take photographs, has always believed that his mind stores memories better, that freezing an instant of his life robs it of the lived experience. That is why there is barely a record of his life in the city, of any of his life lived since he left home. He has always preferred it so.

Now he feels a sudden need to find a piece of Dieter, to acquire a sliver of evidence that he can clutch when his memory betrays him. He tells himself he just needs confirmation, that it is rational to want something more than silence. Yet, even as he dials Sam's number, he knows that it isn't the truth, that it isn't a photograph that he seeks, but a confirmation of his own feelings, his own desire. That he really wants to tell Sam that he has lost something, someone, that the grief he feels will be buried deep within the Arcadia's bowels, in his heart, even when the siege beyond finds a resolution. That he needs Sam to chronicle just one more death before the madness ends, this one not for herself but for him.

THE ARCADIA
ABOUT 20 HOURS AGO

When she returned with her loot to the room, Sam instinctively sought out the sofa where Billy was sleeping. But the sofa was empty, the duvet tumbled on to the floor. She panicked, wondering if he had wandered off into the corridor.

Controlling a sudden, unfamiliar, irrational urge to race out to look for him, somewhere, anywhere, she does not know where, she forced herself to look around the room. The bathroom door was open and she found him curled up on the little square beige of the bath rug, his injured shoulder cuddled by his good arm, shivering slightly despite the air-conditioning being turned off.

'Did you need the bathroom,' she asked him gently, forcing her voice to remain quiet, before carrying him back to the sofa, slightly annoyed with herself for not having asked him the question earlier.

He had wanted water instead. She had not thought of that either.

'Well, you do know you shouldn't drink from the tap, right?' She poured him some of the bottled water, held the glass up to his mouth, and watched as he settled back into the pillows. 'The bottle is right here, if you want it,' she instructed, placing it on the side-table nearest his head. 'And there is food here as well, OK?' Billy nodded vaguely, reaching out for a wilted sandwich from the pile, munching it with little enthusiasm, yawning even before he swallowed another dose of Baileys and valium.

The foraged sandwiches were a bit squashed from being tucked in her field jacket. The lettuce looked wilted, the bread a bit dry, but they were still edible. Sam took a listless bite out of one of them, forcing herself to chew and swallow the little

179

triangle, felt her stomach growl. She has eaten worse than stale sandwiches, she tells herself. It isn't until she has finished that one sole sandwich, leaving the rest carefully wrapped in the napkin, and swilled one measure of whisky in her mouth that she turns back to consider Billy.

He was fast asleep, lying peacefully on the sofa, as if nothing were amiss. Sam swore softly. Yet another glitch she had not anticipated when she had taken on the task of rescuing a child. How could she leave him alone, prone to wandering in his somnambulant state while she went out to document the impending battle outside?

She knows she wants at least one last foray before the end-game begins, while the gunmen are focused on possibilities of an assault mounted in the small hours of the morning and least likely to turn their attention to the higher floors. She sets the alarm for six hours, if only to check on the child. She could feel her mind finally dip into its habitual siege state, she has trained herself to combat the long hours of boredom by forcing herself into oblivion. But the thought of falling asleep with Billy in the room gnawed at her. Not that she is afraid of him, more that she is afraid for him, terrified that he will wake and let himself out of the room, that he will be lost.

It wasn't until she was rolling out her sleeping bag near the sofa, hoping to cut Billy off early if he woke that the solution finally hit her. Moving swiftly, she cut the cord from one of the curtains, climbing on a chair to reach as high as possible, hacking off the long silk loop from its crystal handle with her pocket knife.

Making sure that Billy was asleep, Sam looped the cord around his ankle, fashioning a deft reef knot, loose enough to be comfortable around his socked feet, tight enough to not slip off accidentally, making it nearly impossible for the child to untie himself. Then she tied the other end around the thick lion's claw foot of the sofa. She tucked the duvet around him, checking his brow briefly for signs of fever. So far so good, his skin was no longer clammy.

She calculated the hours till she had to feed him the closest thing she has to medication, and decided he could wait for a few hours. He stirred as she moved him, gave a strangled, barely audible cry, thrashing out suddenly, but then settled back to sleep. Under her wary eyes, his breathing slowly turned deep and steady, his thrashing quietened as he sank back into the drug-fuelled oblivion.

Relieved, she dragged her sleeping bag to the bed, huddled beneath its familiar weight, willing herself to rest, to even sleep a few hours. Before she closed her eyes, she glanced back at Billy. She could deal with him wetting the sofa, she decided, but definitely would not take the risk of him wandering off into the corridors by accident.

***

The room is dark when she wakes, lit only by the diffused glow from the screen of her mobile. Her mind feels startlingly clear. She knows that once night falls it will be time to head out once more, this time not to find food for Billy, and even herself, but to go back to work, to do the only thing she knows how to do well. She decides that she will carry the Mamiya and the Canon with her, knowing that their solidity will comfort her.

In silence, she prepares, washing her face and bare scalp in the sink, pulling on the long sleeved shirt, laying out the jacket on the bed so she can pack its pockets, lacing up her boots. As she lays out her equipment on the table, selecting, planning, measuring, she realises, almost unconsciously, that Billy's breathing has changed, has lightened imperceptibly. He is awake, and watching her prepare, his eyes wide and wary.

'Are you going outside?' his voice is tremulous.

She nods at him, continuing with her preparations, hoping that he will find her gesture friendly, comforting.

'To get more kids? Like me?' Sam lets out a surprised bark, not quite a laugh, just an incredulous, reflex reaction.

181

'Nah…you're trouble enough.' Billy's face deflates, his lower lip thrust out, but Sam has turned away already, too focused on her preparations. The home front! Damn, she should check on that injured shoulder, ask if he needs to pee, or eat, or need a drink, ensure that he isn't going to wander off, or attract attention.

'Can I watch television, please?' Billy has screwed up courage again, perhaps aided by the lack of attention she pays him.

'No, you can't!' A sudden image rises before her eyes, Billy finding a cartoon channel, turning up the sound, loud enough to signal the gunmen outside. 'You want the gunmen to come get you?' Her voice is harsh even to her own ears, and she winces when his eyes well up with tears. 'Oh for fuck's sake!' Sam turns away to pull on her field jacket, patting her pockets in an age-old ritual, confirming, checking, her hand acting as an extension of her mind, even as her thoughts wander off.

'Look, any sound you make will bring the bad guys here. Even the television, OK?' She hates talking to children, doesn't know how to get through to the small being with large tears rolling down his cheeks. She watches him silently, then decides to prepare a fresh batch of Valium and Baileys concoction, telling herself that it would be safer for the child to be incapacitated, asleep, in her absence, that it is safer for both of them that he cannot move or be tempted to cry out loud. Besides, she tells herself, who knows when the pain will kick in again from his injury.

'Can't we turn the a/c up? I am so warm,' Billy pleads.

'No, you just need more medicine,' she growls, kicking herself for forgetting that the power has been switched off. She could have been less harsh, told him that the television wasn't working. Maybe his eyes wouldn't be so large with hurt. 'Bollocks,' she curses softly. Why did she care if he was upset? Why did she care that he was staring at her with those huge accusing eyes?

'You don't smile,' Billy's faint voice is plaintive, as she checks the makeshift dressing on his shoulder. His eyes have stopped wandering to the table where the familiar concoction of Baileys and a ground-up Valium rested and instead scan her face.

'I don't have to smile.'

'Will you smile if I drink that?'

'Maybe,' she sighs.

'I bet you don't remember how to smile. You don't even remember when you smiled last.' His voice grows slightly louder, as she moves him gently back on to the pillows. The bastard! That stung! Sam scowls at him.

'Oh yes I do. And if you drink the medicine, maybe I will tell you.' She grimaces. What the hell is she setting herself up for now? A bloody good night story. No that wasn't it. A sleep time story. Oh what the fuck! Who cares what it is called. But then she notices that Billy's eyes have lit up even through the glaze of pain.

'Really? Like a proper bedtime story? You promise,' his good hand reaches forward to receive the glass.

'Yes, I promise,' Sam watches him hurriedly swallow the concoction, to the last drop, his face scrunching comically in disgust with every gulp.

She settles herself on the floor next to the sofa, one ear to the noises in the corridor. Five minutes? Ten max, till the stuff knocked him out again. Somehow she had to spin out something to tell him.

'So a long long time ago, I was in Jenin, on New Year's,' she began.

'For a party?'

'Not for a party. For work.'

'Not even for New Year's?' he insisted.

'Nobody goes to Jenin for a party. Look, you want me to tell you this?' Under her glare Billy wilted, settling deeper against the pillows.

'There was going to be a big parade, of all the fighters and all their supporters. With guns and missiles,' Sam could see herself, walking through the narrow, maze-like streets, unsettled by the strange impermanence that marked the houses. 'Refugee homes.

183

They all think they will return one day so nobody wants to build anything that means they have settled. That means giving up on going home,' the UN refugee coordinator had explained, pointing to the make-shift foundations of the dun coloured buildings. She was staying in one, a dank, freezing single brick house where the rain seemed to seep through the walls and melt into her chilled bones. The streets were humming, though, as people moved back and forth, with a purpose that she could not identify. Children had fashioned themselves costumes too, relying mostly on old *keffiyehs* and toy guns, and ran about laughing and shrieking in flimsy sandals, seemingly oblivious to the chilblains that looked agonising to Sam's eyes.

She had nearly reached the main street when she had stumbled upon the group. Five guys, possibly just out of their teens, but well dressed, in dark fatigues and proper boots. With semi-automatic rifles over their shoulders, cartridge belts slung casually around their almost frail waists. She had paused, using the Canon to fire off a flurry of shots, instinctively closing in on their faces to emphasise the play of light and shade that gathered around them, the faint shadow of an incipient beard, the sharp blade of a cheekbone. They had not even noticed her, helping each other get the angle of their *keffiyehs* to the right balance of insouciance and military precision, adjusting each other's black balaclavas so they lined up in a precise line across the bridge of their noses. It wasn't until she looked away from the viewfinder that she realised that they reminded her of nothing more than the children she had seen playing in the lanes before, donning their costumes for a performance like children before a school play. She had laughed then, only realising when they looked at her, that she had chuckled out loud. One of them, his face still uncovered, had smiled back at her. The rest had just given a quick friendly wave.

Perhaps that is why she had been smiling as she jostled and wove her way to the front of the crowd, positioning herself to capture all that she could of the spectacle and drama the fighters used to mark their founding. The spectacle mimicked parades of greater military forces, but the desperate fervour of the spectators believing in the fighters who passed before them differed from the smug celebratory spirit of those who turn out to watch bigger armies show off their might.

The noise had been deafening, and after a while, Sam's world shrank to her short focus Canon as she shot the masked fighters parading past, their chants lost in an indecipherable roar of the crowd around her. Which is why she had been surprised when one of them broke rank, watched him draw closer in the viewfinder, adjusting the lens to keep the masked face in focus.

She had sensed the movement of the crowd as bodies had parted around her, the wall of warmth withdrawing just enough to let through a sudden blast of the freezing January damp. The crowd had fallen silent around her and a familiar ache built up between her shoulder blades.

He had drawn closer as her fingers circled the lens, gently manipulating the striations, her nerve endings acting like automatons, keeping the approaching masked figure in focus. He wore a balaclava under the chequered cloth of the *keffiyeh*, his eyes covered with metal rimmed dark reflector shades glinting in the sun. He drew closer, still larger in the viewfinder, until Sam couldn't see past the dark figure clouding her view.

Then something warm encircled her wrist. A hand uncurled her fingers wrapped around the cylinder, pushing it down from before her face. Until the small square of black slid past her eye, only to be replaced by a larger expanses of dark, but with greater texture. Wool, of the scratchy kind, she had noted. Fragmented by the light chequered cotton of the *keffiyeh*. Then as her eyes adjusted, she noticed the glint of metal on the barrel of the AK-56, the matt sheen of the leather strap. A hint of musk tickled her nose, mingled with cheap aftershave. She had looked up just as he removed his shades.

She had watched him, wary as a wild thing, her wrist still wrapped in his warm fingers, waiting till the last moment till she had to choose. Fight or flight. Really, neither were viable

185

options. Her fingers had tightened around her camera, moving it protectively closer to her body.

For a long moment he stared at her. Then bending lower, he slid a single finger under the balaclava to partially slip it off his face. He had smiled then, the exuberance lighting up his honey coloured eyes, before replacing the dark glasses. One of the boys from the alley, she had remembered, recognition flooding back. And before replacing the fabric over his mouth, he had blown her a cheeky kiss.

Sam is smiling as she turns to Billy, an uninhibited grin curving her lips, her cheeks taut with the long forgotten action. But he has fallen back into his feverish, drugged sleep, perhaps long before she had even begun her story.

'So there, you see, I do know when I last smiled,' she trails off. It isn't until she has finished tucking the duvet around him, checking that his injured shoulder is positioned comfortably, has pulled her knit cap low on her head, ready to head out, that she realises that she can still feel the old grin tugging at the corners of her lips.

SOMEWHERE IN THE FOOTHILLS
13 YEARS AGO

Abhi never gets into trouble. Pranks at school, fights in the playground, adolescent acts of rebellion are all Samar's domain. His brother goes through life like a tornado, wildly excited, always attracting attention and trouble in equal measures. Abhi prefers to live on the margins, quiet, self-sufficient, unassuming. He takes on the tasks given to him with the same quietude as always, cricket captain, house captain, mentor. Perhaps that is why the teachers love him so, the principal's firm looping hand always marking the same words on his report card, 'Responsible to a fault but a joy to have in school.'

Sometimes he thinks Baba would prefer him to get into more trouble, be more like Samar. He can feel Baba's puzzled eyes rest on him at times: Abhi always hides deeper, looking away from his father, retreating into studies, or going out for a long run through the valleys that leaves his muscles screaming in pain, his fears hidden away if only for a moment.

Those fears have grown in the past years, with every new class, worsening as he has shot up inches, as his voice has cracked into a pleasant bass, as his body has morphed into a stranger's. He has stopped swimming, even with Samar, in the lake down the hill, afraid that the near nakedness of others will betray what he knows has been growing deep within him, will reveal all that he tries so hard to hide. Abhi fears that what is unfurling within him will mean harsher retribution than any prank he could play.

Perhaps that is why he walks away at first from the fuss in the bathroom, tells himself that it isn't really his battle. It is just a group of schoolboys, some from his own team, even some he gets along with. It is just schoolboy pranks he tells himself, washing his hands in the sink, purposefully ignoring the squeals, and muttered threats, and sobs from the far stall where the boys have gathered. He tells himself it could be him, ganged up on, bullied for something he can't control, that it is best if he remains unseen, unidentified.

He is sweating when he leaves the bathroom, his shirt stuck to his back, can even smell his own fear rising off his skin, like a beacon marking him out. As the next victim, the next one to mock, terrify, brutalise. Behind him, as the door begins to swing shut, he hears the word he has come to loathe, the word that he has heard in the markets and on the playground, the single syllabic slur that he has looked up in the dictionary, dreading yet expecting its meaning. He knows it isn't directed at him, is meant for whoever the boys have found to torment today, that he should be relieved that once again he has avoided the awful slur.

He slumps against the wall, resting his forehead on the cool plaster. He can feel a sudden flicker of anger light up against the unfairness of the tag, of the mockery and brutality it evokes from the other boys. He didn't choose the tag, just like the boy they are bullying back in the bathroom. 'A soldier fights for those who can't fight,' Baba's voice is clear in his head. But would Baba really want him to fight for the fag in the bathroom? Would Baba want Abhi to fight even though he is no different from that trapped, weeping, terrified boy? For a long moment, fears grow large enough to paralyse him, filling his ears with a loud, distant roar. Then Samar's excited voice breaks into his mind, 'Come on, little brother, you could take them on.'

The words push at the weakness that threatens to overcome him. Blinking rapidly, forcing himself to breathe deeply, Abhi knows Samar is away already, off into the mountains with his unit, that the cheerful voice that fills his mind is perhaps fantasy. He knows that Samar's eyes too linger in puzzlement over him at times.

The voices from the bathroom have grown louder, sobs and squeals from the boy Abhi has not seen, not even identified. He can hear the dull thuds of fists or identical school shoes

188

connecting with bruised, vulnerable flesh. And over and over, through the threatening, mocking laughter, that same word he has grown to hate with such passion.

Later, when he tries to explain, Abhi will remember nothing of his actions, will recall only that single moment when Samar's voice was replaced by a sudden haze of red in his eyes. He remembers turning back to the bathroom, will remember the faces of the boys he knows, some even he has thought of as his friends, and between them, crouching on the tiled floor, a huddled figure, made smaller by torment.

Only snapshots remain of the incident on some mental camera, the surprise on the faces of the boys, the anger he had felt pumping through his body, his disembodied voice telling them to stop, and then his own swinging fists, connecting with unidentifiable, collective flesh. He does not remember how long they had fought, knocking into doors and white porcelain fittings, does not remember when or even how he collected a gash on his forehead, the blood intensifying the red haze.

He doesn't remember when someone had raised the alarm, when the bullies had begun fleeing his rage, when the last of them were separated by his teachers. It isn't until he sits in the school infirmary, the old matron carefully treating the gash that the red in his eyes begins to fade. He knows the infirmary, mostly because of Samar's antics, knows the matron has always treated his brother's mishaps, can hear the doctor who has sewn him up already briefing Baba.

'And the kid? Is he OK?' he mutters, squinting through the pain, the stinging antiseptic finally clearing his mind, the sharp tang filling his nostrils.

'He'll be fine,' the matron is blustering about, obviously upset. Or perhaps angry. After all, Abhi never gets into trouble, and the matron's manner embarrasses him. Perhaps that is why Abhi refuses to look up when the principal comes to check on him, to tell him that Baba is on his way to collect him. And because he never looks up, he also never sees the flash of compassion, maybe even understanding, preferring to retreat

189

far into himself, locking out the world. 'That was a brave thing to do,' the principal tells him, his voice deep, authoritative as always. But Abhi knows nothing of bravery, can only shrug in response, his head slumped nearly into his chest.

Baba is waiting by the car, inscrutable, when Abhi walks out to meet him, his eyes silently taking in the bloodied shirt, the bandage swaddled around his head. He has brought a clean shirt, one of Samar's. 'Change into this,' he instructs, 'your mother will be upset if she sees all the blood.'

Abhi's fingers tremble as he tries to strip, reaction finally setting in, coursing through his body in increasingly strong shudders. Baba watches as he fumbles with the shirt, stripping it off his lean shoulders, yanks off the bloodied T-shirt underneath. Abhi can feel his stomach heave, the muscles spasming, the adrenalin pumping undirected in his veins. 'Take a deep breath, hold for a count of three.' Baba's voice is deep. 'Release for a count of five.' Abhi can only nod, focusing only Baba's voice as it counts, slowly, surely, 'One-one-thousand, two-one-thousand, three-one-thousand, hold.' With each count, Abhi can feel the spasms recede. Baba continues counting until Abhi can breathe normally again, until his body grows still, until he can pull on the clean shirt with steadied fingers, until he can climb into the car, and stretch against the dark seat, exhausted but clearheaded.

'Dr Alan says that will be a cracker of a scar.' Baba's voice is light, much like Samar's when he is trying to force himself to be cheerful.

'Yes sir,' Abhi can't think of an adequate answer.

'Women like scars on men. Makes you look tough. Not so much of a pretty boy any more.' Abhi's fears come back in a rush at Baba's joke and he can't think of a way to break the silence, can only mumble something that he hopes Baba will assume is assent. They drive in silence, the gap between them as wide as ever.

In his mind, Abhi can hear Samar's excited approval. He knows he will wait until the evening to call his brother, wait until he has put up his shield again, has found a credible story

190

to cover up all that he fears Samar can sense. He will tell Samar only of the fight, of how he put his full weight behind each punch just as they have practised, that he kept moving and didn't let himself be cornered, that he didn't stay down for more than a second at the most. 'Good job, little brother. Once you hit the floor, they kill you. Stay on your feet and you have a fighting chance,' Abhi can hear his brother's voice, authoritative, protective, even proud.

But it is Baba's voice that finally breaks the heavy silence, just as they pull up home. 'What was the fight about?'

'They ganged up on a kid, sir.' He hopes that will be enough for his father, much like when Samar has come home from fights, just a simple explanation that fits Baba's ideal of behaviour for his sons.

'A friend of yours?' Baba is insistent. Abhi looks up for an instant, noting a new strange closed off expression that gives no clue of his thoughts.

'No sir. I didn't get a look at the kid.'

Baba is silent for a long time, his fingers drumming the top of the car, in an uncertain, unpredictable rhythm. 'Seems we've got another one ready to play the hero,' he finally tells Abhi, a sudden grin lighting up his sombre face.

But Abhi can't meet his eyes, guilt and fear rising again of the lies he has built around him, of all the ways he hides from those he loves. For an instant, his mind flashes back to the bathroom, to a small fragile, terrified face, with eyes red and weeping, hair mussed up by rough hands, collar askew. There had been defiance in those weeping eyes, Abhi thinks, despite the cruelty, despite the horror. And perhaps more honesty than Abhi can manage.

'Good show, son,' Baba pats his back gently as they walk up the steps to the front door.

'Thank you, sir,' Abhi whispers.

THE ARCADIA
14 HOURS AGO

The flashing screen of her phone alerts her. Not a text. Abhi was calling. She hadn't saved his number but the final 3235 digits have grown familiar in the past two days.

'How are you two holding up?' Abhi sounds weary.

'We're OK. What's going on? The channels are just all over the place. Bloody useless!' She flashes another annoyed look at the dead TV screen, then flicks through the multiple windows on her laptop, automatically checking the news channels for repeated useless information and looped images of the Arcadia. Images and information that hold nothing of value for her.

'Yeah, they have been trying to get them to shut down live broadcast but then there is always some that idiot who wants the big story, no matter what.'

'I hope that is not meant for me?' she teases.

'What? No, no, of course not. Anyway who knows if that would help...' his voice trails off, distracted.

'What's going on, Abhi?' she demands, surprised at his sudden wavering. He doesn't answer for a long time, till she almost thinks he has hung up. Only the sound of his breathing, oddly uneven, floats over the line. When he finally speaks, his voice is low, tightly controlled, clinical.

'One question, Sam. Blonde, male, about six two, late twenties. Wearing chinos and a light coloured jumper, sort of purple. Did you see anyone fitting the description up in the Refuge?'

In her head, she scans the images she has collected, her memory flicking through the innumerable shots like thumbnails. 'Good-looking, short hair?' she asks.

Abhi's voice is barely audible. 'Yeah.'

192

Her mind scans back, locking into a series of images from her foray to the Refuge. She had switched from the Canon to the Mamiya, filing away the sharp angled face lying in complete repose for her collection, perhaps to be worked on for an exhibition. Definitely the kind of image that news media wouldn't want, she knows. Too perfect, too blonde, too familiar for the kinds of people who pay for her photos, too similar to their own lovers and sons and fathers to pretend that the world's chaos could be kept at bay. But she had shot off a dozen frames, knowing that she wanted that serene, beautiful face in her files.

'Yeah, I did. On the first trip…' she begins to tell him, half-distracted by the image she has called up in her mind's eye, but a strangled sound on the line makes her pause. 'Abhi?' she ventures, suddenly afraid for him, or for whatever intimacy she has created with him. But he has already hung up.

Sam flicks through her images from the Refuge, from that first foray hours ago. She already knows but needs to calm her churning stomach. There are over a dozen frames of a young man who matches Abhi's description, same chinos, the pale jumper, expensive shoes. Her mind wanders as she flicks through the images repeatedly, dragging them to a separate folder on her laptop, running them on a looping slide show. Her eyes note small details on the photographs, the sharp gilt covered edge of the bar peeking in a corner, the deeper colour of burgundy carpet near the splash of blood on the pale jumper, the shape of an unusual shadow across the man's cheek. She has heard Abhi's grief in his harshly drawn breaths, in his strangled hoarse voice, in the careful way he had picked his words. She counts back to the start of the siege. How long has he suspected? Or perhaps he had seen the man already? She scans the photographs again, frowning as she tries to remember if she had noticed the cameras in the Refuge, wonders if Abhi has been able to see his lover for the past hours.

She can't begin to imagine his grief. Her mind flits back to thoughts of David. Would she feel as bereft for him, she muses for a moment, but dismisses the thought. Perhaps for her parents, though she is increasingly aware, perhaps even reconciled to their mortality, noting their growing fragility on her occasional trips home. Her eyes rest on Billy, still fast asleep on the sofa, huddled under the duvet. For an instant, her eyes soften. She is afraid for him, has worried for his safety, has wanted to ease the pain in his shoulder, hopes that she will not need to see his devastation when he learns of his parents' death. But would she feel that grief that she has heard in Abhi's voice? A part of her feels anger, hurt even, that he has hidden his despair so well in the past hours. His silence over his deepest grief feels a little disloyal to her, as if their conversations of the past hours, the intimacies were not real. Then she scolds herself, telling herself that he has probably been in shock, in denial. Sam knows, with clinical, dispassionate precision, all stages of grieving, even when she can't quite bring herself to feel them.

Most of all, she feels envy, that he can mourn anyone so completely. The emotion confuses her with its novelty. She tends to shut down in face of such overwhelming sorrow, removing herself from the wails and tears mentally, focusing only the square of her viewfinder. Somehow the grief of loved ones always seems slightly obscene to her, something that arouses a queasy pitying in her. Abhi's agony, held so tightly in check, expressed only in the clipped words and tight, harsh voice, seem a world apart from the mourning she has seen and photographed so many times before. Perhaps because she can't see him, doesn't even know what he looks like, his sorrow seems pure, untainted by expressions. Still a part of her is aware of a sense of relief that something is so frozen, or broken inside her, that she will never need to feel his kind of desolation. The strange emotions give her courage and strength to remember their conversations of the past hours as she finds herself looking for the sudden tightening of the vocal cords that would indicate his grief. He has known since the beginning, she decides, or at least since nearly the beginning.

The realisation brings a grudging respect for him, and a recognition that he is not so different from her, bottling up his personal sorrow by turning his attentions outwards.

Perhaps that is why she calls him back, repeatedly on his mobile, until after the sixth ring, nearly an hour later, he finally answers. 'Is it the man you told me about?' she needs to hear him say it.

'Yes, Sam,' Abhi's voice is low, exhausted, strangely distant.

She knows she should say something, anything. In her mind, she can think of all the words she has learned to say in moments like this. After all, she is accustomed to survivors, to the grief-stricken, has long made her way through their ranks, untouched and unruffled, and yet reliant on their wish to give her a clear shot of their beloved dead. But for Abhi, none of the words seem adequate, none of the sentences she has learned by rote seem appropriate. After a long silence, she can only mumble an indistinct OK before hanging up.

It is night when Abhi calls her back, his iron self-control back in place. 'I think they are ready to move. In the next few hours maybe.'

The thought comes suddenly, lighting her up with fierce conviction, lifting the weight she has felt grow on her since learning of Abhi's grief. 'I will make one more trip. To the Refuge,' she tells him, her voice steady.

'No, it will be too dangerous, Sam. They won't go without a fight, and...well, our guys won't know you if you are out and about.'

'So now you are worried about me,' she checks, only half-teasing.

He sighs. 'Of course, Sam. I don't want to lose...' his voice trails off.

'Listen, I want one photograph. I promise, just one photograph. And it isn't even for me.' She struggles to find words that can make sense of her sudden need. She wants to do something for Abhi, give him something, something that will matter, will make a difference. But she can find no words for her

195

irrationality, doesn't even begin to understand her own need to comfort him.

'Sam, you know there are explosives up there. And on the roof above. I am sure they will set them off once the assault begins.'

'So all the more reason for me to go up now.' She doesn't understand the pleading note in her own voice, or why she takes his silence as disapproval, perhaps even rejection. Or why it bothers her so much.

When he finally speaks, she realises she has been holding her breath. 'Be careful, extra careful.'

Her eyes go suddenly misty. 'Super. I will call you before heading out.'

It isn't until she can hear the gunfire being exchanged on the grounds below, the sharp cracks of the bullets echoing up from the belly of the Arcadia, punctuated by heavier, sharp bangs of the grenades that she begins to prepare her final foray. The room is almost entirely dark, lit only by the glowing square of her laptop, and the tiny flickering beam of her small flashlight.

As she checks on Billy, confirming that the dressing is held in place, she worries that he will be afraid of the dark, or that he may cry out in her absence. But then reason kicks in, reminding her that the time for worrying about sounds has passed, that the gunmen will be focused on the threats from the grounds. She knows even she and Billy may have more to worry about if the assault doesn't go quickly enough, if Abhi is right about the explosives on the roof being incendiary. She wonders if she can leave some source of light for the child, but then decides that she would rather keep both her phone and her small wind-up flashlight, that it is better to leave him sedated, unaware of the dangers, of the sounds of the gunfire getting louder with each passing instant.

She tucks him in carefully, refreshing the water next to him, confirming that the cord is secure around his ankle. For a moment, she hesitates. Perhaps she should leave him untied, in case things go wrong, in case she can't return in time to him. But he can't evacuate himself in case of danger, she reminds herself. 'One more reason I better get this right,' she tells herself.

The gear she plans to carry is minimal, just the Mamiya and an extra memory card. She unpacks and packs her flash several times, changing her mind, again and again, until she finally decides in favour of using the glow from the city. Who knows, she tells herself grimly, if the damn things on the roof are truly incendiary, she may even get some added ambient lighting.

By the time she is ready, her T-shirt is soaked in sweat, stuck to her back, the lack of air-conditioning amplified by the lack of ventilation now that the power has been shut off. The thought of pulling on her knit cap in the heat is revolting, but she knows that its cushioning comforts her, gives her at least an illusion of protection. Tucking it into her pocket, she tries to cool off with water instead, splashing it on her face and neck, massaging her bare scalp with her fingers, over and over, until some of the heat seems to recede into the dark.

Just before heading out, her cap in place, pulled low over her eyes, her flashlight still held in her hand, a sole beacon in the darkened room, she calls him. 'Where are they, Abhi?'

'Spread out. Most are down in the arcade, with three groups of two along the lobby. They work in pairs, one going ahead, the second covering. Another two are below, moving around the galleries on the sixth, firing at random, mostly at the grounds outside. The last two are making their way down through the floors. On the thirteenth right now. Seems like the final recce.'

She summons up the floor plan in her mind, marking out the positions on her memory map.

'Sam, I think the explosives up in the Refuge will go off when the assault begins.' Abhi's voice is hesitant, even as he repeats the warning.

'Yeah, I would guess so, probably remote detonation. It will block any ingress from above.' She is concentrated on her mental map, her response mechanical.

'Sam…' he begins, but she interrupts him.

'How long before the final assault, Abhi?'

'What makes you think they'll tell me anything?'

'Oh cut the crap! You know how they think. And you are talking to them. So I just need a heads up on how much time I have. Come on, Abhi.'

He pauses for a long moment. 'Probably in a few hours, maybe early morning. Think it gives you about four hours clear. Maybe less. That's my best guess though. They haven't said anything, you know.'

'Yeah, I know.' She pauses. 'You will still have a visual, right? On me?' She wishes she could explain why it matters so much that he can see her, that despite all the irrationality she is comforted by the thought of him watching over her.

'Yes, cameras are on a separate grid.'

'Good!'

'Sam,' he hesitates again, torn. 'You know what I said earlier? About the Refuge?'

'Yeah?' she knows what he's going to say. That he's had time to think. That he doesn't want to know. That he won't let her put herself at risk for him. Or worse, for a sentimental whim. She is prepared for the argument.

'You don't have to…' he begins, then sighs. 'But if you do, if you want to, if…oh what the hell! Sam, if you go up there, I will be really grateful.' His voice breaks then, trailing into hoarse, strangled, breaths. 'Talk in a bit,' he mutters before the phone clicks dead.

A part of her wishes he had tried to talk her out of one final trip out, if only mechanically, if only so they could argue, so she could distract him for a few precious instants. The sudden well of compassion within herself surprises her. She can't imagine being that bereft for any reason. For anyone. Then she is even more shocked to recognise that it isn't entirely compassion she feels, but a strange gnawing sorrow, a stabbing envy, that she has no memory or recognition of such fierce loss.

It isn't until she is in the fire escape, the sudden drop in temperature reminding her of how hot and stuffy the rooms and corridors have grown in the past hours, until she can feel the cool air against her drenched T-shirt, that she realises that the moisture on her cheeks isn't sweat.

THE ARCADIA
4 HOURS AGO

The heavy thuds – three in a row, closely following each other – sound somewhere above her. The blasts sound duller, thicker. Not grenades this time. Perhaps on the roof. 'Fuck! Double fuck!' Sam tries to frame the shot, to ignore the painful knot throbbing in her shoulder. She knows this is madness, this strange act of sentimentalism for a man she has never met but the thought of Abhi brings a smile to her lips.

'Focus, damn you,' she scolds herself, muttering under her breath. Somewhere not far above her, the explosions have been replaced by a strange new sound, an unfathomable roaring, like a sandstorm. Punctuating the roar are sharp tinkles, loud creaks, the sounds of chandeliers crashing, furniture and doorways cracking like giant matchsticks. Her phone has been vibrating insistently, constantly against her thigh.

Abhi again! Three missed calls and five messages. All within the past few minutes. The first is most calm. 'Roof is on fire. It won't be long till it reaches you. Please get out of there.' The last is just two words: 'Leave now!'

For a second she hesitates, the Mamiya cradled against her belly, the phone in her hand, letting the roar fill her ears. She thinks she can smell the smoke, but then counts back to the last time she heard the explosions. Not nearly enough time. The blonde hair of the young man lying at her feet catches her eye, the pale lilac of his silk jumper stained with red, as if someone has tipped wine over him. In death, he looks as good as perhaps he had in life, his jaw relaxed, the eyes closed.

'Tell me if it gets in the way of the fire escape,' she taps into the phone. 'I'll finish up here.'

200

She has never shot anyone like the man. Dieter, she reminds herself. Deet, as Abhi called him. There is a familiar stillness to him, whatever that lived within has stepped out of the beautiful shell of his body. But unlike the others she has photographed, the stillness shuts her out, as if he has cast an invisible veil over himself, rejecting her gaze, refusing to share any of himself with her. She has mastered capturing the serenity that death brings, but for Dieter she is seeking something different. She wants to find not the stillness, but the luminescence Abhi's voice bestows on him, wants to catch the way Abhi sees him, loved, loving, alive.

For a moment she doubts herself that perhaps, because she has only shot for aesthetics for so long, this photograph is harder to pin down. The dead have always spoken to her, telling her the best angle to capture something of their life, pointing her to the best light to clothe them. The shots have always come automatically, often just aim and shoot, and yet perfectly formed as if by a greater power. But Dieter is silent, sullen even, refusing to give her a clue.

She moves around him, hoping to find a better angle. The lights from the city beyond bounce off Dieter's hair, catch the faint stains of an incipient stubble on his jaw, curl lightly around his dark long lashes. Still Dieter does not speak.

Lifting the viewfinder, Sam stalks around him, repeating the pattern like a beast of prey, hoping that somewhere he will give her an opening, just one chance at taking a shot. The viewfinder limits him to parts, separated into squares and yet somehow indefinably part of the whole. She has set the lens for a close-up and the camera mutilates the man into clean limbs, the lilac jumper, the light coloured trousers, the fashionable suede shoes, the blood-spattered torso. And the face, closed and silent. None of the parts want to speak, blocking her out.

The roar has grown closer, louder, when Sam looks up. She knows this time she is not imagining the hint of smoke in her nostrils. She wonders if the man knows? That the shot is not for him. Sam has always shot the dead for themselves, capturing what she knows is some unique, quintessential part of themselves, for many the only trace they will leave of themselves. But this shot is not for Dieter. Instead, she is shooting for Abhi, to give him a souvenir, a tangible token that whatever he felt for that fleeting instant had been real. Had in fact been a whole lifetime. Perhaps Diet knows that even her camera is only looking for a story for someone else, is uninterested in his own tale.

'Oh come on, damn you!' she mutters. Removing the viewfinder from her eye, she scans the room. She needs more light, or at least the right sort of light, the kind she has used only once before, to transform the dead into the living. She can see it in her mind: a soft pallid glow, almost anaemic, creeping from a far window, crawling across the plush carpet, bathing the boy lying so still on the floor, his closed eyes still facing the horizon beyond. Pushing down the Mamiya, she rapidly starts to re-arrange the furniture, widening the path of the city lights from the floor-length windows to Dieter.

***

Abhi has been watching Sam on the CCTV in growing confusion. The gunmen have moved further down in the Arcadia, disappearing into the fire escapes, turning up on lower floors. He wishes he knew more about explosives and their use if only to be able to tell Sam if they have rigged the fire escapes, if she can make her way back down. But that worry recedes a bit, overtaken by horror at the fire that is raging through the top floor. The luxury 'cottage' has been engulfed in flames, its polished Balinese wood melting into orange, the heavy carved pillar cracking into dust. He feels a twinge of something sharp, another loss. He has used that suite often, to impress, to seduce, to charm. He had seduced Diet there too, not so many days before, clinking champagne flutes as they drank in the city gleaming below, kissing with the backdrop of the sea dotted with glow-worm boats far beyond. He had promised they would be back when his shift finished, after a final drink at the Refuge, to spend another night on that

202

monumental four-poster bed, had even requested housekeeping to ensure the bed was turned down.

On the screen, Sam has not left Diet, though he can't see any of the floor. She is circling, her camera held before her face, pausing to consider, then moving back a few paces. He is reminded of the nature documentaries, about beasts of prey. She moves the same way, cautious, measuring, considering each move. Abhi wishes she would head back down.

The panes of the lounge pavilion have blown out, shattering outwards, sending a rain of glass on to the grounds, onto the troops that are positioned in the shadows. High flames ring the pool, engulfing the diaphanous curtains of the cabanas, tasting the wooden deck, devouring the cane furniture, ringing the gleaming pool like a circle of hell.

He has been told that fire-fighting helicopters are on their way but still cannot stop himself from repeatedly checking if the highest floors are truly unoccupied. The cameras on the top floor are slowly going dead, the screens before him falling blank as they melt. The television channels are on a loop, abiding by the information blackout imposed by security and show nothing more than Arcadia bathed in light, some of its windowpanes blown out and gaping like blinded eyes.

With each dead screen, his vision shrinks a little more, limiting what he can see. Worse still, limiting what he can tell Sam…

Two floors below the roof, Sam is moving furniture around the bar. Suddenly energetic, she tosses away chairs nearest the windows, drags the tables away. Abhi cringes involuntarily as she begins to rip off the snowy tablecloths, sending the polished silver cutlery, the cut-glass, the fine porcelain, tumbling across the floor. He can see she is opening a path from the windows to something that lies below the edge of the frame. He knows it is Diet, and feels a swell of nausea. He has seen Sam's photographs of the dead. Of the corpses that look alive enough to stare out at him accusingly from the canvas, from high quality, glossy book pages. A part of him wishes he had never told Sam that he had no photographs of Diet.

203

He hopes the clatter she is making doesn't attract attention. The gunmen are far below, he can see, but still feels a nervous shudder as each piece of furniture is thrown aside. He wonders if she has noticed others who died up there, the other corpses that must lie on that same plush carpet. But like the beast of prey from the nature documentaries, Sam sees nothing else, her fury channelled only towards the prize she has spotted.

On the line of screens below the flames, Sam is spreading the white tablecloths along the back, lining the high bar, moving the tall lamps to hang the snowy linen squares along the far end of the restaurant, behind Diet. He suddenly realises she is creating an impromptu studio, creating reflectors to catch the meagre light she can use.

Flames have spread to the floor above the Refuge, Abhi can see. The smoke fills the screens and the first of the flames have spread through the corridor, creeping up the shadows like so many reptilian predators, low, fast, with flicking orange tongues. The sprinklers add to the blur on the screen, hissing steam and cool sprays losing the unequal battle against the flames. He wonders if he should text her, but something holds him back, although he can't decide if it is the need to see Diet one last time or to give Sam a few extra moments to work undisturbed.

The cameras nearest the lifts for the Refuge are filling up with smoke. Mesmerised, Abhi can only watch the screens in the restaurant where Sam has returned to her stalking, although this time she seems more precise. The camera has moved again before her eye, its dark case an extension of her face, blending with the dark cap and jacket, making her appear like a robot, or alien. Her movements are like a dancer, muscles tense yet graceful, each step controlled. Even through the blurry image, he can sense her concentration, can feel the sudden surge of power running through her slight frame.

He doesn't notice that the smoke has almost entirely filled the corridors beyond the Refuge doors, that the first flames have begun dishevelling the edges of the carpet before the lifts.

Then suddenly, Sam pauses, frozen mid-stride, the camera held tensely before her. Abhi can almost hear the click of the shutter, can feel the camera judder against her finger in that instant before she brings down the foot that has hovered momentarily in the air. As she straightens up, he flicks a glance at the rest of the screens.

The screens on either side of her are filled with smoke, almost entirely obscuring all vision. The row of screens above the Refuge has gone dead.

Shit! Sam, get out of there. Now! Abhi keeps repeating the words like a mantra even as he punches a message on the phone, his eyes rapidly scanning the screens for information. In the centre of bar, Sam stands still, her eyes bright, shaking her shoulders to release the tension, swivelling her neck to loosen the aching muscles.

Abhi sees her pull out her phone to see his message. She looks up, turning around till she spots a CCTV camera. To find him. Then slowly, her posture switching from relaxed to cocky, a wide grin curves her mouth. She draws up her right hand, index finger extended like a gun. She blows a kiss at the tip of her finger, and aims it at the camera, taking an imaginary shot at him.

THE ARCADIA
2 HOURS AGO

The smoke steadily moves to blind the cameras in the foyer beyond the bar. Abhi knows that the sprinklers will come on soon. Perhaps less than two minutes. In the Refuge, he can see Sam moving swiftly, soaking her scarf in a jug full of water. She wraps it tightly around her face, covering her nose and mouth with multiple layers. Then she pulls off her cap and dips it into the water, swirling it around to let the fibres soak completely. Replacing it low on her head, she unscrews the bulky lens and zips it into place in a pocket. The camera itself she cradles against her stomach, zipping the heavy jacket over it.

'Smoke in the corridors, Sam. The cameras will go out soon. The route to the fire escape looks fine for now.' Abhi taps on the screen. She pulls out the phone to glance at it but responds only by nodding. And then with a last moment of hesitation before the doors, she pushes them open and disappears into the smoky beyond.

***

Sam can smell the smoke creeping silently into the restaurant. Has she taken too long over the shot? She can't pause for doubts, she sternly reminds herself. The key is to get back down to the room. Mentally she charts up her route back, left out of the restaurant, forty-three paces to the fire escape door, thirteen on the marble floor before the lift, the rest in the carpeted corridor. The fire escape is the third on the right, she remembers. The scarf around her nose and mouth doesn't give a lot of protection, but it is something, and she knows the value of an edge, no matter how tiny.

The fire escape will be worse. Coming up in the dark had taken nearly twenty-five minutes of crawling up the steps but she always dreads going down steps, even in the light. She wonders if she can chance using her phone for light. Just briefly, if only to confirm her position.

The smoke building around her, the roar of the inferno above, the screams of furniture and beams succumbing to the flames, are distracting. As she moves to the doors, the knot in her shoulder has built painfully and now gives a sudden spasm, the agony leaving her breathless. Time to go, bitch, she tells herself, and then with one last deep breath, deliberately pushes her way out of the bar.

***

Abhi can only rely on his clock, hoping that the lost visibility will be restored as Sam emerges on her floor below. He wonders if her descent would be faster, remembering the past trips she has made. On the notepad, he has noted the times she disappeared into the fire escape. The last ascent had taken her nearly eight minutes longer than the previous ones. He knows the power outage means she is blind in the concrete stairwell, the pitch dark unbroken even by the glow of the city lights beyond.

The phone buzzes in his hands. 'They are talking about you on TV. You are a proper hero now! Good show, little brother.' Samar!

His eyes flick back to the laptop, one window locked in on a news channel, the images from earlier in the night still playing on a loop. After a few seconds the headline scrolls across, 'The heroic manager helping the hostages.' His photo is pinned to it. A photograph from Arcadia's PR kit. He has always despised that photograph. Great! The one time he ends up on TV, they use a crappy picture!

He looks away, back to the bank of CCTV screens, automatically checking the time counter on the corner. No Sam on any of them, although he hopes she has made it through the smoke and into the stairwell.

207

'Nobody feels like a hero,' he can remember Baba's voice. 'If you feel like you've done something great, chances are you are a liar.' But they had given Baba the medals, the bright coloured ribbons, the shiny roaring lion on crossed swords. He has wanted those for as long as he can remember, telling Baba earnestly that he only wants those as his inheritance. How long ago was that? He doesn't speak to Baba any more, having disappointed him more thoroughly in silence than with any words he could speak.

He would prefer to have Diet instead. Smiling, laughing, kissing him. Or even without Diet, just his normal life, as it was before the madness began. He can see the girl at the reception, the one slumped in her own blood. And after his loss of control, lying still, in his vomit. Surely heroes don't do that? Surely they don't desecrate the dead with such ignominy?

'Stay safe. And stay put!' Samar's text buzzes insistently in his hand. He looks down at the screen, then taps it away to file.

A twisted smiled spreads on his lips. Samar is back to worrying about him, the crisis pushing him back into his childhood role of the elder brother, Abhi's protector, even though there is little he can do now. Even Baba is worried, jolted out of his reserve, by the drama unleashed on international television by a shadowy group of murderers with no goal but killing. Strange that he had done nothing but accidentally ended up in danger, to be adored again, missed again. Even idolised perhaps, for the first time, by Samar. And Baba.

***

The smoke hits Sam instantly, stinging her eyes, pushing past the damp scarf to tingle her nostrils. She drops to her hands and knees, hoping to inhale as little of the soot as possible, feeling the cold marble hard against her palms. Turn left, she tells herself, her eyes squinted to faint slits, as she begins to crawl, the marble still cool under her hands, hard against her knees, scooting forward as quickly as she can, grateful when the marble gives way to plush carpet, softer on her limbs, against her palms.

The problem, she notices, almost instantly, is in pacing her route. She can't judge the distance as she crawls, only recognising the first doorway along the corridor when her finger snags painfully on a jutting doorframe.

In her mind, she must pass a table with flowers within eighteen paces of the first door, but the smoke has grown thick and she misses the table entirely. Bemused, she pauses, wondering if she has come too far, or not far enough. She is still trying to mentally convert her crawl to paces when the sprinklers come on, soaking her almost instantly. The smoke disperses for an instant before descending back, somehow made thicker, heavier. She stays still, hesitating, calculating, pulling up her mental map.

Then making up her mind, Sam shuffles backwards, keeping her scarf in place over her face, her eyes, nearly squeezed shut, crawling backwards until she feels the marble under her knees again. She lowers her mouth nearly down to the floor, forcing herself to breathe slowly, deeply, from the cleanest air she can find in the corridor. Then with an effort, she raises herself to her feet.

The smoke is thicker, darker, filling her squeezed eyes, stinging the exposed skin on her face and hands. Stretching an arm out, she touches the wall on her right. Then she begins to count to thirty paces. Her fingertips brush against the velvety wallpaper. Eight paces, and the smooth of the wood door frame, the slight indentation of the door, then another frame again at ten paces.

The breathing is harder though at her standing height, leaving her struggling with the burning in her throat, singeing her lungs with each gasp, as the smoke pushes past the damp scarf. The sprinkled water seems to coat her with thick gloopy soot, caking her eyelashes, covering her fingertips with oily moisture. She crashes into the table, almost losing count, gasping in agony that shoots up her hip. 'Damn fucker!' Pulling herself together, her eyes still squinting against the smoke, she forces herself to calm down, forcing herself to sip lightly of the soiled air around her.

Twenty-nine, she counts, hoping that the next pace brings her up to the fire escape. She needs to cough, to spit out the smoky filth that seems to fill her mouth. Her lungs are on fire, and her head is throbbing. Her fingers brush against wood again. She moves them down to find the long exit bar, hoping that this is the right one. Yes! One push and she's out, into the fire escape, into clear air, cool and dry in the concrete shaft. She struggles to drag it into her lungs, fighting both relief and lightheaded-ness, pushing back the coughing and nausea building in her.

It isn't until the door has nearly slammed behind her that she remembers the need for silence, and makes a grab for it, pushing her weight against the closing door, easing it shut with as little sound as she imagines is possible. The roar in her ears shuts out most sound, making it difficult to judge if the door has slid silently or with a bang that must surely alert the gunmen roaming below.

But there is little she can do about the coughs that overcome her, bending her double as she gives into spitting and hacking, trying ineffectually to clear her aching lungs. She is too exhausted to care even though she is sure the sounds reverberate right down through the shaft, all the way to the bottom.

***

The phone jolts Abhi out of his reverie, the ring monstrously loud in the silent office. The voice on the line is familiar, the same colonel he has spoken to before. 'We are coming in. Sit tight.' Barely has the receiver been replaced when Abhi hears the first burst gunfire from across the lawn. The final assault has begun.

The bank of screens shows no sign of Sam. 'It is time. Are you back in yet?' he texts Sam, knowingly, willingly breaking the promise he has made to the gruff voice on the phone. But he can't bear to leave her in the cold, can't bear the thought that she isn't safe, that she may be in line of fire. Her grin back in the Refuge had surprised him, the joy on her face so unexpected, so out of character that even the memory of it makes him smile in response.

210

The stopwatch on his phone shows twenty minutes have gone by. Is she in the fire escape yet, he wonders, peering at the screens from around the Refuge, hoping to catch a glimpse of her, of any sign of her beyond the smoke and steam.

Why she matters so much, he can't explain. Just that she does. Kind of the same way Diet had mattered. It wasn't so much him, or his smile, or their conversation about art and politics and life. It was the possibility he held out for Abhi, of love, of companionship, of something more intimate than the friendships that sustain him normally. A part of him recognises that Diet would probably have left, that perhaps he is romanticising what really was another passing romance, the kind people indulge in when travelling, the reality of over there never interfering in their quotidian concerns. He tells himself that Diet would have eventually left, gone back home, that there would have been emails and calls for a few weeks, perhaps even a few months, and then they both would move on, to more banal concerns of daily living, to convenience of companions, lovers, who are available across town rather instead of holding out for or chasing great loves who live a world away. And yet, looking back at their time together, he knows that Diet had offered a possibility that he could be loved. That Abhi could even love back, not out of duty or habit, but by choice.

The sudden flicker draws his gaze. The row of screens from the corridors before the Refuge have gone blank, the cameras cut out by smoke, or fire. Or perhaps water.

***

In the fire escape, Sam is counting her way down, holding on to the guard rail. Twelve steps first, to the shallow landing, then thirteen steps to the next floor, and six floors down. She has pushed down the scarf from her nose and mouth, relishing the cold air of the shaft, letting it clear away the burning from her lungs. Her ears alert for sound, both from the inferno above and the gunmen below, she steps silently, carefully, into the

211

dark. The knot in her shoulder spasms regularly, leaving her aching and tense. She can feel the exhaustion now, the insistent throbbing in her skull. There is a light-headedness that seems to gather around her eyes and ears, dulling the senses, making her feel like she is moving underwater, fighting to stay focused at every step.

Perhaps that is why she misses the step as she turns down the landing, tumbling down the steps, landing in a disorientated painful heap. Winded, dazed, she lies there, too tired for a long moment to notice anything but the agony coursing through parts of her. Her left hand is scraped, and her knees. Her head throbs, the pain now focused on her right temple. And as she regains her breath, she can feel the burgeoning ache beneath her ribs, twinging with every gulp of air she clutches at. Her right hand has instinctively clutched the Mamiya against her torso, but she knows that the camera has smashed against the concrete in the fall, possibly smashed something inside her as well.

She wants to stay there, give in to the pain, to never move until someone finds her. She doesn't really care who. The gunmen, the security, the rescue workers. Even the smoke building somewhere above would be a blessing, if only to give her a chance to sleep.

***

Thirty-eight minutes according to the stopwatch on his phone since Sam left the Refuge. He can't understand where she is. She hasn't answered his texts either. Beyond the office, Abhi can hear the exchange of gunfire. Sharp loud explosions of grenades puncture the night beyond. He can see the gunmen positioned along the main arcade, shooting to delay the entry of troops from the lobby doors. He is sure he has told the colonel that those have been booby trapped, hopes that the soldiers remember his warnings. Dark shapes huddle, crawl, race across the myriad screens, hunching over to shoot, sometimes crumbling suddenly as if in pain. He can only tell them apart because the attackers

212

are positioned inside Arcadia, using its vast galleries for cover, moving little as they defend their positions, fending off the troops who creep inexorably closer.

When the stop watch hits fifty minutes, he calls her. Her phone rings repeatedly. Five, six, then the voice mail message. He hangs up and calls again. Somewhere, he knows the phone is vibrating against her thigh, insisting that she answer. 'Come on, Sam, answer the damn phone,' he mumbles. Again and again, he calls her, cutting off her voice before she can begin the message.

As the stop watch reaches fifty-five, suddenly she answers. 'Yeah?' Her voice is confused, distant. 'Where are you, Sam? They are going in. You need to get out of the way.'

'Yeah, OK,' she sounds weak, completely unlike herself.

'Sam, what is going on? Where are you?'

A deep breath. Then a long pause. 'In the fire escape I think.'

'What floor?' he demands, part in relief, part out of fear, his eyes scanning the screens again to locate the gunmen.

'Don't know.' She seems a bit more awake. 'I fell, I think. Have probably busted something.'

'Sam, can you walk?'

Her giggle comes back weak but oddly reassuring. 'Fuck man, I haven't even tried sitting up yet.'

He forces out a chuckle. 'OK then, bloody well try to sit up please.' He wants to go to her, to find her, to carry her tiny frame down the fire escape to safety, somewhere away. A task for heroes, like the one Samar and Baba think he is. But beyond the heavy re-enforced doors of the operation centre, battle rages on, and there is no way for him to get to her, even if he tried.

He can hear her breaths, harsh and ragged. In his mind, he can see her pulling herself up, her small frame shuddering with effort, her delicate neck straining against the pain, her tiny fists clenching with will. 'Come on, Sam,' he urges again.

'Ah fuck! This hurts!'

'Can you sit up?'

'I can even stand up, mate. With help, mind you. Am hanging on to the bannister for dear life.' He thinks he can hear her sob, her voice wavering just slightly with the effort.

Slowly, steadily, with words that mean little or nothing at all, he coaxes her. 'Get to any door, the nearest one. Go down the steps, not up. If you push ajar any of the fire escapes, I can locate you.'

'Yeah, yeah, wise guy,' her voice is faint still. The sudden hacking coughs sound louder, followed by what he thinks is retching.

'Sam, what's going on?' he pleads, the lack of a visual on her more horrifying than if he could at least see her in one of the blurry grey squares.

'Smoke. Took some in upstairs…the shaft is clear though,' she waves off his question, her voice slightly stronger. He can sense she is moving, her breathing growing more strained with each step as she fight off the pain and nausea welling up within. 'Talk to me, Abhi, just keep talking to me.'

He scans the screens, slowly telling her where the gun men are positioned, where the assault troops are moving, the way the gunmen seem unconcerned about the approaching enemy, that there is a fire department helicopter apparently heading towards the fire on the roof, that there are fire trucks just beyond the dark perimeter, ready to move in the moment the gunmen are taken out. His voice is gentle, coaxing, caressing. 'I am not a puppy, damn you,' at one point she interjects. But he just continues, briefing her on the action unfolding on his screens, one eye locked on to the stop watch.

It isn't until thirteen minutes have passed that he spots a fire escape door edge open slightly, the movement almost imperceptible. The figure that slips through, lurching and unsteady, slumping against the wall bears little resemblance to Sam, and it is not until her face turns up to the camera that Abhi recognises her.

'So where the fuck am I?' her voice is brittle.

Abhi doesn't realise that he has been holding his breath. 'Jeez, you look like shit!'

214

'Feel worse than shit, mate. Tell me where to go.'

Abhi scans the floor, confirming the information twice on separate screens. 'You're on sixteenth. Two flights.'

'And the nuts with guns?'

'Army is clearing the basement but they aren't in yet. The other guys are stationed at the arcade around the lobby. You should be OK.'

'Thanks, mate.' She sidles back into the fire escape, phone still in hand, slipping out of his sight like a shadow. 'And Abs, am seriously grateful!'

The line goes dead.

THE ARCADIA
NOW

Sam slides into 1402, ready to drop to the floor. She slumps against the wall, clawing for breath, struggling to keep in check the heaving coughs that wrack her small frame. Her clothes are drenched from the sprinklers, the Mamiya alone is mostly dry, held protected, cradled, under her jacket, close against her belly.

'Sam?' Billy's voice is hushed, tentative. His eyes are huge, terrified. Sam swipes a hand across her face, unknowingly removing some of the soot caking it.

'Yeah, kid, it's me.' Even to her ears, Sam's voice rasps, the words scraping her throat like razors. She gave him thumbs-up and a wink, as she forces herself upright.

Moving wearily, on autopilot, she extracts the Mamiya, knowing even before she sees the damage that the lens is cracked, the black body dented. She winces as her hands brush against her bruised skin. Maybe there will be a Mamiya-shaped bruise there soon, she wonders, setting up the memory card for an upload, even as she keeps an eye on her lap top, her ears alert for sounds from beyond the room. Despite the exhaustion and lack of sleep, her mind is racing, considering the possibilities.

The dull thuds sound now from somewhere deep within the belly of the tower, punctuated by sharper, lighter metallic bursts. The final assault has begun, she knows, despite the much delayed news blackout. If she can only hold out long enough, the soldiers will get through, will outnumber the gunmen.

On her laptop, a news channel is now showing looped images of the Arcadia from earlier in the night. On the screen at least, there is no explosions ripping through the hotel roof, no fires spreading through the higher floors. Somewhere she

216

can hear a helicopter circling, far enough to not overwhelm her ears, but near enough to be annoying. Hopefully it really does have some fire-fighting capacities. The grenade blasts seems to be moving upwards through the tower, closer each time but not nearly quick enough. She can only hope that the ops will be completed in time; or at least in time for her, for Billy.

Below, the attackers are stalking the floors, now freely shooting, no longer hoarding their ammunition. Abhi's updates on her cell seem to have them moving through floors at a pace that she realises is desperate, or just approaching the end-game. But even he can't tell her if they have rigged up more explosives on other floors. Even had she known the traps, evacuation is not much of an option; she knows can't carry Billy down even one flight of that pitch dark fire escape.

Perhaps, today is not her day? She likes to believe that when she's out in the field: that the bullet with her name, the shell aimed at her, the million and one ways that death can come to her, will not find her. All of them find their target, but just never her. That somehow each day she survives is because of some innate lottery that she continues to win. Of course, one day she will lose that lottery but so far she has won. But perhaps, today is the day she must lose? On her own, she knows she can find her way out. But Billy holds her back, he would slow her down even if she tried to take him along.

A flash of anger, a sudden desperate fear courses through her. She has long known that this is what gets people killed! This hesitation, this need to watch over someone else. This is what slows their steps, makes them linger that extra second longer, makes them look back. She has never hesitated before, lingered before, slowed down before. Colleagues, soldiers, civilians are really not her concern, and when it is their day, she has slipped past them, disregarding the fallen, the wounded, the dying; and that is how she has remained alive, fast, focused.

Damn it! Sam has been always been the survivor; she never looks back, never hesitates, never questions. She always acts on instinct, her feet moving of their own accord, her eye sharp and focused, her finger shuddering automatically when she spots her kill. And now…

Billy is watching her, apprehension clear on his face, sensing the rapid shifts in her mood. 'Will we be OK, Sam?'

'Yeah, of course.' His voice makes her up her mind. Perhaps it is his fear. Or the fact he doesn't argue, or even contradict. She doesn't know if Billy believes her, or is just afraid to not believe her. It does not matter any more.

Pulling herself together, she begins to strip the bed, gathering the sheets and throwing them into the bath. If they must wait it out, then damn it, she will at least fight to even their odds, however skewed they are.

She piles the soaked sheets against the door, then looks around for more. The pillows as well. She shoves them into the half-full bath to be fully soaked, carries them sopping to the door, leaving long wet trails in her wake.

The curtains take some calculation. She has left them drawn for the past sixty-seven hours, knows that broadcasting live may be used to ID rooms with occupants, and moving curtains are a dead give-away. But now the precaution seems pointless. Sam yanks them off the rails, the sound of the heavy metal clips giving way shockingly loud in the silence, the drapes moving slowly and then suddenly, with a huge whoosh, falling to the ground.

The vast dark beyond fills her eyes, a deathly stillness that precedes the dawn. For a long moment, Sam stares, stunned by the sight of the pitch dark sky, the shadowy perimeter, the far off city lights, reminders of a world that she had forgotten in the past days. Beyond the darkened perimeter, the city lights cast a soft glow, obscuring the stars. But before her, towards the left, she knows there is the sea. There, the boats bobbing in the distance look like stars, the night smelting the sky and water into a single vast expanse. Clutching a swathe of fabric in her fist, Sam can only stare, hungry, starved for the vastness, the claustrophobia, the imprisonment of the past hours suddenly washing over her. Like a prisoner who has forgotten the possibility of the sky, of the sea, of everything beyond her cell. It takes a conscious, great effort to pull her eyes away, to fight down the urge to simply undo the glass panel and step across, into the vast beyond.

'I didn't know it was still night,' Billy's voice is full of wonder. It pulls Sam out of the trance. Shaking her head, squeezing her eyes, Sam turns away, reverts to preparing against the smoke and fire creeping closer to the sanctuary, her cell, her prison.

It isn't until the third trip with her arms full of soaking linen that she hears Billy chanting, 'Fuck, fuck, fuck, God damn it, fuck, shit, fuck, fuck, fuck.'

'Who taught you that?' her voice comes out louder than planned, echoing in her head, hanging in the silent, shrouded room. Her throat aches with the effort, as the coughing wracks her again.

'You always say that when you are working,' His voice is soft, slightly abashed. 'I thought it helped?'

She can't stop the smile. 'Yeah, it does,' she tells him. 'Keep going, kid.'

Billy's face lights up at her approval, and he goes back to watching her, his soft voice muttering the words with the intensity of a prayer, a talisman to hold off whatever new danger the soaking sheets are meant to stop from entering.

She can hear his soft muttering as she strips down in the bathroom, washing the soot off her face, leaving her soaking clothes on the floor, seeping black on to the white tiles. Her hands come away black as she washes the soot from her scalp, and it isn't until she dunks her head under the tap for a long time that the water runs clear.

Still wet, she draws on dry clothes: jeans that strangely smell of the jungle, her thickest sweatshirt, a dry pair of socks. She debates about pulling on her boots, but finally decides against them. No need for them now. There is no running now, or even escape.

It isn't until she begins preparing the Baileys and valium concoction for Billy that the tremors hit. It takes Sam a moment to realise that her hands are shaking, rattling the spoon against the glass. She clenches them into fists, breathing deeply. She has heard of this, from colleagues, around mess tables, delayed stress reaction, or just anxiety. Or perhaps this is just exhaustion. She grits her teeth together, squeezing her jaws shut, as the shaking spreads.

Extracting more pills from the bottle takes enormous effort, but she finally manages to extract a handful. Popping them straight into her mouth, she downs them with the Baileys. As the liquid burns its way down her throat, the sweet, creaminess making her nauseous.

She forces herself to prepare another lot, hesitating only slightly before adding an extra half Valium to it. She learned long ago that an easy death is a rare gift, and she hopes the drowsiness will wipe out any terror that may arise from the smoke, or the flames, if they reach past the door.

As Billy grimaces his way through the glass, she leans over her laptop, picking unerringly the final and best image from her last foray. Not her best effort perhaps, not for an exhibition any way, but this photograph is not for her. Attaching it to an email, she waits till it is sent, before deleting the full folder and snapping her laptop shut.

Reaching out, almost on auto-pilot, she grabs the still quarter full bottle of whisky and takes a long swig, swirling it around her mouth, forcing herself to breathe deeply, inhaling the sharp tang, letting the fumes rise into her nostrils, making her eyes water. As she is swallowing, her eyes alight on the unopened bottle of L'Eglise Clinet, the '94 vintage she had swiped from the fat man down the hall, still sitting on the table before her. It would be such a shame to let it go to waste, just because the world beyond is turning full of fire and smoke. A wry smile twists her mouth as she fishes out her small Swiss knife from her camera-bag, uses it expertly to uncork the bottle, then takes a quick approving sniff.

Grabbing the bottle by the neck, she stalks over to the sofa, where Billy lies still, cradling his injured arm, watching her warily. Carefully, moving the cushions around Billy, making room for herself, she settles down next to him. Drawing him close, she can smell the sweet sweat in his hair. That slightly birds' nest fragrance that little boys seem to have all over the world. She smiles as he snuggles against her shoulder, accepting her sudden affection without question. 'So what are we going to do now?' he wonders.

She takes a long drink of the wine, holding the liquid in her mouth, letting the flavours soak her palate before she swallows. Then softly ruffling his hair with her fingers, she gives him the only answer she can. 'Settle down kid. We are going to wait for the sun to come up.'

***

The bank of screens before him has grown darker and duller, corridors full of smoke, the northern edge of the roof flickers with flames. Sprinklers have come on and some of the higher floors are covered in steamy mist, clumping soot over the lenses, making the images blur and twist. Explosions and creeping fires have shot out some of the cameras and the top row of screens has sunk into electronic fuzz. With each passing minute, Abhi knows that the soldiers outside draw closer, their deliberate, measured steps racing against the flames and smoke, and the attackers prowling above. He has been told to stay put, to stay in the operations room, as if he can even drum up any strength to move beyond his chair.

With the power off, even the corridors below are shrouded in shadows. On the tenth floor, around the conference rooms, he thinks he can see the attackers prowling in the dark. And somewhere between the shadows, and fires, bullets and unseen killers, is Sam. He can't find her on the screens; her slight form, the careful, crab-like gait, lost in the smoke and mist. She hasn't answered his texts for over half an hour, even though he tries to update her every five minutes, informing her of smoke on yet another floor that she may need to traverse, of the dull, thumping explosions that periodically shudder down from the roof, through the very bones of the Arcadia, send debris and glass raining on the huddled forms moving through the darkened lawns beyond his sight.

The gunshots sound closer, just beyond his re-enforced door. Then a single heavy thump followed by a long tinkling rain, like hail falling on glass windows. The huge glass front doors perhaps, or the twinkling monstrous chandelier of the lobby? He has told the army that there are explosives rigged to the door. Did they forget? Or was that a disposal gone wrong? Perhaps they just decided to blast it through. The CCTV bank can tell him nothing, as armed and prowling forms blend into one another in the smoke and dark, the attackers and the attacked both clad in near identical clothing of dark fatigues and assault rifles, with the same predatory prowls as they move in an elaborate game of chase and hunt.

His laptop chimes. A single low bleep, signalling an email. From Sam. At least, she has made it back to the room. And to Billy. Relief floods through him, if only for an instant.

'For what it's worth, my friend. Sam.'

It has a single large file attachment. There is no subject, the empty line, the incomplete Re: a silent reproach to the possibility of naming anything, everything. The attachment takes long, weary seconds to download, the fear and horror and terror of what Abhi knows it to be churning all the time, clenching his stomach in a painful grip, twisting his insides in agonising spasms. Then slowly a rich, textured, black and white image fills his screen. Dieter. No, Diet, as in Deet, he had told Abhi to call him. In extreme close-up, his closed eyes forming perfect crescents, the long dark lashes fanning his cheeks. So close, that Abhi can see the faint freckles on the bridge of his nose, the soft bright down on his temples.

Sam has shot Diet in three-quarters profile, as if for a fashion spread. He looks asleep, dreaming, as if any moment those crescents could sweep open to reveal the pale eyes, flashing with mischief and desire. His jaw catches the light, the fine bone defining the lower arc of the image sharply. The first glimmers of golden stubble form a luminescent, near-halo, like vintage

222

studio shots of film stars. So familiar, and yet so alien, like a memory already frozen in a time long past.

The rich burgundy of the carpet is faded to a deep shade of grey, spreading beyond the neatly gelled hair. It forms a rich, grainy backdrop, luxurious in texture, glistening softly, wetly, with what Abhi realises must be a bloodstain. But the moisture gives the image a gentle dewiness, an innocent gloss. He can see the edge of Diet's lustrous silk jumper marking off the bottom of the photograph, a slightly different shade of grey counterpointing, highlighting the background. And the focal point, just off centre is Diet's mouth, the full lips, still moist and shiny, as if fresh from a kiss. The lips are slightly parted, with just a hint of a curve to the edge, in a smile, or a complaint, or perhaps a final cry. There is no hint of pain, or even finality, in the shot. Instead of the smoke and blood and explosives, Abhi can practically smell the Boss cologne he had grown to love on Diet, can almost taste the musky, slightly acrid sweat on his jaw.

Abhi knows why Sam took so long upstairs now. She wanted the perfect shot. Not a Sam-perfect, to be blown up and printed on large canvas, stretched in a gallery. Not a Sam-shot of the final trace of humanity caught in the fragile, ephemeral moment, when death has not yet fully claimed whatever animates a human body. Instead, for once she has shot an elegy, slightly cheesy in its composition, almost clichéd in its sentimentality. It is a gift for the bereft, not meant for use by a news outlet or an art gallery. It is Sam's parting gift, flawed and much less than perfect, but utterly intimate, solely for him.

Beyond the door, gunshots have receded, perhaps moving up and beyond, into the atrium and floors above. Abhi slumps back into the chair, his eyes caressing the black and white image filling the laptop screen. He does not know what he mourns, except perhaps the loss of possibilities. For once the bank of CCTV screens go equally ignored, though his tears blur even the sight of what fills the one screen he has chosen to view. Perhaps that is why he initially ignores the vibrating phone on the desk.

Once. Twice. Then a pause for two minutes. Then again two vibrating silent bursts. A message. Wiping his eyes, he picks up his phone, tapping in the code.

A square photograph appears, aesthetic only in its relentless functionality, taken by a phone camera. A square dark wood frame holds a patch of blue velvet. On the velvet, laid in neat rows, equidistant from each other, and the frame, are Baba's gallantry awards. First row, the three medals for special action, Abhi knows, even without scrolling the image larger. The lowest row with his ribbons, three pinned in a neat row. And in the centre, in the place of pride, the crossed swords insignia Baba only wore on his dress uniform, the highest award for personal valour. Since childhood, Samar and he have fought over these, arguing for the right to touch them, to keep them, to possibly inherit them in some dim, distant future. To even perhaps deserve them.

Samar has added a message. 'Baba says you are the most deserving. He's right. These are yours, bro.'

For a long instant, he stares at the phone in his hand, then glances up at the laptop. Diet's face still fills the screen, a silent sentinel or rebuke. Abhi's lips twist. A smile or frown, he would not know himself. Sighing softly, he reaches out and snaps the laptop shut and begins to tap a response to Samar's text.

ACKNOWLEDGEMENTS

I could not write without the unstinting support, enthusiasm and patience of my family, so first of all much gratitude and love to Mum and Dad. Thank you, Rashmi, for insights into the Global War on Terror. I am especially grateful to Siddharth who read and re-read many versions of this book, and plied me with much food, wine, and critical feedback, and put up with my prolonged absent-mindedness with unfailing good cheer.

I also want to thank many friends, near and far, who sustain, nourish, and encourage my growth as a human being and a writer, and none more so than Sheri Ahmed, Glenn Reid, Dimo Dimas, Berta Sanchis, Marta Roca, and Jo Hogan. In London, a big thank you to the Authors' Club which has given me a literary and intellectual home and I am especially grateful to Chris Schuler and Stella Kane for their friendship and support. A big hug to all my Twitter friends – too many to name – whose insights, views, knowledge and experience continues to educate and enlighten me.

There are not enough words of gratitude and affection for my agent, Laura Susijn, in all the languages that we share between us. I would not and could not publish without her unwavering loyalty, extraordinary support, and absolute faith. She is without doubt the best agent a writer could have, hope for, or imagine.

I am grateful that Naim Attallah just 'got' the book from its first read. Also at Quartet, many, many thanks to Gavin James Bower.

Finally, I want to thank all the women journalists, researchers, aid workers, and activists who are my friends, colleagues, heroines and inspiration. This book is my tribute to all of you.